Harmonie Club

086

ENDANGERED SPECIES

ENDANGERED SPECIES

A NOVEL

SANDRA HOCHMAN

G. P. PUTNAM'S SONS · NEW YORK

Published simultaneously in Canada by Longman
Canada Limited, Toronto
SBN: 399-11912-4
Library of Congress Cataloging in Publication Data

Hochman, Sandra.
    Endangered species.
    I. Title.
PZ4.H6853En   [PS3558.034]   813'.5'4   77-6223

PRINTED IN THE UNITED STATES OF AMERICA

For—William Targ

Acknowledgment

My thanks to these people:
  My daughter, Ariel
  Steve Hochman
  Don Townsend
  Arthur and Alexandra Schlesinger
  Jean Campbell
  Richard and Helga Rosenthal
  Susan and Alan Patricoff
  Mary and John Cheever
  Marc and Susan Strausberg
  Jerry Goldsmith
    who, each in their own way, perhaps without
    even knowing, inspired me as I wrote this book.
                                        S.H.

I was alone like a tunnel. The birds fled from me, and night swamped me with its crushing invasion. To survive myself I forged you like a weapon, like an arrow in my bow, a stone in my sling.

Pablo Neruda—From *Twenty Love Poems*

CELEBRATION
AT FORTY

Helen

Alone. My birthday. A celebration of forty years. I was about to get into bed and enjoy the silence of my own room. Then Helen called.

"Are you alone?" she asked.

"Of course I'm alone."

A drunken pleading came through the phone.

"Tonight it's the eighteenth aniversary of my father's death. His *yortzeit*. There's someone here I want you to meet. Jud."

"No thanks. I don't want to meet anyone through you, Helen."

The lost girl, the sad green-eyed girl began to plead. "Can you come and see me?" I don't enjoy reliving the past with old acquaintances.

Just then a man grabbed the phone.

"Hello. I'm Jud. When your book came out I gave it to Richard Heman to read ..."

"She doesn't care about that," I heard Helen saying.

"Please can I talk to Helen?"

"Why don't you come over—I'll buy you a drink?" the man said into the phone. His voice was loud.

"I don't drink," I said.

"Here Helen. Take the goddamn phone. She has problems. She doesn't drink. She sounds too uptight."

"Please?" asked Helen.

"Where are you?"

"I'm at the Bistro. You used to come here with Sonny. It's on Eighty-first Street and East End."

"I don't have any cash with me," I said.

"Just take the cab and stop the driver in front of the restaurant. I have some cash. Just take the cab."

I agreed to go.

Because twenty-four years had gone by since I first met Helen at Bingham House as a freshman in college. Because I had just been thinking of her on my birthday—fishing her out of the past like a squirming green-finned mermaid who spoke French, once smoked Gauloises, now smoked pot, once drank wine listening to Bach and Segovia, now drank vodka scotch beer—anything—in armpit bars—in flocked wallpaper bars—Helen—is it really you—the red-haired one who welcomed me to Bingham House and wore her hair in a Dutchgirl bob and wore pink leotards and soft black ballet slippers—looking like one of the Picasso clowns in the blue period—*Le Saltimbanque*—Helen—who had abortions, who had lost her virginity in Brooklyn and was the first girl I knew to have "affairs"—Helen whose big fatty saint of a father drove up to college from Pennsylvania—Big Gerald—in a huge shiny black Lincoln car—who smiled behind the wheel—looking very proud—of his daughter—Big Gerald who sponsored composers and the Philadelphia Symphony orchestra—married to a porcelain woman—who Helen used to say always asked her—even at twenty—if she loved her "Do you love me Helen?" her mother, Harriett, would ask like a grownup child herself "Helen don't ever forget I *bore* you" not the bore we would get to know so many years later—the boring Harriett whose hair was no longer combed, Harriett the widow, never having enough money (Big Gerald's money was lost by Helen's old boyfriend and lover and investor—Edgar—who kissed her in the college parking lot on both of their birthdays

and said this is Helen the girl I'm going to marry but never did) –
Harriett of the flesh and bearing of children–now in New York
City living with Helen–briefly in "on a trip from Hawaii" and
Helen, now a holy beggar, crying through the cruel telephone
begging me to come on her father's *yortzeit* to some bar.

I said Yes. Hung up the phone. No. I was too tired. I put on
my old green warm-up tennis suit. Oh yes Helen had said "It
doesn't matter what you are wearing"–as if I cared–and I went.

Helen was sitting on a red leather bar stool. The restaurant was
not the Bistro–it had another name, the Boeuf Bourguignon–
Helen had it wrong–but I got out of the cab and ran into the
bar. Jud–the lug–who Helen had described in her slurred
conversation as "warm and Jewish" came out to pay the cab. He
was holding his dollars carelessly as if they were play dollars.
Always the sign of the really drunk. Dollars fell out of his fingers
on the street.

He slipped as he came to the cab. "I belong to the single
parents association and I give single parties for parents without
partners," he said slurringly to me as he paid the cabdriver.

The driver saw he was drunk. "You owe me another dollar,"
the cabdriver said to Jud. He winked at me. "He won't miss it."

"Leave him alone," I said to the driver. But I supposed he
wanted to be given the money rather than seeing it fall into the
gutter. Why was seeing Helen again always a *nightmare?*

"Jud's my name. I hear you have a child. Enid? Engel? Or is it
two children?"

I'm afraid of drunks. Especially at night. And so I ran into the
bar leaving Jud to follow me slowly.

Helen slid off her bar stool. She still looked doll-like from a
distance. She had red bangs–to cover forehead wrinkles. As she
came closer the drink showed. Her face had now become a
distortion of what it was. One eye squinted the other eye large.
Now she was a different kind of Picasso woman. A one-eyed

woman from the abstract period. She wore black with a rhinestone belt that came from a dress somewhere and white high-heeled bedroom slippers. No stockings.

She put her arms around me and hugged me. "Come," she said, "let us sit down at the table not at the bar." She was princess now in her own court of alcoholics and bloated jesters.

"Kathy. Is it you? You came," Helen said.

"Yes. Your father's *yortzeit* happens to be my fortieth birthday." I lit a cigarette. "I came," I said. "I was thinking about you an hour ago. An hour before you called after all these years. And so I thought I have to see Helen." I was beginning to loathe old times.

Jud came over to bother us. Helen looked at him and began begging. "Please won't you go away? This was my best friend in college. She's a beautiful person. We want to talk privately."

Oh god, twenty years later, for Helen, everyone is still a beautiful person.

Helen began delivering a liturgy for the dead. Edgar had died a terrible death from a tumor. She had introduced him to a Puerto Rican and the Puerto Rican had taken all his seven million dollars. He had left the Puerto Rican before he died. "I was in my tenement. You can't imagine how beautiful it is. I rent it from the hospital. Only a hundred and twelve dollars a month. My mother was staying with me. When Edgar called and told me he was leaving his wife—his Puerto Rican—that *I* introduced him to—he called me when the tumor was coming out to here" (she pointed to her red Dutch-cap bob) "I ran to the back of the tenement while Edgar was still on the phone and I said to my mother—Harriett—what should I do? Edgar wants to come back to me."

"You asked Harriett? Couldn't you decide for yourself what to do?"

Helen ignored this. "Harriett said, 'Be kind to him Helen.

Even if he did lose all of Gerald's money. He's dying.' So I told
Edgar to come over and he did and he said hello baby—and I still
loved him so much—I always loved Edgar—and even though this
tumor was growing out of his head we went to dinner and then
we visited Masha—I love Masha—you must spend time with
Masha—his sister—I love her so much—you would love her—"

"I know Masha. She is lovely."

"Well Edgar was always in love with Masha. He would take
her to a skating rink when they were children. And they would
skate together. And he would say—'Masha? Which girl would you
pick out for me?' You see he always loved Masha. That was his
problem. He was in love with his sister. But to hide this he always
asked her to find him girls. The same thing with me. He loved
me. I think I reminded him of Masha. And when he lived with
me he always said Helen find me a girl. Find me someone.' "

Helen's one good eye opened to a large green circle. The other
eye started weeping. "He died so miserably."

"How did he make seven million dollars?" I asked. "I thought
he was a communist."

"He was a communist. He married a Puerto Rican. That was
his idea of communism. He was an investor. He started out as a
communist but then when he was a counselor in a summer camp
one of the little boys' fathers worked at Payne Weber and he got
a job there as an investor and he was most successful—spook—or
whatever you call what they do at Payne Weber—until they fired
him. But even then he still had his brain. He was a genius. You
remember Edgar? He was the first man I ever loved. I should have
married him. His birthday was the same day as mine. And then I
introduced him to this Puerto Rican dame. Can I show you his
obituary? I have it here. And then before the Puerto Rican he was
married to that pianist—Solovioff—Masha liked her—and then he
died. And you know who else died? Ken. Remember Ken?"

"Of course I remember Ken."

"Killed himself. That's the story that's out. Killed himself. And Toby? Killed himself. And Eleanore? She was married to Bob Nichols—the director who did *Greasy Rider*—you know she had a baby and it drowned. And then her husband who always played around—left her—I introduced her to a cousin of mine because Eleanore was such a beautiful person but nothing happened. And Jane Tish? I hear that she's terribly thin and doesn't look well. She's coming to New York in December."

"Is she still married to the mystic?"

"Not mystic. Midget. He's this high. Comes up to my knee. She's married to this bald mystic midget. You never met him? Well he's into all the religious shit. But not in a *good* way. Her brother sends her checks. She lives in San Francisco. She plays seven hours of tennis a day."

"She couldn't be that broke. If she plays tennis all day."

"It doesn't cost anything to play tennis in California. And she's into her children. And tennis. She would starve if it wasn't for her brother. Do you remember him? Tall and fat and crazy? You once went out with him."

"On a blind date. He took me to play miniature golf. I remember holding a tiny golf club under fluorescent lights somewhere in the suburbs and laughing. He was funny. Like Jane Tish. Only ungainly in an odd way."

"That ugly brother keeps Jane Tish alive. She and her husband make underground small movies that have titles like *Sun-Sea-Wave*. She's still funny."

Was the kaddish over?

"And my friend Cara runs an acting school in San Francisco. You remember her? She was the actress in the Antonioni movie who was big and fat and had black hair. She married Alex—"

"Who is Alex?"

"You don't know him? An actor and they run an acting school. An acting school. And her husband Billy the dentist. He married a psychoanalyst with dark glasses. An intellectual. You know Salvatorre still loves you."

I don't care.

I leave Helen. I go home. Birthday. I love Helen. There's nothing I can do. I think I can't see her any more. I always *say* that. I'm alone. A birthday.

Fear and Nurturing

What happens to women's lives amazes me. Here I am—Kathy Kahn. My name. We may rationalize or anesthetize we women who live on the edge of dream and reality—but the odd turn of a life—the death of the soul—the absurd maze of today bewilders me. Is it today? And the swift wrinkle and endless risk—all of this amazes me. I sniff under my past for who I am.

*

I am an odd person who hates background noises. My ears are sensitive. Too sensitive. So is my nose too sensitive. In fact all of my senses seem to be always overextended. I would describe myself as a woman who is always reaching out for someone—for I learned somewhere that to communicate is the beginning of understanding. I think I do not understand myself. I know that I am forty, I have two children, and I am petrified of closed-door panic. The sudden realization that death and age are not zeros to be written on someone's blackboard. I fear age. The crinkle in the thigh, the nipple that gets brown and does not turn like a thorn to prick against the finger—the chin that is more round—the newly seen lid that hangs over the eye like a dough-white pattycake of flesh—this is new to me. I must get my eyes fixed by

Doctor Converse. The lids hanging are not attractive. It doesn't matter. Fearful and happy I pretend nothing to myself except that I hear the deafening rumors of angels. Alive in the seventies—me in my forties—I have tried many beginnings and many ends. Anger chokes me. Often I find myself saying "I live for revenge." For example—the two-hundred-dollar child-support check which comes every month from the chartered bank did not arrive today. Instead I received a yellow debit—a piece of paper that was mistakenly put in the envelope and mailed to me instead of to my ex-husband which infuriated me. Another mistake. It was as if the bank was especially there to harass me. I spoke to the bank manager a certain Mr. Doldrums—that was his name. Dear dumb doldrums I wanted to scream—my ex-husband is an ex-ecutive in ex-cellent condition using ex-lax in Ethiopia where he dispatches orders for the ex-ecution of my soul. But of course the doldrums gentleman at the chartered bank had no understanding of all this and proceeded to explain the mistake. He will be calling me. Meanwhile—money is a problem. Raising two young girls is a problem. My heart goes out to women who are divorced in their forties with children and never quite enough money. And hear the truth: If I could only get back to the earth all would not be over for me. I was born in the country. In Ossining where the red leaves fall like tongues jabbering from the autumn trees. I used to take long walks in Hiawatha woods—and look at the herons and sparrows chattering in the autumn. I used to walk around the woods of the Kress estate when I was very young. I envied the peregrine birds who lived high above the sea and longed for sea as a child—I too wanted to be one of those peregrine birds who never had to come down to earth—but rested instead on the momentum of clouds. My girlhood. I remember being in love with fronds of green palms in the Florida world my mother and father traveled to each winter. My mother, a great lady, and my father from Russia—a rich clown with a world of his own—a businessman and a violinist as a matter of fact—whose life ended with a dum te dum and a clatter of drums. How they hated each other—and yet I knew they loved me. My parents divorced, I lived with my grandparents. What then? Boarding school—actually a sort of health-oriented Swedish boarding school where we all carried hockey sticks. The Bennington College in Vermont I still call EdenSchool. And all my chums—Ellen—Carole—Helen—Nancy—Sara—Lois—now swimming like fish in the life pool. The human loneliness. The thinker, me, in my odd apartment surrounded by children's drawings—thinking good thoughts among all the murky masonry we take for remembrances.

Dear Uncle Eddy:

Today I'm forty. You're someplace out in California now and for the moment you've disappeared. I guess you won't mind me writing about you although I too hate family confessions but I hope you'll take it as a compliment that I lie in bed thinking about you and the warehouse and what a wonderful idea you are for a movie. It seems strange that you're out under a palm tree background somewhere in Beverly Hills trying to write scripts, I've been told, for movies and here I am sitting in New York City thinking of what a wonderful movie your life is. Or is it your life? Or my way of piecing you together—fixing you like a shadow in my night mind that keeps boxing with my imagination. But you're here all right and I can't get you out, so let me elaborate a little on what I'm seeing.

I see you first as a photograph. You were a handsome man in a photograph in a frame. You sat on my grandmother's bureau and smiled at everyone. You were in California then—this was before the war. I think you had run away from New York and frankly I can understand why. Even though I was three years old I think I could look at your photograph and understand why you had gone.

You were out of things in the family. I remember when I was four you made your appearance back in the city and someone led me into the living room and said "Do you know who this is?" What a faker I was even then. It took about five guesses out of my baby mind before I came up with the shout "Uncle Eddy" although I knew all along. Okay. That's a long time ago. But I was pumped full of how you had taken me out of the hospital in a carriage and how you had loved me when I was a baby and how you were my favorite uncle. Then you disappeared. My parents were divorced. I went to boarding school. And you emerged as a photograph again. This time in a captain's uniform. I followed your whole career in the army (it was wartime) through a series of photographs in my grandmother's bedroom. I really took your career as a soldier seriously. I listened carefully to the letters you wrote home from India. They were brilliant and funny although no one but me really got them. For example, grandma (you always called her by her first name, Rose) had said to you to write home two words once in a while. You wrote home "Dear Rose, here are the two words: I'm fine" and other letters talking about how you were caught up in "red tape." I imagined the Nazis had bound you in yards of red sticky tape somewhere in India. Such was our ignorance of the war—American babies. The hammered gold Indian ashtrays you sent home were also displayed. And the heavy necklace of green jade that you sent me went over in boarding school. As did the pocketbook with silver stitches. I missed you all through the war and prayed every night "Dear God, keep Uncle Eddy safe in India." As far as I was concerned war was a victory garden, no men for mommy to go out with, and you in India which I imagined to be somewhere in Europe. Those pictures of you in front of the Taj Mahal with you smiling into an imaginary pool made me want to leave school and join you. Also the pictures you sent home in a scrap book called "India: Land of Differences" interested me so much that I decided my life would be devoted to going to India, getting there, and making a scrap book like yours. To me you were the spitting image of Tyrone Power. Speaking of Tyrone Power I remember, when the war was over, I was living with grandma during my school vacations in the maid's room. I remember, out of great loneliness, I pasted pictures of movie stars all over the green bathroom. There were pictures of of Tyrone Power (because he looked like you) and also pictures of other stars especially Linda Darnell and Lana Turner, and Greer Garson. You said, "Jesus, I'm embarrassed to piss in that bathroom with all those gorgeous girls looking at me" and I thought that was funny. I also thought it was funny that we were the only two single people (except for Aunt Polly) in the house. Everyone else, including Mother, and Uncle Tony had gotten married. You had a room in the back of the West End Avenue apartment that you built up with bookcases and radios and all sorts of things. You were so handy. Also you spent most of the day playing the grand piano in the dark living room. By that time you no longer loved me. I used to sneak in and look at what seemed to me a very romantic language: the sheets of music. I loved "Come Back to Sorrento" which, for some reason, you played over and over and over. Grandma used to complain in the kitchen it gave her a headache. Why did we stop loving each other?

The Life Scales

Because I'm forty I want to change—but I'm afraid. Sing the scales. Doremifasolatido. Sing the joy of it. The madness of it. Warm the throat muscles. Head high.

What's in a life? The long of it and the short of it—is that one tries to survive. More than that—to make oneself as wise as possible. You may remember the letter written by Rimbaud to Paul Demeny, in which he said

> It is necessary to be a seer, to make oneself a seer. The poet makes himself a seer by a long, immense and reasoned unruliness of the senses ... He attains the unknown.

Let me say an intermediate word about my life–that I live very deeply in the irrational. A beginning word? Childhood takes too long. Let me just tell you that my name is Kathy–I was born in New York City in nineteen thirty-six. Recently I have been suffering from a panic about getting old. Closed-door panic I once heard it called.

That is what I must tell you about.

It happens–suddenly you are lost. Your childhood gone. You run away from old friends. It is *they* who have aged. You, still a child, now have turned. Turned to an old person. Unprepared you hide from the mirror. The lead behind the glass is black. Looking in the glass a new face is there. Wrinkles like leaves around your lips. Tiny record scratches in the eyes. Try not to look. But suddenly–the youth marketable apple face becomes the tired fruit not good enough to eat. Juices gone. Only poetry is the cure of the mind. Poetry is a health. But age is there anyway. That's it. You're no longer the young poet. The young imaginative girl in the fine pink elastic girdle. Reality is the spirit's true center. And what you see frightens you. The closed-door panic. Doors close— to what? Open them. But where are the knobs? Your friends, like Helen, feel it too. You know they do. The revelations of appearances are there. Only originality can help you escape from repetition. The newness of life. There in music. Children. A green map with pink and blue spaces that you might travel into. The pink and red roses mixed in a white vase on the ledge by the window. A rented outdoor tennis court on the Upper West Side where you run to find the body of the girl you used to be. The ball high in the polluted city sky—the yellow tumbling ball—you raise your arm and slam down the ball on the gray court—the daily necessity of hitting back. But the truth remains—you will die. You are serving the ball towards death. "What goes up and doesn't come down?" your eight-year-old daughter asks "Age!"—but at eight—does not know the meaning of the word. In the long run the word doesn't matter. Closed-door panic? The door is closing.

*

Open the door.

Scene from Childhood

FATHER:
What's that thing on your head?
MOTHER:
It's a cloche. I just bought it on sale.
FATHER:
Take it off! It looks like a piece of shit. It's the kind of hat that even the maid wouldn't wear. You embarrass me in front of my friends.
MOTHER:
I don't dress for your friends. I think it suits me. It's understated. Something you couldn't possibly understand . . . with your background.
FATHER:
Would you cut that crap! So I come from the Lower East Side.

I'm not ashamed of it. You think you're better than I am. Well you're not. Big deal—your old man's a producer in show business. And sent you to college. Don't forget—*I* paid for your master's degree. All I do is pay. And then I have to listen to you tell me how illiterate I am. Where has all your education gotten *you*?

MOTHER:

It COULD get me a job. If you would only agree to let me go back to teaching. I never asked to be a showpiece wife. All you want is someone to show off, who will put a lot of expensive clothes on their back, and entertain *your* friends elaborately. But I'm tired of being choked to death on this silverspoon existence. I could just—regurgitate. I'd like to get out of this house. I want nothing more than to go and work with handicapped children and do something worthwhile with my time.

FATHER:

How can you teach the handicapped when you're so handicapped yourself?

MOTHER:

What is that crack supposed to mean?

FATHER:

That you're a scatterbrain. If you didn't have me you'd be out on the street.

MOTHER:

That's a lie. I was teaching before I met you.

FATHER: *(Ignoring her remark)*

And if you want to help kids so much how about helping your own daughter. Look at her. She's dressed like an Indian. She runs wild.

MOTHER:

That's why we put her in a progressive school so she can learn to cultivate her imagination and express herself and not be inhibited to extend the boundaries of her mind. She's my daughter and I want her to have all the opportunities to grow.

FATHER:

That school is full of shit. Fingerpainting. Making pots. Eurhythmic dancing–how's that gonna help her in life? I don't want her to be educated and useless like you.

MOTHER:

That's the whole point. I don't want to be useless. When I married you I had to give up my career as a teacher. Now I no longer have my old friends with whom I could discuss political and creative issues.

FATHER:

But none of those smart alecs could support ya. Now that you are a mother–why should I put up with your running around? Why do you need museums? Stay home. Be a mother. You might even like it.

MOTHER:

Why do I have to stay home? That doesn't make someone automatically a good mother. I take Kathy to the museums with me, I take her to puppet shows and the ballet. I'm opening her mind. You're so goddamn lazy you don't take her anywhere. It wouldn't kill you to get up on Sunday mornings and take her to the Botanical Gardens. Or the Cloisters.

FATHER:

Why do you have to always DO THINGS? Can't you just sit home and relax? And STOP PICKING ON ME. You're goddamn lucky to be my wife. I'm *very* successful. Didn't I just buy you a mink coat? You have a maid. A nice apartment. I put up with your passion for books. And paintings. I put up with your high-class family. I listen to your daydreams about helping people. I'm GOOD TO YOU, AREN'T I?

MOTHER:

You don't understand. I don't want things. I want a life. This may come as a shock to you but I have other aspirations besides wearing a mink coat. As a girl I always yearned for an exciting and interesting life in the arts and politics. I was always a bit of a rebel–I should have pursued my life. But the Depression came along ...

FATHER:

And you were scared. You couldn't find a teaching job. With all your socialist ideas– So your old man told you to marry me. Or else.

MOTHER:

And I listened to him. But I did the wrong thing. I realize now. So, here I am. Locked up on Riverside Drive. With a successful baboon ...

FATHER:

You'll be sorry you ever called me that. You bitch! *(He walks over to her and gives her a slap on the face.)* Shut up! She can hear every word you're saying. She may be a child. But she's not stupid. Believe you me she understands.

Ceremony of Misery

Christmas was always a ceremony of misery. I remember boarding school blues–all year long we were preparing for the holiday. There was the build-up where we tried out for the Christmas pageant, learned the carols, and it was always a time of excitement. Christmas was coming–Christmas was coming–every day on the calendar brought us closely in touch with the time of miracles and enchantment. Around the Christmas season Dr. Lindstrom, the dean of the boarding school, invited us into her "home." Her home was a large brown building on the end of the campus, a building made out of large worried brown bricks that had the stately air of suitcases piled one on top of the other, suitcases left in the Gare St.-Lazare. The home of Dr. Lindstrom was like a recovery ward for me. The institutional buildings of the boys' house and the Manor House and even the Fine House all smelled of lonely children's urine—children from broken homes wept themselves to sleep in the dormitories. The Fine House—where I grew up—was an institutional little madhouse—a place where we slept in open dormitories—and went into the cloak rooms to smoke and show off our brassieres which none of us needed. But even the Swedish Pavillion—a small white dormitory that was supposed to be "cozy" for girls in the eighth, ninth and tenth grades—had that odd smell of cigarettes and the centuries of a child grieving—that odd grief that I knew all through my nine years of boarding school—where death was waking up each morning and still being in the same school—with housemothers and wet beds and rules and bells and hash to eat on Thursdays, fish on Fridays, chicken Sundays, tunafish on Mondays—every day of the earless eyeless senseless year, where the tongue had nothing good to taste, where the face was never kissed, the boarding school where I dreamed of getting out of that place—a prisoner's dream of being free. But Christmas was the time when Swedish Lindstrom—our beloved eccentric on horseback—who came from Stockholm and had a husband named Dr. Sasha who was a translator at the United Nations and a blonde daughter named Anya whose boyfriends always wore sneakers—Dr. Lindstrom whose large behind barely fitted into her riding pants where she went kaplop kaplop—whose fat legs barely fitted into her riding boots as she mounted her groaning horse Strawberry and rode around the campus with her blonde ringlets and her riding cap—charred brown bricks of her solid house seemed to be groaning at Christmas—as the wide doors were thrown open—the doors to candles, flowers, mysteries, thousands of watts of pure light—the pure and somewhat foreign world of straw Swedish angels and wooden plaques—and beets and anchovies and herring—the world of golden angels tooting little gold horns twirling around and around the golden disc where the energy of candlelight propelled them into the psalms of spurts of light—the open yellow world of Doctor Lindstrom's house—where her husband—Doctor Sasha—mosied amongst the hungry bratty students all pushing each other for cider and grog—saying "Skol" and "Merry Christmas" in his sad breasted Russian accent—himself the skeleton of some bygone time when everyone including him more than others wore a monocle. Was Doctor Sasha born with a monocle? I often wondered. There in the organpipe world of stars and straw horses and Swedish cookies and grog and wooden spoons and Sabbath and requiem—where the servants were all "volunteer" students in white aprons—everyone trying to bite into cookies and burning herring. Christmas was the time when the Swedish crackers crumbled in the weathercocks' molten mouths, when the children found the altars of oven-hot breads in Doctor Lindstrom's buffet tables, when the legends of Christmas all seemed to burn in our throats. But then—Misery. School would be over for the holidays and we—the orphans, the under and over privileged, the rich and the nouveau riche, the Arabs and Jews and South American and Chinese rowdies—the unwanted children from every corner of the earth's sad breast—were forced to go "home." Even if we had no homes.

I had no home.

My Russian grandparents were my caretakers. My grandfather and grandmother—Russian immigrants who had done nothing in life since they arrived in America except be pushy—had me. My grandfather had gone from plumbing into show business. He was an "angel" who invested in Broadway plays. He had white hair and looked Mongolian. My grandmother had black hair and sang sad Russian songs. She was a great lady. But I hated going to their home. No one really spoke English very well. My Aunt Polly was always drunk—secretly. She wore fox coats and spent a lot of time on sleep-over dates. My uncles were off at the war. One in

India. Another in Alaska. My two handsome uncles. I missed my Uncle Eddy–although he used to call me little poison, or poison brat, and had forgotten me.

I remember one Christmas–I was still in the Fine House–I must have been in the fifth grade. My father and mother–who were divorced and were truly devoted to insulting and hating each other–each sent Christmas presents to me to give to my teachers at boarding school. My father sent me a big package filled with manicure sets. Beautiful little objects of happiness–those manicure sets with shiny silver buffers and silver scissors and red alligator cases. I kept them. My father never gave me a Xmas present so I took all the teachers' presents and pretended they were mine. My mother also sent presents–not as nice as my father's–she couldn't afford fancy nail sets–but the whole idea behind the presents was that the teachers were "impressed by presents" from the parents. I kept all the presents. Those from my mother and those from my father–and was delighted with my Christmas haul. I threw away the phoney little notes written by my mother–"Dear Miss Morgan, thank you for all your kindness to my daughter in spelling" and other notes written in her loose handwriting that no one could decipher anyway. Going home on the train for Christmas I was painfully aware that there was no home to go to. Who met me at the train? Usually my grandmother. Or a maid. That year my mother came to the Grand Central train station–that little wheatfield of anxiety–where we all were deposited into our loving and unloving parents' arms. That particular Sabbath of the Christmas holiday I cheerfully moved out of the train, carrying my big satchel of clothes, and–stupidly–and not at all like a good detective–wearing the present my mother had sent to Poppy Morgan, the dance teacher. My mother had sent Poppy a kerchief made out of chamois cloth and bordered with a bright aqua color. On the chamois cloth were dancers–Cossacks–printed in bright red and blue and black. I had sat on the floor of the Fine House and opened the silver wrapping of the present–tearing off the ribbon–throwing in the waste-basket the little "thoughtful" note (my mother's thoughtfulness extended from smiles and nice words to thoughtful notes–she had a note for everything–birth–death–Christmas–Easter–Valen-tine's Day–my closet was still ringing from the clack clack of all the words in her notes which I saved in the back of my closet)– the kerchief! When I got off the train I came bobbing into Grand Central wearing the kerchief which I had forgotten to hide. My mother greeted me with a hard smack across my face. My two uncles, in war uniform, had come with my mother to the train. My uncle Eddy–the one who once loved me but now hated me backed my mother up–"the little brat" he mumbled in a whirling accent of glee–but my uncle Tony–his eyes burning like brandy–hugged me. "She didn't mean it" he said–holding his arms around me. Towering over me.

"The little thief," my mother said. "That was meant for her dancing teacher. Did you ever hear of a child keeping a present meant for a teacher–at Christmas?"

"Little poison. She's grown into a terrible brat," my Uncle Eddy–the one from India murmured–snapping the rims of his lips as he spoke–bursting with the silent center of a nasty egotist–ho ho we now hated each other. Uncle Tony the good held my hand in the taxi. We were going to go to Macy's where my mother had promised me a bicycle for Christmas–but in the taxi my mother announced that since I had stolen the kerchief there was not to be any Christmas present–and certainly no bicycle for me this year. We rode back to my ugly grandparents' ugly apartment where everything was old fashioned and colored maroon and brown. How I dreaded that place–where I would spend Christmas in the maid's room. The maid–a large dark woman from the south wearing always a bandanna and green felt bedroom slippers in the house–and huge high heels and girdles when she went out—used to spend an eternity getting in and out of her pink girdle whaled with white bones. The room after she left smelled of violet and quite violent cologne. And cheap talcum powder that was odious and odorous and reminded me of flour left in sugar.

At my grandparents' in the maid's room I would try to create a Christmas. My grandparents weren't really religious but out of spite became outraged at my Christianity—and denied me a glowing Christmas tree. I had to buy my own little miniature Christmas tree at Woolworth's which I put in my room. It glittered all silvery on the table. And I was so alone at Christmas. Forced to visit my mother and father from the base of my grandparents' dark cherry red and brown apartment. And so once below a time it was Christmas time and I would be accompanied by the sweaty sweet smelling maid Henrietta and would venture to my father's apartment in the Sheraton Hotel. There, lying like a fat walrus on a murphy bed, he looked at me and offered me candy. The big fat blubber of a man was always crying. He recited the catechism of his complaints and agonies. He was a wounded bear. I sat on a Hotel Sheraton rocking chair and rocked back and forth in astonishment of all his ills. He was almost blind. He was lonely. No one loved him. Ever since my mother left him he was sick. And miserable. Once he was a millionaire. Now he was poor. He was bankrupt. The war had ruined his building-material business, brick by brick. Why wasn't I a boy like my cousin Winston? What did I want to do with my life? Be a poet? That was hardly a profession where I would make any money. Why didn't I think of becoming a judge? They were the people with the power. What was I wearing? Why did my mother dress me in my aunt Polly's bloomers and clothes? Why was she so fucking cheap? Why didn't I wear nice clothes at least when I came to visit my father? Could I get him a Taryton? Could I turn the light on? I froze in the hotel room. My finder's keeper's loser's weeper's world was a nightmare. I was revolted and fascinated by my father at the same time. I loved him too much.

Visiting my mother at Christmas was also difficult. Her husband would scream "Get her out of the house Mae—I told you I don't want her sleeping over. She's nothing but trouble, the little brat." "She's my daughter and I want her sleeping on the Castro convertible. Why did I buy a Castro convertible if not for my daughter to sleep on it?" "I don't give a good flying fart if you bought a Castro convertible," my stepfather would say (I rather liked him). "She belongs with her grandparents. We have our own children." And off I would go on the endless subway which was a rocket of loneliness and filth—downtown—to be deposited back at my grandparents' lonely apartment building at 441 West End Avenue. Once below a time I hated Christmas in New York. I had no one to play with. I never talked to my grandparents. My mother was busy with her new family. She was always "going away for the weekend" with her husband, leaving the "babies" with her mother-in-law. My mother was on one long permanent weekend. My father was always about to "die." He lived to die. Oh don't die daddy please don't die and abandon me. Please, I will never be able to survive without you daddy—the hardship of the boarding school and grandparents' grotto of maroon and brown—and the maid's room with its little stink—and mother's apartment where there is never a toothbrush for me at the sink—all of these places will not be so bad as long as you're alive, dear beloved conglomerate of tears and loneliness. Don't die daddy. Please don't die and leave me alone.

"You're not the daughter I wanted," my father would say. "Why weren't you a son?" Summoning a child's voice from the webfoot stone of my stomach I would say "I love you pappa" and claw my way through the dark empty days of the Christmas holidays. The gong would ring. It was winter. And schooltime again. I was always glad to escape the shabby streets of

Manhattan, father's lonely hotel room, the crowded apartment uptown of my mother's family—or my granparents' West Side monument to show business—and arrive safe and sane back in the crazy wilderness of boarding school. The Fine House. The Athletic Field. Doctor Lindstrom on her horse Strawberry. Lying down in boarding school on the pillow of shabby little girl lonely tears I wept for the ceremony of Christmas that was supposed to be a miracle. But—for me—Christmas was always a time of disappointment, loneliness, and streets of snow quiet as a bone. What we didn't tell our teachers was the misery of our bad experiences. The sexual mysteries. At boarding school the sexual mysteries were carved in our minds. My mother had told me once, when cousin Les jumped on top of me in my grandparents' apartment, that he would like to take off my undershirt and pants. "Never let anyone do that to you" my mother would say. "Do what?" My mother looked at me. "Touch you." The way she said touch made me wonder—why not touch? Was I an untouchable? Unluckily for me Les did try to touch me. "Your father doesn't touch you, or does he?" she asked. Does that mean my father should not stride out of the bathroom in his shorts and hug me in his damp little mortal hotel room? "Does he sleep with you?" my mother asked, making my whole life even more mysterious. "When you visit him at his hotel—does he sleep in the same bed with you? Because you're too old to sleep with your father. Make sure he sleeps on the couch." My mother had told me when I was about nine about menstruation and intercourse. Without meaning to she made it sound like a monstrous set of bad things—bad blood—bad body—the duck-billed platypus penis was out to get us all. "No. No. I won't let anyone touch me."

At Cherry Lawn, in Fine House, all the girls lived in a dormitory. It was painted pink.

At Cherry Lawn in girls' quarters—there was one girl called Flora Roberts. She was called "Heart-throb" because she was in love with all the boys. I was called Tut-Tut because I was always looking in the mirror. Heart-throb told Tut-Tut one day that her boyfriend was—you won't believe it—holocaust of flesh and taste—Rufus—the chef in the kitchen. Rufus? He was one of the black men who stared hungrily at the little girls as they carried their trays in to the kitchen, passed through the counters to the big bowls of food to which we helped outselves. The only thing I knew about Flora Roberts was that she wasn't clean. Flora Roberts had brown streaked underpants. Flora Roberts had dirty underpants and that was that. I, on the other hand, was compulsively clean. I washed my face so often the teachers who were called our housemothers claimed I would wear out my skin.

Flora Roberts and Rufus once invited me into the dining room—and my date was James—the second chef. I was scared to death. I didn't like James—and I didn't like Rufus—and I really hated dirty Flora Roberts—but there was something exciting too about breaking the rules and "fraternizing" with the chefs. Tall and unhappy black men they were out to smile their great gold teeth. And to attack. They wanted to caress the little girls (us) in return for giving us Hershey bars and forbidden ice-cream. They had the key to the boarding school freezer. James played the bugle. This all took place in an empty dining room. Rufus banged on the piano. Open as the air to the naked shadow—I sang along during these music sessions that would end in sex sessions for Flora—and Rufus. Terribly excited—Rufus would get up from the piano and carry on with Flora in the cloak room where they would never get caught—since no one used the cloak room on Saturdays. Left alone with James—I began to get the jitters. As a child I wasn't at all sure of the sexual mysteries. Suddenly this large black man pressed me to him and put his huge lips down on mine. "Please don't do that James" I said—and he laughed a laugh as sad and as deep as the bugle that he played. Then I ran away—and he ran after me. After our "Kiss" I was too frightened to ever "pass" by James again in the kitchen. Since each child at the table of their designation was obliged to "wait" on tables–I knew that on my "day" to clear the dishes I would have to see James. I began paying other children "to wait on table" for me–so that I was not in the deadly kitchen for very long. I began to stop eating–or ask one of the other girls at the table to get my food for me. "I just don't feel like going in the kitchen." I would say without offering an explanation. But I would always be frightened to meet James–frightened to "bump" or "bunk" into him. Forgotten was the feeling of "liking" the kitchen help. Now–at nine–my attacker was one of the chef's assistants–tall black James–who was after me and would press his lips on me. I didn't tell anyone. I was petrified that James would kill me.

On vacation–a Thanksgiving vacation–when all the schools let out and we were dumped into the aimless existence of prisoners on bail–I was in New York City living with my aging and rather boring grandparents and being shuttled, as usual, between my father's hotel and my mother and her second family high up on Dyckman Street. In my father's hotel I asked my father for some candy. "Please can I have a box of candy to take back to school to one of my teachers?" I asked. "Since when do you give candy to your teachers" my father remarked. He was suspicious. But gave me the candy box–huge dark bonbons of chocolate with syrup and cherries bursting out of the chocolate baskets–back in boarding school I ran up to James when I saw him walking from the help's quarters and said "Here. Here is some candy. Take this. It's a gift. My father gave it to me. Take this candy and never come near me again. I'm not mad at you. And I hope you're not mad at me." I ran away. Later Rufus and James were fired. I was so happy when James left the campus. My attacker was gone.

That was the beginning of the sexual mystery. A frightening one. How did people become pregnant? I had it all wrong. I thought it was during your period. Someone had said "The only time you can't get pregnant is during your period" but I had thought it was the other way around ... The sexual mysteries of Cherry Lawn–the samba with Ned Blassberg–. Unluckily for life ... once upon a time ago the sexual mysteries got all confused in my head. Kitchen chefs attacking seven- and eight-year-old girls– the parents ignorant–the cool mortal gardens around the dormitories–and me with my large green eyes–crying for the world of social dancing and Blassberg boys doing the tangos–the war over–father blind in his hotel–mother busy in the country on her weekends in the leaves–me–walking by myself–trying to discover who I was–the mysteries of sex a heaven and a hell–large green eyes–the peasant body of a girl whose grandparents came from Russia Gebernia–whose grandparents came on cattle boats–whose grandmother–father's mother–was a janitor–whose grandfather– father's father–died in a poor house when the catering business didn't "pan out" and his wife–El Janitoress–kicked him down the stairs and out of the house sweeping him out like a large piece of dust–feh–and telling him never to come back. My father the middle boy. Always a little blind. The younger boy in school. The older boy on the road–far from the Puerto Ricans squashing seeds with ripe feet on the Lower East Side–one boy dying for lack of medicine–all boys undernourished–laundry hanging down in back of the house–a holocaust of laundry–and the streets of the Lower East Side spilling over with prayed-over flesh–the old women in aprons–the girls in tears–the apartments little graves for the children–who just wanted to get out of childhood–away from the herrings and boring radiators that thumped all night– away from the radios and the brooms and the ash cans and the aprons of emptiness and the nagging failed parents who never had the joy of life in the shape of their palm–and me–the child of a father who had wooed my mother in a Pierce-Arrow–my mother–a fairytale girl with curly hair and large blue eyes–finding herself moving out of Brooklyn–the thief of adolescence had robbed her of her books and now she was married to this odd man who spoke such bad English in the forgotten dark–and then me–a dangling participle that fit into no one's grammar–a she bird in the bright yolk of Riverdale and my mother finding me alone always reading the Bible–or playing theater with myself the audience and the performer–crying for a nurse–thoughtful of the nursie at the end of the house–childhood were you only all that? And mother talking always of the sexual mysteries–which led from Riverdale to my grandparents' house–(parents rest their pulse and divorce).

Oh for the sexual mysteries.

Cherry Lawn. School of perverted kitchen chefs. School of little girls too frightened to tell–all old memos to myself for the book of secrets, dreams, favorite things to do, bad habits. Sex was in the boys' quarters in the secret nights of Arkie Larkin sneaking off on the grass with Virginia Belle. Sex was Beverly Nomsen making love with James Manachotti near the lake and leaving a condom behind–a sperm-filled flower which grew luminous on the field of grass. Sex was Letty in the English classroom playing up to Mr. Wilbut. While Billy Holiday sang on our record players into our dreams. Sex was playing strip poker at the age of thirteen and everybody looking at ebony pubic hairs–the first hairs under arms and sex was shaving–constantly shaving–sex was the mystery.

There was no escape from our adrenal glands. No escape from menstruation. No escape from wanting to make love. I had no boyfriends. True–at nine I sambaed with Ned Blassberg in my new dress and won the samba contest.

Sexual Secrets Revealed

"It's like horseback riding" says Harriet Neuberg.

"Like sitting in the bath with running water" says Arlene Faks. My mother seeks to enlighten me. "Intercourse is a natural function of the human species"–talking about the patchwork quilt of vaginas, breasts, nipples, scrotums and hairs. I wonder if sex is funny. Will the arterial angel laugh at me? Is that possible?

I enter into my first two sexual disasters.

The first is with Edward Greenberg. The second is with James Brosnahan. They both center around *proms*. What is a prom? you ask–I glide back to the prom world. The prom is the great big sexual harvest at Cherry Lawn School. I experience "Junior Proms" in the lower school. My first evening dress is a long apple-green taffeta dress. A boy takes me to the prom. He is "assigned" to me by my housemother. I wear flowers. It is all innocent.

The upper-school prom–this is more serious. You have to be asked. Each one has to mate. To be invited. Boy must ask girl. The sex game. In the upper school I do not pet. Or kiss. Ergo I am not asked to the prom. As a freshman in the upper school I am the only girl who has no date for the prom. Neither does Wayne Rodgers. We are both considered intellectuals. Therefore we are mated to go to the prom.

The evening dress. I come to New York and go with my father's girlfriend to buy a long white and pink net evening dress. With net gloves. It is miraculous covering my breasts and stomach and thighs. All net and glowing. The study halls are decorated for the prom. Balloons hang over the lights. The bookshelves are covered. Waxy crystals are scattered on the floor.

Tara! To the prom are imported some strange boys from Mt. Vernon. Friends of one of the boys at school. I meet Edward Greenberg. It is the firstborn sexual moment of my life. Edward the Dark. Edward the mysterious. Who has a slight fuzz of moustache over his lip because he does not shave. Who has a dimple in his chin. Thin. Wearing a black suit. With slow slinking eyes that almost slant and brownish skin. He must be Russian too. Into the innocent world of the upper school that is not so innocent–is Edward. Tara! Tara!

"Who's your date?" he asks.

"Wayne Rodgers."

"Who's that?"

"A boy in my class. No one likes him. We are both smart and equally unpopular" I confess.

"Do you think we can sneak out? And go somewhere and talk?" *Yes.* We leave the Manor House. Take a long walk. I drink in the smell of Edward's foliage-scented cologne. We walk to the Fine House. We go up the stairs. We enter the empty dance studio on the top floor. Suddenly I am afraid. Edward kisses me. Ancient minutes chime in the cuckoo's mouth. Folly chatters in my teeth. A hand on my breasts. Edward's hands. He bites his nails. So do I sometimes. Kisses.

I snap.

This is paradise. Nothing more. We separate.

I see Edward in "the city." My father is now letting me live in his depressing hotel where there is no furniture. Edward visits. I never see him again. He remains a dark stranger. I dream about him.

And later. James Brosnahan. A blonde ringer brought to our boarding school for basketball. I am now a sophomore. He is a senior. He is from Queens. He is one of the five athletes brought to the school to play "ball" for the school. Everyone at Cherry Lawn is just a so-so athlete. We are all weak. The ringers are strong. They are "street" people in a fancy school. They stick to each other. They are the only interesting people on campus. My best friend, Dolly, goes with one of them. A tall giant with bulging eyes. A boy who is called George. Another ringer is Skip. He always laughs. Then there is James Brosnahan. Tough. Blonde with blonde eyebrows. They are always playing poker. James is Catholic. I am in love. He askes me to the prom. The prom again. But now with the most popular boy in school, captain of the basketball team. We take long walks after the prom to the lake.

Behind the lake he kisses me near a shack. I smell his smell. I feel something under his pants. I feel close to him. We have our secret bond. Nothing "serious" just a promise—a hand that is held. "You're my girl" he says. We go steady. Then—disaster strikes. James leaves Cherry Lawn to join the Navy. I am desolate. I cannot study. Another separation. I cry. Doctor Lindstrom asks me why I am always crying. I tell her that I love James who is no longer on the basketball team but in the Navy. He sends me a huge white satin pillow cover that says Sweetheart. During vacations he takes me to baseball games when we are both "on leave."

There was that time. That good time. Then James disappeared, and his letters stop. End of the sexual mystery for the time being.

But is it really the end? Does the sexual mystery ever stop? I want to take you to my side of truth. In the odd place of a woman's life—What is Helen to Ulysses? Simone Weil writes that the "art of war is the art of producing transformations"—I am forty years old. This morning I'm at war with everything.

Could there be a celebration with such loneliness? Loneliness for what? The mother never found? Or the father—dead. The flesh that was so close and now is strange. All the lovers now strangers. The husbands strangers too. I am Helen reborn. I am Eve. I am Joan of Arc. I am who I say I am. But who am I? I am a naked woman hardly yet suffered for. A girl of common thread. I summon a child's voice from my past. I lie in bed in this bedroom with white pillows and an orange chair where I seat myself. I lie down quiet as a bone. I am Kathy the coward. My younger daughter calls me from another room. I comfort her. She's having a bad dream.

I go back to my own bed. I hear—the boats of my childhood and the honk of the Staten Island ferry. I hear the morning waking. When I wake my key opens my door. My head opens. My life speaks. The clocks have funny tongues and I ring all the bells. The door opens and closes. And the years are only shells. I lie still in bed. I suffer my old wounds. I open myself to girlhood. To the drowned days when I obeyed what my mind said was the trembling flesh. Life passes so quickly. I lie still. I am born again. I celebrate myself. The bride I was—twicefold. The child I was. I celebrate myself as I used to be. In college when I melted my self down from Helen to a fumbling student new-born.

Bennington College. Specific courses are not required at Bennington. College passes in its own way. I meet all different girls at EdenSchool. Joan Slivotize—the human one. Sara—who is funny. Sara the jester. Specific courses are not required. Honey is beautiful with long blonde hair. Jane Tish is zany. Specific courses. Helen is artistic and French. Helen is the one I love best. Joanne is quiet. And mousey. Specific courses are not required. Lois has black hair and sculpts. All girls who join in the odd world of EdenSchool college. We study philosophy. The relevant works of Hume, Kant, Schopenhauer, Nietzsche and Sartre. Open to first- and second-year students.

Philosophy and Film. Specific courses are not required at Eden-School. This course will introduce students to theory of film. To some methods of interpreting film. A number of papers will be required.

South American Indian Ethnology. A survey of the native South Americans, with a particular focus on tribal societies from a variety of theoretical perspectives.

Courses. I live in Stokes house. Specific courses are not required. I write. I "go out" with Williams boys. I talk to my friends. I act. I paint. I discover a lot of things. Teachers that I have crushes on: Howard Nemerov. Danny Shapiro. Long walks. I hate the boys' schools. Frightened of winter carnivals. Don't want to make love. Helen talks constantly about sex. So does Joanne. Linda Kesselman my best friend. Visit her in Boston. Write papers on Proust. Wallace Fowlie and Ben Belitt ascetic teachers. Time passes in the slow slipshod way. I think I have forever to live. But I don't. Graduation. Paris. Marriage. Divorce. Affairs. Poets. Novelists. All of this is in front of me.

Forty Years Old

Good evening life. I have led a woman's life. It has been speeding ahead at many miles an hour. How many miles an hour? Forty. Sometimes sixty. I have met many interesting people. Stravinsky. Sartre. Picasso. W. S. Merwin. Robert Lowell. Saul Bellow. Philip Roth. Miguel Arerola. Rene Leibowitz. Thousands of women. Millions of women. My best friends are women. Suddenly I am forty years old. Lives have been shed. Husbands have been shed. Friends have been shed. I have worn many shoes. Many stockings. Many pairs of supphose. Thousands of tears. Thousands of Tampax. Many hours of soul-flinching. Loving life. In contact with force. Many lunches. Many memorable afternoons. Years and Paris. Years and Hong Kong. Junks. Many junks in Hong Kong Harbor. Long sails in the Bay of Sai Kung. Picnics at Lantao Island. Sails into the New Territories. Buying flowers in Hong Kong. Jade. Visits to Macao. The children of Hong Kong play in the street. I sit in my house on the Peak waiting for my husband to come home. I write. I ride the tram. Poetry is published. Brush drawings. I have visions in the markets of Kowloon. I wander into the sitting rooms of Chinese families. Eat oranges in the courtyards of refugee housing blocks. See war-lords, bankers, courtesans, emperors, merchants, princesses, impersonators, peacocks as a spectator at the refugee theatres in Kowloon. And return to American hugging my jar of orange kumquats.

One winter when it snows a lot I am divorced again. This is where my new life begins. I find through pain and suffering if I am fit to survive. I find that I have two children—both girls. They have blonde hair. Both of them look like redcheeked tomboys. A lot of bills. No husband. A baby nurse. And a will to survive. I come into my own. Why am I forty years old? I am a refugee from childhood. I have constructed an enormous tent in which I live. I create performances. They are called dates. And dinner parties.

I am living in the odd tent of my own secrets. I lie awake at night and on the ceiling my whole life is, in a shadow play, revealed to me again and again. I remember my life. I remember the divorce of my parents. I remember boarding school. I remember Bennington. I remember non-resident terms. I remember my first husband in Paris. I remember poverty. Affairs. Green and white cafe cups of coffee. I remember Greece. Chios. I remember returning to America. Divorce. An affair with a poet. Another affair with another poet. Tired of poets. My father's death. Writing some books. Marrying again. Going to Hong Kong. Returning with my second husband. Giving birth—the miracle of birth. The enormous tent of memory. It's warm in here. I live in a world of feathers and memory. I hug my plump children. I'm panicked by age. One morning I wake up and I am forty years old.

> Oh Helen—mommy—daddy—uncle Eddy—
> Intricate womanhood.

> Shear sleep. And sleep. I shear
> My life and childhood in my sleep.

Hong Kong. Explosion of sweat.
He was racing for his life's sake.
Riding the horse as dangerous as a wolf.
The crowd in the Hong Kong Race Track stood on their feet.

All of the women had stopped being bored and eating their melon. The men were screaming.

Michael! Michael—

Almost all of the people spoke English at this British Crown Colony Race Track.

Some spoke only Chinese

Around the bend. Sweat pouring out of his nose, his eyes and down his face. Under his arms the silks were sticking to his bone. He kicked his feet into the horse's belly. Riding for a prize that never matters.

Riding for his life's sake.

Out front.

A winner.

Hong Kong.

Squatters' shacks made out of tin roofs on a hill.

Water thrown out in a tin bucket.

Hong Kong. The China Sea. The sampans bobbing up and down and scuttling like small straw mice across a blue floor. The shops in the harbor quiet as whales.

The English Consul General and the American Consul General and all the other consul generals asleep in their beds. Clean sheets.

Hong Kong. Island of loneliness and power. White new buildings shine in the sun. Across the bay on the Peak Sun Tong, a tailor, rides on his motor bike delivering dresses—the early morning tailor.

Amahs in black pants and black shirts and cotton black shoes carrying fruit on their back as they trudge up the Peak like mules. Mulberry trees. Frozen flowers. The flame trees upon the hills. Conduit road. Pollock's Path. The China Sea so blue as you climb the Peak.

"What do you expect?" Mae took the dishes off the table. Her only delight was being with her husband before the servants woke up. She hated servants.

"I'm getting tired of Hong Kong" Mae complained. "We can't even see the Oscar Awards here."

"I know. We'll go back to the States soon. I just have to finish a two-year contract and we'll do whatever you want darling."

Peter was dressed. Kissed Mae goodbye. And as he drove his blue Jaguar down the Peak to his office waved to Michael who was jogging past the hospital and Peak Road.

"Sw-eet guy" Peter said to himself as he drove on.

*

Michael rode his own horse at the Hong Kong Race Track. Dressed in his colors–green and blue–he was dark and handsome in an Irish sort of way. His hero had always been the Pan American jockey–Braulia Baeza–nicknamed Buddha on Horseback. Baeza actually looked like a Buddha. Michael had traveled to Cambodia and seen in Angkor a stone Buddha that really was Baeza.

Because he spoke Spanish Michael had become friendly with Baeza when he was riding in the States. Baeza's father had been a jockey in Panama and his father before him. Michael wanted to be a jockey since he was a kid. Now he was riding in his favorite track–

Galloping past people, hunched and galloping, riding for his life's sake, as he rode he tried not to think of anything but winning, of the horse–which became part of his body. Sometimes he had slept with the horses in the stables, sleeping beside his horse like a quiet spoon. When he woke from dreams he would groan and nuzzle against the nose of his own horse and go back to sleep. Mornings would bring sunlight and he'd walk home only to go back to the stables later. He rode for his life's sake.

And won.

This was his last race.

Michael had made up his mind to be a student. To be a student of the great books.

When he took his saddle off his horse it was for the last time. He went to the locker room. Joked around with the other jockeys. Most of them were Chinese. Some were Spanish. Then he left the locker room and had a drink with the Toles.

Went home to the Peak.

Packed his bags.

And left for a vacation.

He had friends to see. Odd people he had known. Slept with. His father. His father wanted to see him. And then? Back to Lantao Island.

He wished he wasn't alone.

"But I'm a crazy son of a bitch?" he said to himself. "Who would love me?"

Sounds of hooves, water beating against the ferries, the sound of Chinese—all of this sounded in his ears. He was leaving the place he loved. He'd be back.

Alone.

Or perhaps not alone.

Something inside him told him he was going to find someone to bring back with him to Lantao Island.

He felt happy as he took the ferry to the airport. Tomorrow seemed easy. Everything was possible. He was a jockey priest—a mystic rabbi with an enormous imagination and a great desire to love someone. Anyone. He knew he would meet someone in the not too distant future. He had to. He couldn't stand not being loved—the explosion of loneliness—for too much longer. He grew curious. Who would she be? Did he know her? Would he meet her—in a crowd? At a party? Through an introduction? He laughed. The ferry stopped.

He was leaving. He felt strong enough to face anything. And he knew he would miss riding for his life's sake.

But there was a time in your life, he thought, when there was no more winning.

Just living.

Living was winning.

The Zone of Light Ends at Six Hundred Feet

Katherine Jaksforth studied this fact carefully in her notes. She was studying the sea that summer—a hot summer late in nineteen seventy-two when she and Mr. Jaksforth and their two children as well as one governess lived in a summer house in Ossining. The house was large and white and spread over the lawn where giant peonies and begonias bloomed. They were cared for by a gardener called Annuciada—a huge gnarled man from Palermo whose face was covered by wrinkles that grew like weeds around his lips. Katherine was trying to write her summer poems. Studying the zones of the sea she realized suddenly that she was living in the *Zone of Perpetual Darkness* herself. Suddenly in Westchester she would wake in a cold sweat. Lying next to her would be Mr. Jaksforth breathing evenly—sleeping in his jockey shorts. They were not making love that summer. At first Katherine had tried to "understand" the problem. They had talked about it. "I just don't feel like it" Mr. Jaksforth would say. "You don't feel like it? You mean the rest of my life I'm supposed to remain a nun because you don't feel like it?" Mr. Jaksforth was not a complex person until one got really down into the realm of perpetual darkness. Then Katherine knew something odd happened. Was it that his mother had over-smothered him in Bangor, Maine where he had grown up hating his normal childhood? Had he become

an emotional cripple at college? Somewhere a kraken of distur-
bance had crawled around inside Mr. Jaksforth. Katherine had
read that "no adult crocodile should be kept in a room." Mr.
Jaksforth was that adult crocodile. He was obsessed by jogging
but once in the bedroom he withdrew completely. No touching.
No kissing. Every night that summer in Westchester they went to
sleep in silence. She often suggested that he see a doctor about the
"problem."

"It's not a problem. I don't want to discuss it."

"It's very rejecting. To have a husband that just isn't *interested*
any more in you as a woman. I feel like a widow. I mean as far as
I'm concerned you're dead to me and I'm dead to you. You don't
even notice me. I still love you very much. I wish you'd be more
supportive."

"Why do you have to use words like 'supportive' all the time?
So what if I'm withdrawn? Does everyone have to be outgoing?"

"No. I respect your privacy. But I'm alone in the country with
the children all day. I read. And write. But I wait for you to come
home so I can talk to you and just love you. I don't think we're
friends any more."

"Were we ever?"

"I thought so. When we met in Asia I loved you very much."

"That was Asia."

"I think we should talk it over with someone else if we can't
talk it over with ourselves."

"I have to go. I'll talk to you later."

"Don't you have anything more than that to say?"

"Yes. I think you should learn how to drive."

*

That was Westchester.
Loving was over. Making love, once basic to her life, was over.

Katherine would lie in bed with her husband. She would listen to the crickets. Cold sweat would pour down her face and she would close her eyes. Slowly the memory of another summer would come back to her. She would be sleeping once more with Romano. Romano Erba. Katherine would say his name before sleep and he would swim back into her memory. She had met him after her first divorce when she was in her early twenties. She had been a school teacher then–teaching poetry and mathematics in a private school in New York. She had saved her teaching salary and spent the summers traveling around Europe. In London she had met a young Italian girl on the subway who had taken her to a discotheque where young Italians met at night and danced and wriggled like worms in a jar. She loved to dance and suddenly found herself with a blonde, suntanned boy who didn't speak English. They spoke in French–his French was better than her Italian. He walked her back to her hotel. He told her how he had come to London for a holiday–to spend the summer. He was studying architecture at the University of Milano and lived with his family in Milano. They were very strict Catholics–and he could barely stand being home, but he had no choice until college was over. She remembered that she was moving the next day to an apartment and he said he would come and help her. He carried all her suitcases the next day and after he helped her carry the suitcases up the stairs she asked him simply if he would like to spend the rest of the summer with her. He was earning some money working as a dishwasher in an Italian restaurant. He said yes.

She remembered making love with him.

They would drink some red wine and lie on a large shaggy white rug in the living room, listening to classical music. She would let her long hair loose and he would play with her hair and rub his hands–which had callouses and felt very strong–over her body. It felt good. She would play with him until he started kissing her, and then he would carry her to the bedroom and they would laugh until suddenly he threw her on the bed and suddenly he was inside of her. Romano. In the kingdom of lust where loving was not getting even.

He would kiss her so many times and she could still remember the smell of both of their bodies. The moisture that came out of her legs. The smell under his arms. His teeth were straight and very white and he always laughed. She remembered his laughter. His smooth skin that seemed very burned by the sun. A blonde Italian boy with large blue eyes and rough hands.

Romano Romano. Was that the only happiness she would ever know? A candle lit by the bed. His body on top of hers and hers in his, rolling together. Making love on white wash-and-wear sheets. Making love against the wall. Making love by the moment and hour and never wanting to leave that room. The feathers of the pillow heightening her body. Who are you? Who are you? And he would say his name over and over again. Romano. Her soul wandered, happy, sad, unending. In the moist night, love made quickly, love made slowly. She remembered Romano in her mouth. His kisses all over her body. Until she would laugh and say "Enough—I'm exhausted and can't any more—" and they would make love one more time. He came in her body—her body totally open to him—slender and silent. She remembered him in Westchester with her soul clenched like a fist. She would touch him again—but he was lost to her now. Where was he? Somewhere in Canada. Married. Perhaps he also had children. Romano—how could I lose you? Once, when she had smoked hashish for the first time, she had relived the two summers that she spent with Romano in one moment. Now she lay in Westchester her marriage bed—remembering him—trying to touch him against her body—trying to be him and her at the same time. The salt poured over her face. She would never find him again.

Mr. Jaksforth lay sleeping next to her, cold as stone. He was a stone. His face was a stone. His hands were stone. Stones in the bedroom. Cinnabar and stone. This was a kind of death. To lie in bed at night and remember Romano. His eyes. Romano. Romano. You occupy everything. You occupy everything. Romano. Swim back to me. Lost fish. Swim back to me.

She remembered that summer closing her eyes. But never being able to find Romano. Not in Westchester. Where all night the crickets continued to make noise on the lawn. She would listen to them and think how one kingdom was made to witness another.

THE COMPANY

The Company

After she parted from Mr. Jaksforth, Katherine assumed her
single name, Kahn, and took the children and went to live in an
apartment on the West Side–a much cheaper apartment. It was
the kind of place that smelt of janitor's dogs in the hallways. The
main elevator was always broken. And the tired Costa Rican
elevator man who ran the service elevator could never remember
her floor. The apartment was nicer than she had expected. The
windows looked out on Amsterdam Avenue. The shopping was
good. Between Amsterdam and Columbus were so many stores
filled with pyramids of oranges, lemons, apples and persimmons–
mounds of rinds in bright orange and bright yellow and red
fruit–she often felt in some odd way that she would like to open
a grocery store. She yearned to spend the entire day amongst the
lettuce leaves, the cauliflowers, the great red cabbages whose heads
were ripe for a salad, the carrots and their ferny tops, the runny
beets that bled all over your fingers, to spend a lifetime amongst
the vegetables and fruits was preferable to the erratic places where
she must look for a job. "I am an earthworm" she wanted to
shout as she traveled down winter streets. Job hunting.

Katherine Kahn's feelings about the divorce were mixed. She
was relieved and desperate at the same time. She had met Mr.
Jaksforth in Hong Kong. She had been traveling with her dear
friend, Jane Tow, a Chinese painter married to an executive who

worked for the Esso Coporation which soon became Exxon Corporation. She and Jane had taken a summer off to look at scrolls, meet painters, and explore the places of the Orient where neither of them had been. At that time she was teaching poetry at Fordham University and doing some writing. Verse had been published under her maiden name—most of it verse about the sea—and had caused some little attention. Her father had died leaving her more money than she knew what to do with—and so she had put it all in the bank and continued living modestly in an apartment near the University.

Traveling with Jane had been the highlight of Katherine's life. For the first time she had seen the world as a child—each morning was another panorama of new things. New faces. Temples. Stores. One morning waking up in San Francisco, the next in Tokyo, the next in Kyoto. She had eaten noodles in tiny Japanese restaurants in the mountains and felt for the first time in her life the sense of freedom that money can give. Noodles and freedom. Katherine and Jane visited many Japanese temples, collecting the temple-stamps, and eating in the temples on the red felt table cloths the Buddhist foods. In Hong Kong Jane and she stayed at the Mandarin Hotel. It had all been a dream but a miraculous dream. Jane was not talkative but spoke slowly. They had long talks at night about aesthetics. In her whole life she had never talked with anyone about aesthetics. She had never been able to say to her first husband—who she married at nineteen—"Isn't this beautiful?" He had no interest in beauty. He had been an American bowling ball salesman who represented bowling balls in Europe. The whole thing had been a mistake. She had taken his crumbs of love at the altar, grateful to escape from America—and possibly from her parents. "Bowled over" she had been more or less grateful to escape from the responsibility of being a writer. She had been a writer at Bennington—winning the Silo Magazine award—and publishing poems in little magazines when she was sixteen—but the "responsibility" of writing terrified her. She could never take her place with the "great" writers—"so why bother?" she thought. For nine years she had led a quiet life in France keeping house for her husband as he took his bowling balls over Europe and opened up bigger and better bowling alleys. After such fighting as the weakest know, after bickers and headcolds and a slight nervous breakdown, she had come home to America to go into analysis, live with her father who was now living on Park Avenue and still—as always—needed company—and take her doctorate at Columbia.

Columbia Graduate School had proved to be unbearable and dull. After all of that she had lived alone, continued writing, and started teaching. She had met Jane at an art opening. They had become art buddies. Kathy recognized that Jane was neither competitive or overly friendly—she was a perfect companion— almost like a huge cat—and they would often have Chinese tea together and talk about writing, mantras, and stupas, about the history of China, about silk, about jade, about history, about so many things. Kathy would read Jane her poetry. Jane would show Kathy her abstract orange and black paintings.

And then they had decided on the trip. They had planned it for a year. Jane's husband was in favor of Jane being "independent of him" and Kathy admired Jane's desire to broaden her outlook on bones and paintings and blood ties—and they both mapped out on the huge atlas that was so mysterious their trip. Kathy felt again like a wild and curious child involved in the ceremony of planning a party. For the trip had been just that—a longitudinal visual party—with Buddhas, and scrolls, and mountains, and seas— a sinew of paradise. And it was in Hong Kong that she had met Mr. Jaksforth.

They had met at a dinner party. Kathy had been given an introduction by a friend, Mu Yhap, to a Susan Chew in Hong Kong. Susan had turned out to have once worked for Time-Life magazine and was now running the *Reader's Digest* in Hong Kong. A member of the foreign correspondents club—she seemed to know everyone—she sped around downtown Kowloon and Hong Kong and up at the Peak and around the New Territories showing Kathy the sights in her red MG. It turned out that Kathy knew quite a few people in Hong Kong. Her best friend Alexandra had a cousin called Justine—who was almost a look-alike. Kathy met Justine while going up the elevator of the Hong Kong Hilton. Justine was wandering around in a straw hat and Kathy recognized her as Alexandra's cousin. Justine introduced Kathy to Judy—a young American girl who was from Connecticut and had worked for a literary magazine in New York—and all three of them went to parties with good-looking young Aus-tralian bankers who all had words like "super" as part of their ho-hum vocabulary, and who all tooted around Hong Kong in small foreign cars as they traveled back and forth from the Hilton to the Peninsular to the Mandarin. They all played tennis.

Kathy did not particularly like the Australian gentlemen. They were all "limited" and did not seem in any way to be "supportive" to the person they were dating. They all seemed as mindless as koala bears and terribly proper. But they were fun. The truth was—Kathy managed to tell this truth to Susan as they walked on the beach—she had been very much in love for the only time in her life—with a married Borscht Belt comedian whose name she would not reveal to Susan. It might be considered off-beat by some to go as far as Hong Kong or the black hole of Calcutta to get over a Borscht Belt comedian but that was truly one of her intentions on the trip.

Susan seemed to Kathy to be a nice unfocused girl. She struck Kathy as one of the young Chinese swingers—who was a dilettante. She had no particular respect for the jet-setty Hong Kong girls and Susan, who lived with a boring and limited journalist, seemed to be the very kind of person she would have avoided in New York. But she was in Hong Kong. And Jane Tow was spending a lot of time with her family and Kathy, not knowing anyone, was at the mercy for once of anyone who would be kind to her. And for what calculated reasons she wasn't sure, Susan was "nice" to her. She offered to make a party in Kathy's honor, which was where she met Mr. Jaksforth. Kathy had expected the party to be made up of Chinese people. Instead the entire dinner congregation was of Americans who worked for the American Embassy. Either Susan had no other Chinese friends—perhaps she was too sophisticated—or she was "showing off" her new friend from New York—but that evening Kathy met Mr. Jaksforth. He was her dinner partner.

Her marriage to Mr. Jaksforth came as a great surprise to the Hong Kong community. Mr. Jaksforth, a handsome bearded New England gentleman with fiery red hair, was attached to the Embassy as a special diplomat. He drove a Rolls-Royce convertible. He had a Chinese servant called Lee and lived in an elegant apartment in Kowloon. He confessed that he dated rather skinny young Chinese girls from rich families whose clothes all came from Christian Dior in huge gray shiny sad boxes which were immediately welcomed in Hong Kong. One of his dates had been a young Chinese girl from a wealthy family who married a water skier in a water-ski ceremony. Mr. Jaksforth was quiet. Diplomatic. Funny. Well groomed. Well educated. And weltering in his own inability to do very much with his life. He seemed to be the kind of man who was continuously taking *Contacts* for sinus and consequently seemed always a little bit sleepy. What attracted Kathy to Mr. Jaksforth were his qualities of thoughtfulness, modesty, and a certain malicious normalcy that Kathy found most appealing. Her first husband was an eccentric, her recent lover a terribly neurotic narcissist bordering on being a psychopath—Mr. Jaksforth did seem to be a good man. "Is it ideal to marry a man as charming as Mr. Jaksforth and leave America and settle down in Hong Kong where no one knows me and I can build an orderly solid life?" Such thoughts ran through Katherine Kahn's head.

One person almost deterred her from that marriage. A certain Mike O'Neil whose father was a famous broadcaster. Mike worked as a jockey–he was a playboy–and seemed to have a bad-boy Irish quality about him that Kathy enjoyed. She went out dancing with Mike O'Neil and was almost in love with him. But Mr. Jaksforth seemed so much more "reliable" and the thought of bouncing all over Europe with a bowling ball salesman and then going from one race track in the Orient to another with a jockey–it didn't seem to make much sense. She really preferred–sexually speaking–Mike O'Neil. He brought out that maternal quality in Kathy which often becomes sexualized and she fantasized making love with him although she never did. Instead she gave in and had lunches with Mr. Jaksforth; later she married him. She went back to teaching at Fordham where Mr. Jaksforth reached her by long-distance telephone on a cold winter morning and proposed. She accepted. They were married in a month. Mr. Jaksforth flew to America on a special government permit and married Kathy Kahn in an Ethical Culture Ceremony and they both returned to Hong Kong. Kathy spent many curious afternoons going to consulate functions and diplomatic teas. She studied Tai Chi Chuan. She studied needlepoint. She collected the work of Cheung Yee–a Chinese sculptor who lived in the New Territories. And she behaved as "normally" as possible.

She had two children. Girls. They were the high point of her marriage. She invented normalcy as a romance.

One day Mr. Jaksforth and she moved back to America. They moved to a large apartment on the East Side and Mr. Jaksforth went into public relations. Kathy was terribly disappointed. She hoped he would do something interesting. Join the peace movement. Work for consumers' rights or the civil defense league. He had pretended to be political when he courted Kathy. But he was more materialistic then ever Kathy had imagined. He counted the cost of everything. All of his friends had a lot of money. He was terribly impressed when Kathy invited Norman Mailer to dinner. "Why are you only impressed with Norman Mailer?" she asked him. "How about my other friends who aren't famous but that I love?"

"Norman is special," Mr. Jaksforth said with a grin. They both had enjoyed talking about the Marines. Mr. Jaksforth's favorite time had been when he was in the Marines. He was often caught saying "My favorite time in my life was in the Marines." Was that a clue?

Kathy began to feel uncomfortable with him. She disliked Mr. Jaksforth's insulting sly remarks. His smell. Most of all his silences and his ability to disturb her by ignoring her. His favorite trick was to only pay attention to "the children" and to her through them. When he married her he had said, "I love you Kathy because when you come in a room everything lights up. You're *fabulous*. You're so creative." Now he only said, "If you weren't so creative and did a little more to make my life pleasant, everything would be good between us again."

Mr. Jaksforth, as it turned out, spent all of Kathy's money. She watched the figures in her little blue savings book go down slowly like mercury in a thermometer. What did he spend the money on? That was questionable. One theory that Kathy had was that he was building a bank account in Switzerland. Another was that he was investing the money in certain poker games where he did not come out the winner. Perhaps he just spent it on nothing. He worked now for a Japanese public relations firm. He was not really interested in making money for the Japanese. He began spending all his time with the children. Now he never talked to Kathy except through the medium of the children. He combed his red beard over the sink. She saw small curly red hairs on the porcelain.

So she left him.

Mr. Jaksforth retaliated by moving to Ethiopia. He wanted the girls. He wanted visitation rights. He wanted money for the apartment. (Kathy had bought their coop apartment and put it in both of their names.) And so Mr. Jaksforth, sure that Kathy could not support herself, said, one winter morning—"I'm going to fix it so you can never buy flowers or books again."

What he meant was—if Kathy wanted the children—she would have to bring them up and pay for them. All of his training as a diplomat went into insuring a settlement in which Kathy received two hundred dollars a month ... he had quit his job as a public relations consultant during the divorce proceedings so that the judge would rule that since Kathy had some income she was responsible for the upbringing of the children. From Ethiopia—where Mr. Jaksforth went into oil development—a lot of presents arrived for the girls. And no money.

And so it was around the time of her fortieth birthday that Kathy moved into a West Side apartment and began looking for something to do to support the children, and begin all over again—a life—an identity—to try and make a career-change at forty was depressing.

A few months later she was even more desperate. Nothing had come along. Money was tight. A career must be found, she said to herself. But what could she do? Nothing. Career opportunities? What were they?

"You're a scoundrel," Mailer had said to Kathy. "No, not a scoundrel—a wastrel."

"Why do you say that?" she had asked.

"Because you have all this talent and you throw it away—you don't use it—"

"I need a job. Something to do to make some money. Not every writer gets paid a fortune for what they write. Besides, my work isn't selling. No one is interested in stream of consciousness poetry."

Mailer sat in his usual vest and crumpled shirt. He squinted—smiled—drank gin and tonic. He was wearing a velvet suit. Once, when she gave birth, it had occurred to her how marvelous it would be to have Norman Mailer as a godfather. She had befriended his daughter, Susan, who now lived in Mexico and it seemed that if *she* could have picked a godfather—she would have wanted him to be—the greatest and most impossible writer there was. Mailer had agreed and had sent a gold cup with lines from her poems to her daughter. He had often come to visit and taught the girls how to box. Now, describing himself as a "bad-weather friend" he was sitting in the living room sympathizing and offering his advice.

"I would get an office if I were you. And just start writing again. Tell your secrets. Write another book of your poetry. Sell the poems to magazines." But she was unable to write anything.

Mailer had been a good-weather and bad-weather friend. His favorite expression, which he borrowed from Voltaire, was once a philosopher twice a pervert. She had changed it to once a philosopher—twice a poet. What did all these things mean? She had dinner to get on the table for the girls. She had a lot of bills. She had a slight gift for writing verse which she could not turn into a living. She had a baby-nurse who quit. She had only fair-weather friends—and most of them were couples who were friends of Mr. Jaksforth's. She had a body that was falling apart. She had bags falling over her eyes. Yes, she was interested in politics. Yes, against Mr. Jaksforth's will she had run as a delegate for Shirley Chisholm. Yes she believed in career opportunities for women. No. She had absolutely no talent.

Her friends from Bennington consoled her. Elizabeth King, who lived in Palm Beach, was a widow. She was taking the "I.U.D.'s" for law school. Kathy detested lawyers. Was it because Mr. Jaksforth had been a lawyer and had managed to turn his Harvard Law School training into foxing her out of child support? Most of the law was so filled with the helium of power.

These were the power brokers–the power peddlers. They were usually people with divided souls. No the law didn't interest her.

What else was there?

Dance? Don't be ridiculous, she told her friend Mary who lived in Ossining. At forty it was impossible to make a career as a dancer. How about a dance therapist? Therapy yes, but dance wasn't her specialty.

Through a friend, Jacob Felcher, she had become interested during her marriage in psychotherapy. It had occurred to her that if she ever took the girls and left Mr. Jaksforth–she would need something to do. Jacob had been a screen writer and had actually conceived and been the main writer for *Yellow Submarine*. Then he had gone into therapy. So she had investigated, the way you investigate the medicine cabinet–the different schools for psychotherapy in New York. What it came down to–was that to become a psychoanalyst took about fourteen years–just for the training. By the time she would be ready to practice she would be a geriatric case. Jacob had suggested the APA–the American Psychological Association, as a place to train.

Soon after the divorce Kathy investigated the possibility of a career as a *psychotherapist*. She had heard that the easiest institute to enter was the N.Y.C.P.A.–the New York City Psychological Association. To enter you first had to have an interview with a Doctor Kaufman. You had to get past her to be "admitted." Doctor Kaufman was a fat flabby woman who was obviously self-centered, narcissistic, opinionated, obnoxious, and consumed by her own importance. And she was the doctor who interviewed for the New York City Psychological Association.

Doctor Kaufman had a charmless apartment on the Upper East Side. It was filled with plants and reproductions of Klee. It had need of a good cleaning. Kathy went there for her interview. She sat in the office. She noticed that Mrs. Kaufman had a mean little face, bloated and pockmarked, that her hair hadn't been washed, and that she had fat ankles.

Dr. Kaufman looked with hostility at Kathy. It was as if she *owned* all of psychoanalysis. "Why do you want to be a therapist?" she asked Kathy at the beginning of the interview.

"I would like to have a career in which I would come in contact with people," Kathy said. It was disconcerting to have to be a computer and spit out the "right answers"—it was a heady feeling to think of answering "because my grandmother was a hippopotamus long ago in Egypt and this is my destiny"—but she decided there was no point in ruining her career—or possible career—because of Dr. Kaufman. Dr. Kaufman jotted down the information given to her carefully on a lined notebook. She stared at the flabby little hands.

"Also—say that I want to help the troubled," Kathy added to her answer. Dr. Kaufman looked questioningly at her. She smirked at the word "troubled."

"Are you in any kind of trouble yourself?" Mrs. Kaufman asked—a cruel grin stretching across her mouth like a slash. She had tartar on her teeth.

"Yes and no. I've just gotten a divorce. And I have two children to support. I was trained as a writer. But I have never had a career. I've published some verse. Nothing very important."

"You were trained as a writer? Then why do you want to be a therapist?"

"I want to help others to make a living. I was also trained as an abstract painter. And a musician. I played the gun, when I graduated, in one of Henry Brandt's symphonies. When I graduated from college I could shoot and drip. Then I got married. My husband was a salesman. We lived in Europe. What does this have to do with anything?"

"What kind of salesman?"

"Bowling balls. Bowling alleys."

Dr. Kaufman wrote this down. "And then?" she asked. Poised to write.

"I came back to America. I was used to living in Paris. I had to relocate myself in New York. I lived with my father–that was when he was still alive–and I studied literature at Columbia Graduate School. I never got my doctorate. I taught for a while at Fordham and then I took a trip to Asia."

"Why did you go to Asia?" Dr. Kaufman asked in a monotone, repressing but not quite, her actual hatred of Asia.

"To study Buddhist scrolls. Just to look at things. It was there that I met my second husband–Mr. Jaksforth. We were married. We had two children and we moved back to America. I took my job as a mother seriously. My children are now in school. I would like to do something with my life."

"What is your relationship with your children?"

"I love them. We are affectionate. I would say it was a good relationship."

"And your relationship with your mother?"

"Good. I visit her almost every other Sunday."

"Are you interested in feminism?"

"Yes, I am."

"Do you realize that many feminists have unjustly accused Freud as a male chauvinist? Do you realize that the essence of feminism is to discount Freud?"

"That's ridiculous," Kathy said.

Dr. Kaufman was now able to get into her true subject.

"Paradoxically enough the great *conquistador* of the subjective world, Sigmund Freud is the one psychological thinker whose work leads us back to the actual social base of the psyche. The root is however fissured, the historical splitting between body and society, out of which the mentality is generated–this appears as a profound grasp of paradox and contradiction, the sense that what is truest in men and women is the irreconcilable conflict between desire and civilization. But this sits ill with the needs of many modern feminist therapists who chafe under the limits that he has set." Dr. Kaufman was breathing heavily. Her hands quivered.

"I don't know anything about this. I am not chafing. I am applying to your institute to learn something."

"But it seems to be apparent that you do not have the personality of a psychotherapist."

"How can you say that? You bitch. You have no right to judge me because I am applying to your school!"

"When you start using language like *that* it is apparent that you are not an adequate candidate."

"Listen. I've been to your school. Any moron can enter if they have a master's degree. I have attended and audited classes and I am sure that I am qualified to enter."

"Not in my opinion," said Dr. Kaufman. She got up, indicating that the interview was over.

"Wait a moment," said Kathy. She stood up in Dr. Kaufman's office.

It was apparent that Dr. Kaufman expected her to hit her. She ducked. "Get out of my office," she shouted.

"Please. Listen to me. This interview has gone all wrong. I simply want to see if I am qualified to be a therapist."

"You are a potential revolutionary. This means that you do not have the personality of a therapist," said Dr. Kaufman still crouching.

"But you are accusing me of something that isn't true—I am able to tackle a great range of subjects—Freudian, neo-Freudian, post-Freudian—or human potential—behavioristic, Langian, relationships between psychoanalysis and Marxism—the fate of individual intimacy in industrial society—the conduct of feminists in radical politics—all with a depth which makes up for a lack of comprehensive detail."

"Get out of here," Dr. Kaufman said.

"You're crazy," said Kathy. And slammed the door.

As she went down in the elevator she decided that she was not really interested in the N.Y.C.P.A. She was outraged and decided to write a letter to the president of the N.Y.C.P.A. What was the point? She'd write to the director in Albany and try to get the goddamn place shut down. Still—that didn't solve anything. She still needed a career.

*

Kathy Kahn woke up one morning when the children had already gone off to school and put on her bedroom slippers—reaching for the vacuum cleaner which she had left by the bed. Into the vacuum cleaner went all the dust. It would be interesting she thought to use a vacuum cleaner to suck up all the dust of her life. Wouldn't it be wicked and wondrous to vacuum out all the problems? She began to dress. It was time to go for the usual morning walk in the neighborhood to do the household shopping. Oh it would be lovely to vacuum out the need for money. Money had begun to obsess Kathy Kahn. The savings book—the blue book with its assets—deposits—and withdrawals—was a keepsake of her ups and downs. She had problems with time. She had problems with reality. She had problems with money. She hated background noises. She was getting really fat. The bags were hanging over her eyes. Well she would never take a cab again. That would solve something. She could ride a bike around Manhattan. If she didn't get injured that would solve everything. But what if she did get injured?

The door bell rang. A suspicion came in her mind that she had invited someone for brunch. But who the hell had she invited? Now she remembered. Agatha Papadendris. A miraculous Greek.

Agatha, the daughter of a shipping king, had loved her second husband dearly and had just been widowed. Agatha was the ex-sister-in-law of an old love—a certain Mr. Peter Livanos—a shipping king who had courted Kathy after her first marriage. She had adored him and had met Agatha at a charity luncheon.

Agatha was in her late sixties and still looked miraculously young. When Kathy had expressed sorrow at her husband's death she had said "Just one of those things" in her English accent. Agatha's son was the head of a shipping empire and was starting a new business sending cruise ships–which he ran–around the world. She had asked Kathy if she would help her with three things although she did not say which three things. All that Kathy could think of was how messy the apartment looked. She had called Delphine, the woman who cleaned, four times on the phone but she was out. Suddenly it occurred to her that she might pretend to *be* Delphine and say that she wasn't in. She was embarrassed to have Agatha see her apartment. The girls' shoes and socks were left in the living room. Dead flowers were in the vase. Oh god. The bell kept ringing. She had to open it.

Agatha came in and took off her nutria coat. They sat down on the couch.

"My son Mikos thought you were ever so nice. It's so kind of you to help me. My ex-husband–his father–has bought this property in the north of Greece–it's so lovely there–rolling hills–very clear water–well I want to help them get it started. Kisias is an extraordinary place. Unfortunately they ran out of funds to develop it at just the last moment. But more important than the land is the sea–the boats–my dear–the cruise ships. I do want them to go well. I personally can't understand why my son Mikos wants to run *cruise* ships when he's so brilliant in human relations and political science–but that's his bailiwick–he loves finance and of course I'd do anything to help him. Now I'd like to ask of you three things–what were they?" Her sad eyes filled with water.

"The boats?"

"Yes. The boats. We've hired this dreadful public relations firm that didn't tell anyone about the cruise ships. I fired them. I thought perhaps you might know editors–and writers–we could invite them to a coctail party. Could you make up a list for me?"

"Agatha—I'd be happy to. It's easy to find out who are the editors of the travel sections—and perhaps with a cocktail party—and a press kit—when would one of the boats be docked so that people could visit them?"

"What a good idea. In January."

"You could send out a letter with our names."

"Good. I need to do things with other people. It's dreadful to try to be a self-starter. Especially in shipping promotion."

"I understand."

"And you think a little party would be the thing, do you? How about a fork buffet?"

"What is that?"

"A fork buffet—you know—forks for dinner would be nicer."

"Yes. I think it would be lovely."

"Now the second thing is my special pet and it means so terribly much to me. I just have to say I'm a Mediterranean girl. I loathe the Caribbean. I loathe the humidity. The last time I was in the Caribbean I put my foot plop on a sea urchin which certainly didn't endear me to the Caribbean. I loathed the people living on the backs of all the blacks. How can anyone have a vacation in the midst of that poverty is beyond me. However the Project HOPE Winter Cruise Benefit—sailing in January—is so worthwhile. It's one of Kostia's boats. It's really a first-class ship—it will be a benefit cruise and that is something I do believe in even though I just loathe the Caribbean."

"How can I help you?"

"Tell your friends about it. We must make this thing go."

"Frankly my friends are all busy, working, or have children, or are involved in something or are too poor. I don't know anyone who has two weeks' leisure time to cruise in the middle of January. And it is expensive."

"Right. And you know—I think the time of cruises is over. Why do you think that is? You know a psychiatrist friend of mine in London said if more people took off from land and went to sea—where they could be reflective—he wouldn't have any patients. What do you think of that?"

"I think he's right."

"But that's just it—people don't like to leave the land. They are not sea people the way we are."

"Or they can't afford it."

"You know I think cruises are finished because people have summer homes, or their children are in school. I don't really know why cruises are finished. Do you?"

"I don't. But I would love to go on a cruise. I just don't have the time or the money."

"The second thing—no the third thing—is a dinner which I think is terribly important. It's for this new method they have of shrinking cancer. You know one in every four people has this damn thing—it's just terrible—this is the most important thing."

"I have a list of about three hundred people. I keep their names in a file cabinet and whenever there's something really worthwhile I use the list. I don't give it to people but I'd give it to you Agatha. I'm sure whatever this process is—if you're involved it's going to be helpful. Why don't you send an invitation to Ralph Nader? He went after the Bar Association and I'm sure if this is an investigation of the American Medical Association he would be interested. He's the only person really investigating the rip-offs of medicine and law that means anything."

"Marvelous idea."

"You know, Agatha—I'm very happy to help you with anything. But I bought this book for you because I wanted to say something—which is now that you're alone—you'll need to reach out to friends. And I'm your friend. You know when I was married—I didn't know how important friends were. I always had my husband. My children. I was so busy giving to them. But since I've been divorced—this is hard to admit—I live from one day to the next and one friend to the next. Each helping hand is another way of holding on."

"Kathy—can I tell you something? I feel that each day I have to just get through. You know when my husband first died I felt that I was physically unable to bear it. People forget that suffering is not just mentally draining—it's physically draining. I felt I just couldn't move my body. It was as if I had an octopus in my stomach. A great big octopus that kept eating away at me. Oh people invited me to lunch. I got many invitations. It wasn't that. I just couldn't eat. I had to eat lemon soup all the time."

"I know. And I've been divorced a year and I still feel that way. Of course being a widow is easier than being divorced. You don't end in a drastic hostile way."

Agatha's eyes grew red and moist. "When I had my son Mikos at home it was different. You see you're always giving out when you're with a child and your husband. Suddenly they're gone. Well—I must admit that my second husband was the love of my life—now that I'm alone I have to give to myself if you see what I mean and I'm not very good at that. Of course Mikos is married and I'm always welcome to be with him and his wife."

"What is she like?"

"A terribly feminine girl. Yummy. A very good housewife and looks marvelously after the children. Well someone has to, you know. And she makes him terribly happy. Which is all I care about. As a mother-in-law—I must say that I find her terribly boring. She's young. I guess that's her excuse—most people don't have much to say until they have lived through a lifetime. Of course when I was her age I was different. At twenty-eight I had a lot of living past me. But I lived through a war you know. A war—life—and death—that's something. You know what my good friend Maurice Bowra said to me once in Athens? He said loving and death are the only two things that interest him. Don't you think that's good? Loving and death. I wish there was more

loving and less death. Well, I must not speak of death. Kostia
lives in a charming house in Athens. Right under the Parthenon.
It's the smelly part. The old part of Athens. You know that I hate
Athens because it tries to be so chi-chi. Well where he lives—it's
built on three terraces—he has the peasants in front of him and
the Parthenon in back of him. It's lovely."

"Do you think of living in Greece?"

"Oh no. I couldn't live in Athens. Do you know why? Do you
know those plants that climb up a wall—the plants that are so
very beautiful? They have little tendrils and they climb one tendril
on top of another to reach the sun?"

"I do."

"Well that's what Athens is like. Only it's not beautiful. The
doctors and the lawyers climbing on the backs of the poor people.
The peasants are all the poor people supporting those climbers.
It's hideous. And Athens always trying to be so chi-chi. It's only
in the north of here—in the country where you meet the good
solid people. The peasants are so much more interesting than all
those doctors and lawyers—like the sea-going men who go on the
boats. The sailors. They're really jolly and nice."

"Your ex-brother-in-law often invited me to Chios."

"Peter did? Oh yes you told me. What did you make of it?"

"I loved it of course. The mountains. You went inland and saw
all those old people whose grandparents had come from Mongolia.
And the Byzantine monasteries. And the Egyptians who fled from
Alexandria and turned their homes into museums. And the
bouzouki. And ouzo. And flies. There was no airport then. Peter's
house was like a voluptuous fairy-tale house. All the beds had
mosquito netting around them just as they did in the fairy tales. I
wrote a poem about Chios."

"Do you remember it?"

"Yes I do. It was called simply Chios." Katherine recited it
quite naturally. "In the stone banks of Chios angry words burned

like the bright melon seed. The piano played all day. I sat on a barrel sun-struck by the sea, and Bach poems flew into me. Village without roosters, village with golden flowers and golden crosses. There was a boy with a violent temper. He threw a hive of golden notes at me."

Agatha lit a cigarette. "That's lovely Katherine. Did you ever show it to Peter?"

"No."

"You know since my husband died I feel as if I've been drowning. Each day is such an effort to stay alive. I feel as if I've entered that realm of the sea where there is no light. I feel as if I have entered that portion of the sea called the zone of perpetual darkness. Here there is no light to support the grass of the sea. I feel as if I have left the zone of light and must live in this darkness perpetually. Well my dear. Thank you so much for your help. Then we will do three things together won't we my pet?

"First we will send out invitations in your name to the journalists and editors—secondly we will do what we can to sponsor that cruise of HOPE. I know it's too expensive for most people—but just by chance you might know of someone who wants to get in the sun. Tell them the ship is called the *Alexandria* and it is truly a remarkable vessel. You know—palisander woods, china from Bavaria, table settings from Italy, fabrics from Belgium, swim in a swimming pool with water almost as blue as the Mediterranean—not that anyone gives a damn. Most people who can afford to go on the cruise have their own swimming pools. But HOPE is an international organization dedicated to better health care throughout the world. And it *is* worthwhile. And then your list for the cancer evening. You are a darling. You are a very nice girl Kathy. It's really a pleasure to see you. It's too bad Peter died before you could marry him. Now I have to go. I have my own work to do. You don't know of a good secretary do you?"

"No I really don't. I've had part-time secretaries when I've worked on dinners and things but they are all hopeless. I use a secretarial service if I need anything typed."

"Well goodbye my darling. I was happy to have a chat with you this morning. And do keep in touch with me. I'm having a little party on the seventh and I'd like it very much if you can come."

"Thank you Agatha. Keep surviving."

The door closed. For the first time in a long while Kathy felt like going back to bed and crying. She was also at the bottom of the sea. Suddenly Kathy remembered the kraken. The kraken, a fabled creature at the bottom of the sea was said to have swallowed sea vessels. "Some kraken or other is swallowing me," Kathy thought. "I am being swallowed by a kraken every morning of my life." No point in tears. The house had to be cleaned. The girls both needed shoes. Books had to be set aside for the Walden Fair. Why had both of the girls insisted on Walden? It was so expensive. And then there was a gym class. But she could skip that. It was terribly expensive. Every penny asserts itself like a thorn.

The sun came through the window. "I have to wash the windows" Kathy thought as she dressed. She looked in the mirror and noticed her body was changing. Yes it was definitely getting fat again. She had to devote her entire life to being thin and it was worse than the plague of locusts. Every day brought another pound. Fat large breasts. Fat stomach. Thighs bulging. Being fat and almost broke—wasn't it enough to break your heart?

*

Somehow Kathy wanted to say—to get it across to the girls—how important it was to be close to each other. To talk to each other about problems. The girls—Julia and Jeanie—looked so much like their golden redhaired father. They played in their room. They fought. They were jealous of each other. They loved each other. Kathy thought it would be a nice surprise to buy them some roses.

Kathy made a cup of coffee for herself and looked out the window. She was thinking of the words "orange trees" remembering the time she had planted little orange trees in Hong Kong when she had first married Mr. Jaksforth. And now—in the cold of the city—there were no orange trees. She would go shopping for flowers. That was it! She would go shopping for flowers on a cold winter morning in New York City when the desperation was beginning to eat away at her stomach. What was it Agatha had said? An octopus in the stomach. She would go shopping for flowers. Flowers could make everything better. One lives for candles. Flowers. Books. Music. The children. A fire in the fireplace. Wasn't that why she had taken the apartment? Because it had a fireplace. Oh goddamn the shoes needed heels. The shoes needed heels. She needed new stockings.

Kathy said "How much are the bachelor buttons?"

"Three dollars the bunch. Bachelor buttons are expensive at this time of the year."

"And the pink carnations?"

"Eight dollars a dozen."

"Eight dollars!"

They were magnificent pink carnations, large pockets of flesh that opened and seemed to look at her and beg to be taken home. Suddenly Kathy remembered the carnations in Spain when she had just been married to her first husband. They had gone to Torremolinos where he was trying to conquer the entire section of Málaga for bowling territory. They had visited some friends of his in Torremolinos and she had seen them—the huge fields of *claveles*—red carnations stretching out—a sea of red carnations. She had seen them and always remembered the smell. What was the poem she had learned in Cherry Lawn?

Si me pierdo por el mundo
Buscadme en Andalucía—

Claveles. Claveles. I love *claveles.*

"Give me a bunch of carnations" she said impulsively. There was never a time when she bought flowers that she didn't remember Mr. Jaksforth's warning "You'll never be able to buy books or flowers again." The hell with Mr. Jaksforth. He could choke to death in Ethiopia with his postcards and his two-hundred-dollars-a-month child support. She would still go on buying brown almonds, she would still go on buying poetry, she would still buy roses and jonquils and lilies and carnations. The carnations looked strong. They might last a long time. She took her last ten-dollar bill from her bag. "Oh god!" she thought, "I've got to go to the bank."

After she deposited the carnations in the living room she decided to telephone Jonathon Leeds. He was the one person who was always able to help out other people in emergencies. He had handled her insurance problems. He had listened to her literary problems. Her romance problems. And so in an odd way his office was open to her for visiting, or insurance, or any kind of problem. When she talked to Jonathon romance and insurance and money got all mixed up. He was the one person she could truly give her confidences to. He was very discreet. He lived in a small townhouse on the Upper East Side with his wife and five children and a large beagle dog. "Sometimes I think the only person who understands me is my dog" Jonathon would say. But of course everyone understood Jonathon. He had had a very fortunate life. Born on the Lower East Side, he had discovered insurance at the time that most young men of his age were still in high school. He had never finished school, but instead married his beautiful childhood sweetheart, went in the Army, went in the insurance business, had children, made money—and always looked at the world with the curiosity of one determined to have a good time. He always wore brilliantly colored ties. An odd bird, Jonathon. She telephoned his office.

*

When Katherine Kahn sailed into Jonathon Leeds's insurance office on Fifth Avenue she went immediately into the big office. The receptionist knew her. They were used to seeing her arrive with her two daughters on her hands—their faces covered with whipped-cream tracings or candy.

"Come in Kathy" said Jonathon. He often listened to classical music and at that moment was listening to a new Vivaldi record.

"I have to get a job" she said.

Jonathon turned off the music.

*

At this moment in his life Jonathon Leeds was tired by insurance. Many of the boys from the Lower East Side that he knew had gone into the rackets and made a lot of money. Or into show business. That was another racket. All the buddies of his who were agents were now producers. He had somehow missed being where the action was. He had plenty of money. He had plenty of security. It was now time for him to do something else. On that particular morning Jonathon Leeds was waiting for an idea to hit him. But something odd had happened. Katherine Kahn recently Katherine Jaksforth—mother of two children—with a house to maintain—a husband who beat it to Ethiopia—and not very much of a promise of an income had come into his office.

Katherine sat silently in his office. "I need a job" she said. "But I have an idea."

Jonathon said "Your ideas are good. You had an idea to make a film and someone else made it. But your ideas are terrific. You should be in the idea business."

"No. I should be in the insurance business."

Jonathon laughed and said to his secretary through a dictating machine "Hold the calls."

How may a man live in Manhattan in an office without a secretary? How may a man live without pictures of whatever family he has on his desk? How may a man live without talking to his secretary and saying hold the calls? How many calls must be held? These were all intangibles going through Katherine's mind.

Jonathon Leeds who loved Vivaldi. Jonathon Leeds who loved his country. Ho-ho for Jonathon Leeds. Who was kind. Who was generous. Who adored his wife. Who liked to be where the action was. Who was looking for something he couldn't quite define. Who was faithful. Who was considerate. Who was fed up with his job. Who was bored. Who was good-natured. Who liked to help people out. Jonathon Leeds who had a sense of humor. Jonathon Leeds who found life to be like a vaudeville show. *Yipeee.* Jonathon Leeds who read Katherine Kahn's poetry. Who liked Katherine Kahn. Who felt that Katherine Kahn should not go down the drain was about to listen to Katherine Kahn's idea to make a fortune.

"Listen Katherine, I'm ready to listen to anything."

"I need a job" Katherine said. "And I have an idea for a company."

"Go on. Let's order lunch. Send me two cottage cheese two hard boiled eggs two fruit salad. I know you're on a diet too, right?"

Jonathon said "You sure you know what you want for lunch?

You sure you don't mind eating the same lunch I do?" Jonathon Leeds who was also a sea person, who was also in his own way desperate, who was also in some odd way at the bottom of the sea—in his own way—sat back and little Katherine Kahn who was now big Katherine Kahn—little Kathy Kahn with little problems—now big Kathy Kahn with big problems—began from the bottom of her stomach to unreel her idea for a company.

Jonathon was a camera freak. Katherine looked at the cameras on Jonathon's desk.

"You see Jonathon—every day is a new day. And this morning I was thinking that my idea—is something that might interest you."

Jonathon laughed. "Dear Katherine—" he said. He was toying with one of the cameras. "My money is on you. Mostly because you always have creative ideas. There is so much in you wanting to come out. What have you been thinking about?"

"I've been thinking—" Katherine began to laugh.

"Your ideas are always passionate" he said.

"I don't want to go back to writing. I find it too difficult. I don't mind the interviews, the occasional journalistic biography; I rather like the miniature patterns that one arranges as honestly as possible for interviews. I always feel as if I'm making a tiny telescope in which I peer into the oddities and terrors of a human life. But there's no money in it. And in some minor way I find all of this questioning painful. I mean I hate digging into a stranger's privacy."

"I see what you mean."

It took a few moments of courage for Katherine to continue.

"I remember when I first started writing journalism. I wanted to interview Leonard Bernstein more than any person in the world. I was in love with him. His cape. The way he conducted without a baton. I remember this so vividly—I was a student at Beaupre summer arts camp in Lenox, Massachusetts and I was only fourteen years old. I had sent for the catalogue from the *New York Times*—I had seen an ad in the Sunday magazine section. Beaupre, said the ad—was a music and arts camp where you could study acting and painting and music and dancing. Well, to be honest, I was positive I wanted to be an artist—I just didn't know what kind. I was in love with dancing—acting—I wanted to paint—to compose. It was all so heady. I remember going to that camp as the very happiest time in my whole life. Dr. de Lorenzo, the head of the camp, met my father in New York. They worked out a deal where Dr. and Mrs. de Lorenzo could stay at one of my father's hotels for nothing in return for my tuition at the camp. It cost about three thousand dollars to go there and my father—who was never terribly sold on the arts as a profession—thought it was a terrible waste of money. But when the 'deal' was worked out—I rode up to Beaupre and I almost fainted when I saw the lawns. The large house that we lived in had a huge piano in it. There were dance rehearsals in the barn, painting classes on the lawn. I felt as if I had died and gone to heaven. At night we listened to the music students play the piano. The food was good. The students were all nice to me. It wasn't at all like boarding school where everyone was so neurotic and banged their heads against the wall at night from loneliness. The girls at Beaupre were from wealthy families. They were well brought up. And most of them came from families that were truly cultured. To them playing the piano was as natural as eating. My first visit to Tanglewood— where we sat on the big lawn and listened to Mozart and Beethoven was—what can I say? It was the first moment of truth in my life. I had read about paradise and I had found it. On the lawns of Tanglewood. Of course there was a sexual excitement to all of this too. The girls at Beaupre—'dated' the musicians at Tanglewood. Although I was fourteen I fell madly in love with a bassoonist. Matthew Ruggiero. He now plays the bassoon in the Philadelphia Orchestra. I saw him once in the pit—he's old and has gray hair and a hunched back. But when I met him at Beaupre– he was tall and we took long walks. He told me a great deal about the bassoon–and how it was like the human voice.

"But Leonard Bernstein was my hero. He was way beyond Matthew Ruggiero. I had no illusions that I would ever 'go out' with him. I wanted to only talk with him. The true hero, the true subject of my fantasy was Bernstein–and I can't really tell you why. Perhaps because I had seen conductors stand like penguins on the podium–whereas when he conducted Mahler and Brahms he moved his arms and body like a dancer. At the same time 'action painting' was developing with Kline and Pollock in New York City Bernstein was practicing action music–his whole soul seemed to rattle in the purest way when he conducted. I had to meet him. Finally I came up with the perfect way to have a chance to talk to him. I decided to ask him for an *interview*. This was difficult. Interview him *for what?* I invented a magazine called the *Beaupre News*. Then, aware of the fact that my voice sounded girlish since I was still going through puberty, that my voice didn't sound 'grown up' enough–I asked one of the counselors–a girl called Ethel Gottesman who went to Beaver College–and was sixteen–if she would come in on this adventure with me. I explained that she would call Blantyre, where Bernstein was staying–I had checked all of this out over the summer via my sources at Tanglewood, and that she would take notes as my assistant. We would pretend to be from a magazine called the *Beaupre News*. And I would pay for the taxi cab to and from Blantyre. Well, Ethel was in love with Bernstein too. Her crush wasn't as deep as mine, but the idea of taking a hero who was a *stranger* and actually humanizing him–finding out facts about his *ordinary* life–this appealed to her. She made the phone call. I am not sure whether she talked actually to *him* or someone else but she arranged for the interview. The day came when we were to go and talk to Leonard Bernstein. I felt absolutely nauseous, I was giddy and sick at the same time from excitement. I think I had stage-fright. At the last moment I confessed to Louise Arnold, one of the girls studying piano at Beaupre, that I was actually too frightened to go. I wanted to call the entire *interview* off. I began to throw up.

"It was too late. The cab arrived at Beaupre. Ethel Gottesman and myself were dressed for the special occasion—I to look older than my fourteen years. We had our props. Paper-pad and pencils. I wore glasses I could hardly see through to look older. The big black cab sped us past Haggard's drugstore in Lenox, past the tiny white houses and the green lawns newly clipped, up the winding majestic runway of Blantyre. It was an inn, a sort of castle cum tourist home with a restaurant. I had once eaten there and was impressed with the fact that they gave you free cottage cheese. At Blantyre castle we were told Mr. Bernstein would receive us in the garden. I excused myself from Ethel. I went to the bathroom and threw up quietly. Then I returned looking 'ready' to interview. He sat there in the garden. Next to him was a beautiful young woman with short hair and a low voice. He introduced her as 'Felicia Montealegre.' The leaves in the background of the garden framed their faces. Everyone spoke in low voices. I believe he had a cigarette holder. The sight of a human being pushed to such an extreme of talent and graciousness moved me. I think the only other person I admired as much as Bernstein was Sigmund Freud, and since he was dead I could never *interview* him. I took a breath and began my interview.

"'Mr. Bernstein, where were you born?' I asked. It was absurd to ask this question. I knew perfectly well where he was born. In fact—I knew his life better than he did. 'Where did you go to college?' I had to ask this. Because in my fourteen-year-old mind I thought that was what an interview was. I knew he went to Harvard. I knew who his teachers were. I knew everything one can know about a hero—because that's all you have—the facts which you collect like tiny pieces of mica sifted out of the waters. Facts. Not one question did I ask that I didn't know the answer to already. However he did say something which amazed me. He told me that at college he never studied the things he knew. Only the things he didn't know. I always remembered that. When the interview was over the beautiful lady spoke to me privately; she asked me what I did. I could not tell another lie. The *Beaupre News* was a lie but I had to be honest about myself. 'I am a student' I said quietly. 'At Cherry Lawn. I want to be an actress someday.'

"She looked at me with such sweetness and said if I ever came to New York I should 'get in touch' with her and she would 'give me the name' of her *agent*. The very word agent was magical and filled with the promise of the future. I wrote up my interview but I had nowhere to publish it. And I always remember that interview as an experience when a prayer was answered. I had followed my impulse and I had met my hero. But—now this seems odd—I always feel like a bit of a fake and an intruder during an interview. I think that in some odd way it is humiliating to oneself to be prying into another person's life. Peoples' lives take place in their fantasies anyway. And in the very act of being born one begins to shield one's life from the *others*."

Coughing, Katherine stopped talking for a moment. She quickly added— "Interviewing people is a way of meeting others. But it is a very false way—because there is no communication. No interaction. You must eradicate who *you* are. Naturally I couldn't have said to Leonard Bernstein—I'm a fourteen-year-old-girl who admires you. I want to *be* you. The beautiful woman with him at least *acknowledged* me and to her I admitted my own fear of the *future* and told my ambition. But the point is—I now hate interviewing people. I can't write poetry, except for myself, and I have to find something to do to support myself. I've come up with the idea of starting a company."

"What kind of company?"

"A woman's insurance company."

"What made you think of that?"

"I just put two and two together."

*

What happened to Katherine Kahn was then told quite easily to Jonathon Leeds. She had been invited to a cocktail party by a certain Ryan McFarlan who had once been an editor of a magazine and from time to time Katherine had written a column for him. At one of his annual cocktail parties Katherine had arrived and seen a lovely woman in a pink dress that she had wanted to talk to. The woman, it turned out, was Joanna Harris, a charming executive who had just left one company and was in the process of finding another. Katherine—it turned out—discovered that they were both recently divorced and both had children at the same school. They had arranged to meet for lunch.

*

When Joanna came to Katherine's for lunch Katherine at once said "Perhaps we can think of something we can do together."

"That's not possible" Joanna said, "because I'm being considered for another job. But I might be a consultant to a company. God knows I'm on enough boards."

"What do you think of a woman's insurance company?"

"Good idea."

"The reason I thought of it—" Katherine said across the table as she was eating her lunch, "was I said to myself—there's women's magazines, women's banks—almost everything for women. But not one place have I seen a woman's insurance company. It just seems to me that now that women are the heads

of households and have different economic and security needs—
that they might also need life insurance of their own to protect
their families. I mean—suddenly—here I am with two children to
raise and to take care of. If anything happened to me—what would
happen to them? I've read somewhere that there is a fortune in
insurance. That *life* insurance is in fact—a great big numbers game.
Well my idea is to *market* the company correctly. It's not the fact
that it's a company run by women—it's also a company where
women sell to women. A sort of in-home selling program—where
women salespeople come into other women's homes and sell them
protection and security in the form of life insurance. Just like
Avon did with cosmetics. Only it's not cosmetics but life
insurance."

"Sara Coventry did the same thing with jewelry. It's a good
idea. An even great idea. I wonder why it was never done before?"

"The main thing is" Katherine continued, "I have a very close
friend—Jonathon Leeds—who runs one of the largest insurance
broker agencies in New York. He insures all the people in show
business and he's a very creative guy. Would you meet him? I'd
like to get his idea about this."

And the lunch ended.

"That's how I got the idea" Katherine said to Jonathon.

*

"You are strange" Jonathon said to Katherine. "First this long
story about interviewing Leonard Bernstein when you were
fourteen. Then your concept about a women's insurance company.
It's nuts. But I like it."

"You do?"

"Yes I do. I think it's a good idea. We would have to put it
together with an actuary. He's the person who puts together the
numbers. Then I have a friend at Payne Weber—Irwin Boodlin—

who is an expert at insurance investment–he'd be a good person to raise the money. So we could form a small group. Joanna as a consultant could be the marketing person. You could be the conceptual person. Who works with training the agents."

"You mean we could set up a school for training women insurance salespeople?"

"Right. And Irwin could raise the money. He could help us get the charter. And I'd like to bring in my lawyer, Leslie Cummings, to put the whole thing together."

"How much do you think it would cost to start such a company?"

"I don't know. Let me think about it. Let's meet in a week or so. But I like your thinking. My god we could all be millionaires."

"You know Jonathon" Katherine said, "I've been a tycoon of the imagination for so long. Wouldn't it be funny if it became a fact?"

"It wouldn't be funny–it would be terrific."

"Is it possible?"

"Everybody starts at a beginning. Everything starts from an idea."

"I guess that's what my business has always been–giving ideas away. I've been doing that since I was a kid."

"Me too."

"We have nothing to lose do we?" Katherine said.

"Absolutely nothing."

"And I would much rather have my own company–run my own store–than work for someone else."

"That's the idea."

"Desperation has led me to think."

"What a crazy thing to think of–a woman's insurance company."

"Well it's really because I know you. Because of you Jonathon

I thought about insurance. I suppose if my best friend had been a sailor I would have thought about refrigerated shipping. God knows in my life I've thought of starting a school to teach poetry to children, starting the first woman's film company, creating a college to learn about media, doing a film out of Dylan Thomas's *The Doctor and the Devils*–inventing a camera that would take pictures of the backsides of women in slacks–creating community hotels for women with children to live together–a million thoughts cross my mind every day. Once I went out with the man who invented frozen waffles. I asked him how he thought of it and he said 'I don't know. I just thought about waffles. And one day I thought that TV dinners were catching on so much why not TV breakfasts? And then I thought it was quite easy to find a way to reduce the waffle to powder and then distribute them.' Well Jonathon, if he could think of frozen waffles I guess I could think of a woman's insurance company."

"What would we call it?" Jonathon asked.

"Woman's Life. The Woman's Life Insurance Company. It's got a marvelous ironic ring to it. For the first time women can take their own life and death into their own hands. Woman's Life."

"To life," Jonathon said. And showed Katherine his new camera.

A Gentleman for Dinner

The girls were coming home from school at three. The place was a mess. And it took so long on the bus. It groaned to go. Tonight she was having one of those "semi-blind" dates that divorced women with children are so prone to. She had to clean for the semi-blind. Gregor Heitzink was someone she knew, but didn't know. It was half a blind date. She had seen him for the past ten years in god help her—the Hamptons. That awful place. The palindromes of anxiety all began and ended in the Hamptons. "Nothing good ever happens in the Hamptons," Jack Richardson—the playwright—once said over a game of poker. She had dropped her cards and kissed him.

What did she know about Gregor Heitzink? He wore glasses. He was a writer. People said he was "brilliant." She had never read anything he wrote. Other people said he was bizarre and crazy. He was once known to miss a shot on a tennis court and ask his opponent, "Do you think I have multiple sclerosis?" Katherine had seen him on the Montauk tennis courts. He always wore torn clothes. Tattered shirts. Sneakers with small strings. The kind of clothes you trip over. He was a tall man with black hair and a beard and round jovial face. She had seen him bouncing up and down at cocktail parties. He had once been married to a girl he had met in an airplane. The girl turned out to be Julia Winnoker—a roommate at Cherry Lawn. Divorced. He had been married again to a dentist. Divorced. Then he was married, she had heard, to a tall blonde faith healer in San Francisco. He was now divorced again. She had seen him at various political campaigns—Gregor Heitzink—he had worked very hard for McGovern and professed to be a friend of the women's movement—although that seemed doubtful. Once he had spoken up at a Tom Hayden meeting on health insurance: "Why should anyone have health insurance free? I'm a writer and I have to stay healthy. If I don't stay healthy I can't work and pay my rent—and if I have to pay my rent by staying healthy I don't see why everyone else can't."

He had also bobbed up and down like a tire on the sea at several Phoenix House and Fortune Society cocktail parties. She really didn't know him at all—except that he seemed knowledgeable about current events. She had called him and invited him to a drink when she discovered that they were both Virgos at the last fund-raising cocktail party for the Circle Repertory Theatre. He had an extremely lovely voice. She even fantasized having a love affair with him. She could close her eyes and forget the flabby stomach, the hairy arms, she could pretend he was quite attractive. After all he was an *intellectual.* He had a nose that was nice. And for godsakes it was time that she started dating. She couldn't go on being frightened of men forever. Just because Mr. Jaksforth had tormented her with his frugal emotional outlay–and Harry was a generalissimo of stupidity–she could after all make an attempt to try again to find human warmth. If not warmth–at least understanding conversation. She sprayed perfume all over her dress.

Ding Dong, there he was. The gentleman caller. Not exactly. She had called him but it didn't make all that much difference. She had ordered liver–the easiest thing to cook–from the Venice Market. She could handle liver in a hurry and still keep on being the hostess. And then she had set the table–with candles. And bought those madly expensive candles from France–Gigoud candles–the sexual green little cups of wax that gave off a heady odor of pine. Now the whole house smelled like a goddamn pine forest. The food was laid out attractively. She had shaved her legs for this occasion. The girls, unfortunately, were fighting in their room.

"Girls. Close the door." The door slammed. The noise was terrible. They were screaming above the television. Katherine began to sweat under her arms. "The children know, instinctively, that *I need to get laid*–they are determined to ruin everything." *Oh God*–she began to pray–*please let them be quiet.* She could have murdered them.

Then an odd event happened. Gregor Heitzink just came in the door. She had forgotten to lock it. "Good evening," he said. He was holding a bottle of wine in a paper bag. He had obviously just showered. His turtle-neck sweater was dapper. But he didn't smile.

And then the children's door opened. Both of them came screaming out of the room. Screaming? Screeching. Tears. Screams. Yells. Indian war-path yells.

Katherine smiled and tried not to notice. "Good evening Gregor."

"Who's that?" one of the girls asked. "Is he sleeping over mom?"

Shhh girls. Excuse me Gregor. Door opened. Child spanked. A bath given. Beds turned down. Television turned off. Half an hour later Katherine emerged from the children's room. Still the hostess. Trying to carry on the conversation as if she had just been interrupted in the middle of a sentence.

"I haven't really seen you alone in years," Gregor said. "In fact I've never seen you alone. We always seem to meet each other at parties. What have you been doing for the past twenty years? I think I met you twenty years ago at Lois's house. That was before each of us were married."

"Yes. And you have a daughter the same age as my oldest. I remember Julia and I were pregnant at the same time."

"That's not possible. Mine is adopted."

"Oh I'm sorry. I didn't know that. I remembered him as being very sweet. I once saw him in the park."

"If you don't mind—" Gregor said, fixing himself a drink, "I'd rather not talk about children. I absolutely have the willies when we talk about children. I hate children."

"When *we*. How can you say that? I don't really know you Gregor and *we* have never talked about anything."

Another drink is poured.

"I said I hate children. You know coming up here in the cab I kept thinking to myself—are she and I going to have a thing together? I mean—really Katherine—you are terribly attractive and

I kept thinking—will we have an affair? And my answer was—no we won't. Because I hear she has two children. And I couldn't stand another woman with children. I've just gone with two women. Actually *gone* with them. Each of them had two children. Girls. Girls the same age as your girls. Isn't that odd? And in both cases I broke up with them. I just couldn't handle the children. Oh—they tried to manipulate me with the children. And then—as I walk in the door—all my nightmares come true. You actually have two screaming girls. Just what I can't put up with. I frankly find it too threatening."

"Well now that we know we won't have an affair—would you still like to have dinner?"

"What are you cooking?"

"Liver."

"I love liver. Nothing better. I just can't stand it raw. When I was a boy at military school they always served raw liver and I threw up."

"Well I'll make it well done."

Gregor sat down on the couch. As Katherine swept past him in her bare feet and long flowing striped at-home dress her skirt brushed by one of the green candles. It had been burning all afternoon to make the house piney—and another disaster happened. The fragrant soft green wax spilled all over the table and over the rug—spilling unfortunately on Gregor Heitzink. Katherine looked at the huge fragrant splotches of green wax. They were everywhere on the table and on Gregor Heitzink's suit. Large green patches of unwashable green were all over him.

"Oh god" Katherine said, crossing herself—a leftover from saying grace at Cherry Lawn. "I am sorry. This is just terrible. I'll send your clothes to the cleaner."

"You don't have to. They're ruined."

"That was such a stupid accident. These candles come on little aluminum steel tops that you put on the bottom but one of the girls must have removed the bottoms. What can I do to make this up to you?"

"Just fix dinner. Forget about the wax. These are old clothes."

Katherine went obediently into the kitchen. The green-splattered man followed her.

"Are you hungry?" She tried to sound cheerful as she was setting the table. This evening was ruined. Gregor was definitely not the suitor who would sweep her off her feet. How dare he tell her not to talk about children? No point making a scene. Just never see him again. With the wax all over his corduroy pants there was no worry about that.

Finally dinner was served. Wine opened. Salad made. He sat down. "Do you have any bread?" he asked.

"I don't eat bread." Suddenly Katherine remembered the rolls that came with Colonel Sanders chicken she had brought home yesterday. Were they stale? She went to the ice-box. Yes they were stale. She called to Gregor "I'm afraid I only have stale buns."

"Bring them out."

The buns were produced.

"Do you have any butter?"

"No."

So hers was a household without butter. The look of disgust crept all over his face. An unbuttered house. With screaming kids. And smelly wax. Gregor began drinking the wine. He looked wistful. "What have you been doing for twenty years?"

Why was he asking that question, Katherine wondered.

"I have my children. I worked for politics. I've written a few poems. I've been living in Hong Kong. What else? I'm thinking of trying to create the first women's insurance company."

"That woman's thing? The woman's movement is all over."

"But women aren't."

"The bank isn't doing so well."

"Well it's just an idea. I have no idea if it will work. I just need to make some money and I've thought of it as a concept. What are you writing?"

"I'm becoming very famous. Nobody knows about me really yet."

"Don't be silly. Everyone knows you."

"My name. But not my work. I don't see myself quoted in the *New York Times Book Review*. Ads for my book, yes. Quotes. No. To be frank I'm in the process of making a million dollars."

"How?"

"By writing. By popular fiction my dear. I'm not a literary snob the way you are—"

"What makes you think that I'm a snob?"

"With your fancy poetry readings at Saint Mark's Church—or is it the Judson Church—and your references always to your friend—Saul Bellow—is he really a friend? Or merely an acquaintance? You don't really *know* him—besides he's not in the same category as *Camus*—"

Katherine flashed back to Camus walking down a street in Paris.

"What are you writing about?"

"Oh, I'm on to something sensational. But I can't tell you about it. You'll steal it."

"How can I steal it? I'm not writing any more."

"This idea is so hot. Mailer only wishes he had an idea like this for a novel. The name Heitzink is going to be as big as Mailer and Bellow. Maybe even as Camus. I'm writing a new book—all right I'll tell you—called *Fire*. It's about the world reaching burning temperature—one day the temperature of the world goes soaring. It's an ecological problem you know. Historically we lived once in a sun age. Is there any reason to think that this couldn't come back? My agent is selling it to the movies. Actually I'm writing three novels at the same time."

"That's marvelous. What are the others about?"

"One is a fictitious study of Hegel. It emphasizes ritual. You know Hegel's theory of identity is what is really the basis for modern relationships."

"I didn't know that."

"I suppose you're not interested in relationships any more?"

"Well, to tell you the truth I'm not. I have my children to bring up. And I have work that I'm in the process of creating that interests me."

"And no more love? You're not going to fall in love?"

"No."

"You're not as romantic and sentimental as I gave you marks for. As for me—I'm looking. I'm looking all the time for a relationship."

"What kind of relationship?"

"A partner. The ultimate partner."

"Excuse me, but haven't you been divorced three times? You've had so many partners."

"Yes. I know I'm a man who has been married many times. I often discuss this in group therapy. But now—I'm looking for someone I can really fall in love with. Identity is spiritual transcendence. I'm interested in ecology, sex, orgasm, identity, and psychic phenomenon. There's no commercial fiction dealing with these subjects. You'll see. I have a woman editor. Just to show you that I'm not against women editors—they're taking over publishing by the way."

"That's good."

"What's your sexual life like?"

"It's private."

"Are you really a private person? Or is this a put-on? You seem so outgoing."

"Actually I am a private person. I was rather frightened of this dinner. Semi-blind dates can be frightening. Especially at my age. I find it easier to relate to younger men."

"Is that meant as a put-down?"

"No. It's just that I have more fun with people who don't have marriage or love affairs preconceived in their minds."

"I love you when you're like this. Just straight. None of the bullshit."

"You like me when I tell you I'm frightened?"

"Yes. I'm afraid I have to leave now. Thank you for a lovely dinner. The liver wasn't half bad."

Katherine rose ceremoniously. Gregor walked over and kissed her. A little good-bye kiss. "I'm not a leaver. But I have to go. I'm really not a leaver."

"Then why are you leaving?"

His coat was on his back. "I just couldn't possibly get involved with a woman with children. And to be honest I find you attractive."

He was out in the hallway and rang for the elevator. "Look for my books" he said. "And remember—if you shift your identity pattern—to another which corresponds to a more sexually aggressive and less domestic pattern—let me know. I'm glad to see you Katherine. There are so many people I haven't seen in the past twenty years. It's hard to keep up with people."

She could hear the elevator coming to her floor. She was going to be saved by the elevator. Hurry up!

"That's all that counts in the end. One's humanity. Politics. Old friends. And sexually aggressive women."

He stepped into the elevator. She blew him a kiss.

*

Katherine Kahn had found her semi-blind date disappointing. She found herself drinking alone in the middle of the night. The children were in their dreams. The wax had been scraped and now she washed the table with ammonia.

"No possibilities there" she thought to herself. And went into bed.

Her bed had a large tented sheet over it. She felt like a sultana at night. She was reading books on the Middle East. She was also reading the studies by Ralph Nader. Suddenly she remembered her last *bad* experience. Bad experience. Bed experience. Deep down. Oh I have grown tired of the water-tap—what was that—a poem written at Bennington:

> I have grown tired of the water-tap
> The bowing maids, the telephone messages, the crap.
> From now on I will praise the water
> That runs down me and to me and from me. I am
> only embarrassed by the wealth of my own freedom.

Freedom. That was so long ago. Bennington in a sea-world a long time ago. The lawns running to the pine forests. Pine needle crescendos. She could put her special ear against the kiln in the fiery ceramics studio. Or sit all day, strumming her fingers—the high tide of slow wishes. The lost faces of all her old friends whirled in her mind—Shirly Bonway now working for New York Hospital—and making training films on death. "Why are you doing this Shirly? You were once a brilliant writer at Bennington."

"Once a writer. Now a mother. I'm doing it for the money. What else?"

"But what *are* training films on death?"

"You can read about it in my death handbook. That's a handbook that goes with the film. I've been working on death so hard I'm exhausted. But the handbook is written with a light touch—I now have to put into easy words—how to get used to Death."

"Isn't it odd—you Shirly trying to support your kids—making training films on death? And me—trying to support my kids—trying to start a life insurance company? What would Helen think?"

"You mean Helen from Bennington?"

"Helen the drunk. Helen would give it some mystical significance. You writing a pamphlet about death. Me starting a life insurance company. Remember at Bennington—that was so much like being in a garden. I called it the EdenSchool."

"I know" said Shirly. "By the way—I hear Helen's become a complete alcoholic."

"I know" Katherine said—" 'the garden was not ours.' " She remembered Helen saying that.

Katherine put down her books and fell asleep dreaming about the company. Helen, the gentleman caller and Shirly as a young girl at Bennington moved in and out of her dreams.

Camus

Jump out of bed. Comb hair. Put on bathrobe. Make breakfast for children. Eggs to be beaten. Cold milk. Cold frost on the windows. Hot coffee and soap. "Yes" thought Katherine—I am a sensualist. Joy is in the oven. In the soap. Sometimes it took so little to be truly happy. A bright shining apple. A painting of the body. Pink carnations. The poinsettias had arrived. She had brought them home lovingly in the cold, holding the plants under her cape—two twins with soft tender bejeweled red skin. That was joy. And tangerines to be peeled and smelling the scent of the tangerines on your fingers. Life. Joy. Was it only all that?

In the kitchen the eggs seemed to say "Time to hatch your life."
"But where do I begin?" thought Katherine.

Memories of Paris in the morning. The children off to school.
Their blue canvas satchels on their backs. Their hair in ponytails.
The private world of just the right *kind* of satchel. The right kind
of elastic for the ponytail. The girls practicing their carols:

On the first day of Christmas my true love gave to me—

My true love.
Let's see who was he really? Romano? or her first husband?

Katherine pulled the heavy gray vacuum cleaner out of the
broom closet. Some days she investigated her life as if it were a
great secret thing she kept in the broom closet along with the
rags and the duster and the dust-pan and the great yellow wicker
laundry basket. That's it. Her dust was dust. Dust to dust. Sweep
it all out. Get life all clean. She thought of Paris.

"Why am I thinking of Paris?" Katherine wondered as she
pulled the vacuum as if it were a prehistoric animal throughout
the house.

She remembered arriving in Paris. Twenty years old. Up-stairs
and down-stairs looking for apartments. Meeting all the people
she had only read about at Bennington. Wouldn't her teacher
Wallace Fowlie have been jealous? She had been studying Cocteau
and here she was being introduced to him at one of the salons in
Paris. Her first husband's mother was French and insisted on
taking her son and his American wife to the parties she went to.
Cocteau with his flowing white hair and little rosette. This was
real surrealism. Vacuuming and starting an insurance company.
Trying to start one. Would Cocteau have understood? And
Camus—his eyes burning holes in the faces of strangers. She
remembered being on the street when Camus was killed in a car
accident. The workers buying the paper. One street worker

saying—"One doesn't drive like that with Mr. Camus in the car—"
And afterwards. Venice. His girlfriend weeping tears at the
Biennale. And all of France so lonesome for him. Albert Camus.
Insurance. Pablo Neruda sitting in a small house in Paris.
Neruda—her life-hero. Driving Matilda and Neruda around Paris
in her husband's small white car. Finding him a tiny apartment on
the Ile St. Louis. Going with them visiting other Chileans. To see
the film Neruda made on Macchu Picchu. Pablo reading nursery
rhymes in her living room. And the great big poems. The great
pearls.

> Thinking, tangling shadows in the deep solitude
> You are far away too, oh farther than anyone.
> Thinking, freeing birds, dissolving images,
> Burying lamps.

> Pablo Neruda dead.

> Camus dead.

> Cocteau dead.

Katherine Kahn, age forty, gives up on bodies, poems, seas, and
rocks—to vacuum home and look for any kind of employment.
Children must have braces. Piano lessons. Gymnastics. Ballet.
Leaning towards afternoons she casts her sad nets towards—the
Woman's Life.

Memos

Katherine liked Jonathon Leeds's face. His manner. To Katherine Kahn he was a true life-hero. Here, in the middle of this city, on Fifth Avenue, was a man whose radiant smile was genuine. It was interesting to go to Jonathon's office. He liked to hunt butterflies, especially certain whites in the mountains of Iran and the Middle Atlas. One year it would be butterflies in South America. Another year butterflies in France. Now the woman's life insurance company. She sat in his office, looking at displays of butterflies. She showed him her memo on the company.

"My dear Katherine this is brilliant. I admire the way you put things together. What I want to do now is arrange for a meeting with the actuary and with Louis Naturman, the gentleman from Payne Weber. He's the one who's going to raise the money for the charter."

"Do you want me to read you just the outline of the proposal I've typed up? The whole proposal is twenty pages. You better have your secretary photocopy it," Katherine said.

"By all means. Read it out loud and then we will go over it." Jonathon spoke into his voice box. "Hold the calls."

"Report—" Katherine began. "Confidential to Jonathon Leeds. Re: Woman's Life—An independent Insurance Company. Concept: Selling and Training Women about their own security and protection needs. Concept includes: Why Women? What kind of woman will be selling? How long will the training program be? Where will it be? How will it be set up? What is the program? Guest Speakers. Field Trips for students and Student Training. How many women in the training program? What else will the Company offer? Adult training classes for policy holders. How will the women be recruited? How will they be selected? What kind of degree will be offered? A suggestion for evening workshops."

"Excellent" said Jonathon.

"Now what happens?"

"It's just a question of our man raising the money."

*

The next few weeks passed happily for Katherine Kahn. With the promise of the new company starting she prepared for Christmas. Apricots. Nuts. She bought dollhouse furniture. And encountered another gentleman caller. Only this time she called on him.

*

Bernard Jafee. An odd-ball corporate banker. He had been introduced to her by the husband of a friend. He was divorced. Long white hair fell around his shoulders. Clothes impeccable. Large eyes. Bluish green. He was riding past the divorce-land, riding for his own sake, riding a new life—that was what he had told Katherine Kahn when they had met briefly at a bar to look each other over, size each other up, look each other up and down. Katherine found his voice sensitive. He seemed intelligent. She asked him if she could spend an evening with him talking about Woman's Life, her concept for a company. He had a little Mona Lisa smile. Did he know everything? The world of stocks and bonds and numbers and returns? Was he king of that world? She called Bernard Jafee up one evening when she was alone with the silence of a pre-Christmas evening and the children were long ago in bed.

"My daughter and son are visiting," he said. "But why don't you come over? They are going to leave soon to go home to their mother. And we can talk. I'm interested in your company. At least I'd like to have a chance to chat with you about it."

Katherine remembered that Joseph, the neighbor's son, would happily baby-sit. "All right. If I can get Joseph to stay here in the house I'll come and visit you. Where do you live?"

He told her the address. He lived on Park Avenue.

She could have guessed that.

*

It was a cold night. The frost made her face red. Katherine arrived at the small discreet office building cum apartment house. One had the feeling that the entire house was filled with business men who worked not only in their offices but in their homes. Their homes were just another kind of office. Business was never done. The doorman in a monkey suit admitted Katherine to the lobby and rang upstairs to see if she was expected. She rode up in the elevator looking at her face in the mirror. It was bright red.

Bernard Jafee greeted her in his bathrobe. He was smiling. "My children have gone home" he said. "What would you like to drink?"

"Oh anything" Katherine said. She looked around his apartment. A blue carpet was on the floor. A bare Christmas tree was in one corner of the room. There was also a pinball machine (for the children?) and an imitative modern painting in the worst taste was above a fireplace that had a fire going with a fake log. There were no curtains in the windows. The couch was cheap looking. The walls were depressing. It did not look like a home. Or an office. It looked like a corridor somewhere in a transitional place. Not a living room.

"Can I show you the rest of the apartment?"

Katherine Kahn found herself saying politely "I'd love to see it."

He led her, barefoot in his robe, into the "children's rooms"—a place with games and a double-decker bed—into his own bedroom—which had wallpaper of brown and blue flowers—bedspread and blinds out of the same material—a library without books—back into the living room.

They both sat down on the couch. He began rolling a joint.

"Do you smoke?"

"No. I used to. I really don't any more."

"Well I do." He lit up. One joint was followed by another and another. The story of his life tumbled out. His father was a pilot in the war. He was stationed in the Philippines. He grew up in the Philippines. His mother played Mah-Jongg. He lost his mother in a hurricane. He became an oceanographer. He sailed the Gulf Stream. Then he went into business. Now he wanted to make love.

Didn't he want to discuss the company?

Suddenly he reached out his hand and ran his hand over her breasts. She noticed the nipple growing larger. She was attracted to him.

He bent over and gave her a long kiss. His mouth was moist. She was entering the ocean again. She breathed him into her. His large lips were soft and began kissing her neck. He lifted her sweater and began kissing her breasts. She wanted suddenly to make love with him. She lay back gently on the couch and let him run is hands over her body. Slowly she found her hand under his robe.

Romano. Romano. She remembered him as she began kissing this odd stranger. In a way—he looked like Romano. Same full lips. Slanted eyes.

Bernard was now kissing her cheeks. Her face. He took her hand and put it inside of his mouth. He was biting her fingers. He was kissing her again. She really had not come to make love.

But she could feel her body becoming excited. Heat started inside her arms and legs. She felt warm and moist. She looked at his white hair as he put his tongue on her breasts.

He began to caress her thighs. This too was making her so warm. Katherine had forgotten–truly forgotten–the excitement of touching and being touched. She kept very still as he kissed her breasts. She wanted him. His tongue was her tongue. Then he pulled away from her.

"I assure you this is not the time for insurance." The poetry of the bedworks. "My dear Miss Kahn. I assume you did not come here to only talk about insurance. I like you. I wish you would continue this conversation with me in the bedroom."

He rose and led her like a lord in a silk robe to his boudoir which was a mess. More marijuana. Brandy. A few more details about the Philippines.

Katherine went into his bathroom. She was inclined to stay in there forever. After all she was forty. Did she want to make love with this man? "Not really" a voice said to her. "Try" said another voice.

Wearing one of his terry-cloth robes she emerged from the bathroom. She realized, with a certain weariness, that he was an aging hippie.

"I really like younger girls" he said.

"What can I say to that?" Katherine asked.

"Nothing. I like your skin."

It was all absurd. Memories of Camus this morning with the Windex and vacuum cleaner. Chats about insurance with Jonathon. She had to hurry. The baby-sitter! Oh my God. She'd better hurry.

"I'm terribly sorry. But I have a sitter waiting for me."

"A what?"

"A sitter."

"Please" he said.

"Please what?"

"Please spank me" he begged. He started crying. He was in the fetal position. Was he joking?

"Forget spanking. That doesn't turn me on."

"It turns me on" he said.

"How would you like it if I took you over my knee and started a great spanking so you began to howl?"

This man was crazy. Perhaps he thought this was exciting. Out of his nakedness he became a stranger.

"Katherine. I want you to be my nursie. I want you to take me over your knee and spank me. I want you to be my mommy. Ever since I first saw you looking at me I saw the mother in you. I wanted to say mommy mommy. I lost my mommy when I was a little boy. Now I want you to spank me. I'll be good mommy. I'll be good."

How depressing, Katherine thought.

And still—maybe it wouldn't hurt to spank him. If it really made him so happy. How would she do it? She never spanked anyone. Not even the girls. She had heard about the bars in New York by the waterfront where there were leather thongs and people beat each other. It was all a symptom of a crazy society where pain was pleasure—the inside-out world where people drove each other to death to feel life. She had heard about it. But this man was not a sado-masochist. He was a businessman for godsakes. He didn't want whips or boots or thongs. He didn't want anything except an innocent spank. Couldn't she give him that? Would it be so terrible to just give a little potch on his tookis? Potch on tookie? Baby world of potch potch. Deep down in the spank world of babies. This man was a baby who wanted to be beaten by his elders. A little boy needing mommy to make love with. Suck suck suck spank spank spank. Oh no. This is too ridiculous. I don't *want* to spank him.

"I can't spank you. I'm terribly sorry. I really would like to oblige you but I am afraid I am unable to take you over my knee. To begin with you're too heavy Bernard," she heard herself saying. Was she really saying it?

He was not a man any longer. But a whimpering crying screaming infant. "Spank me. Spank me mommy."

"Shhhh."

"Spank me. Spank me. Spank me."

Either she had not heard him correctly or she was going insane.

"Katherine. Please—" he began to whimper. "How did you know?"

"Know what?" Katherine asked. It was now a question of how to get out of this place immediately. She didn't have a baby-sitter at home that she was paying two dollars an hour—to go out in the middle of a cold night and spank this maniac with his stories about Mah-Jongg and the Gulf Stream. And the Philippines.

"Spank me—Spank me" he begged. He was now whining.

Katherine bolted from the bed. Took off the terry-cloth robe. Got into her own clothes.

"Where are you going?" Bernard Jafee asked, surprised.

"Home."

"Without making love?"

This man ran a corporation. These were the wheelers and dealers of the corporate structure?

"I must leave."

"I want you to come back Katherine. Katherine I need you."

He had changed into a total baby. It was probably his pinball machine in the living room. Or was that for *afterward?* His adolescent period?

"Take care of yourself."

Compassion was needed. Goodnight Goodnight.

*

Out on the streets. Snow flurries. Couples walking home. Scarves around each other. What if the insurance company didn't work? Then a job. But what kind of job? Spank him indeed. The whole world was nuts. Let him spank himself.

*

The next day Katherine met with Jonathon and the actuary. Tables were being drawn up. The actuary was from the south. He thought the company was a good idea. He had his doubts. The actuary said he thought Katherine was a "brilliant girl."

*

Months passed.

*

A meeting was held with Louis Naturman from Payne Weber. The actuary was there. It was in Jonathon's office. Drinks were being poured from delicate crystal decanters, under the butterflies. The gentleman from Payne Weber once had played baseball for the Kansas City Athletics. His wife, he said "was an outstanding teacher in the field of science." He wore a sad look. Entering the room he took out his briefcase.

"The news is not good" he said in a monotone voice.

"What is it?" asked Jonathon.

"I can't raise the *financing* for the independent women's life insurance company."

*

She looked at this man. Was he going to tell her there was not going to be a *Woman's Life?* Was it *possible* that her "partner" had failed? She wanted to cry.

Louis Naturman continued speaking in a cultured but helpless voice. "Katherine," he said, "I received a letter that was personal and confidential from the U.S. Life Corporation. It was sent to me by T. U. Clutterman, chairman of the board and chief executive officer. I will read it to you."

He adjusted his glasses. His voice became more cultured. It was his cultivated letter-reading voice.

"Dear Louis.

"Several of us have independently reviewed copies of Miss Kahn's proposal which I have made and distributed.

"Let me share my personal observations with you first. I do not agree that the need for a woman's life insurance and retirement income policies is not being addressed by the traditional insurance industry, at least insofar as U.S. Life Corporation is concerned, nor do I concur with the statement that the nation's insurance agents are trained to sell insurance products only to the man-in-the-family. Of course I cannot accept the statement that the major companies are so large that changing both procedures and sales policy orientation rapidly are difficult if not impossible tasks and I believe we have proven this by actions taken within our corporate structure. In the same vein I have to take exception to some of the commentary which follows the caption 'The void: Direction of Insurance Selling.' Although it is possibly correct that no conventional insurance company in the past has targeted the women's market, I do not believe that assumption is any longer valid, at least for some carriers.

"Where I come out on your proposal is that conceptually, Louis, you may have gathered something that is pretty sound and you certainly have gathered together a prominent group of talented individuals, but I believe a better course of action would be to devote that talent, time, energy, and money to the formation of a general agency which would represent a major company attempting to tap this market rather than forming a new life insurance company.

"I imagine these are not the comments which you would prefer, Louis, but am assuming you wanted a candid and professional opinion of your proposal.

"With warm personal regards"

The letter was over. It wasn't *so* bad. Jonathon, the actuary, and the gentleman from Payne Weber poured themselves a drink.

Jonathon spoke first. "You can't raise a cent can you on Woman's Life?"

"I'm afraid not."

The actuary spoke. "I think it's still a good idea. But we don't have the start-up dollars and without them we can't form a company."

"I'm already in the life insurance agency business. Besides you don't get that rich from an agency." Naturman was pulling out of Woman's Life.

There was nothing more to say.

Katherine Kahn spoke slowly. "A women's insurance agency will of course be started by someone else. The target market of women is in need of a women's insurance company. I am sure that a direct mail campaign, plus leased counter areas in major shopping centers—is bound to work. However—I have researched a breakdown of media and marketing expenses—and I am equally sure that if well marketed this company could work. However—I can't do this alone. Nor am I able to raise the desired capital."

She sat down. She was happy not to have cried. She stared at the butterflies.

"Money is hard to come by today" the actuary said.

"Insurance stocks are depressed" said the gentleman from Payne Weber.

"Media prices are high. So is rent. And a quarter of a million dollars isn't even seed money" said Jonathon.

It seemed inevitable.

"I suggest we table this company until the time is ripe" said the actuary.

"Agreed" said the gentleman from Payne Weber.

Everyone said goodnight to Jonathon and Katherine and took their departure.

The actuary had a car waiting. The gentleman from Payne Weber was playing tennis. Jonathon and Katherine were left alone in Jonathon's office.

"It was a great idea Katherine. Really it was. I don't think you should abandon it. The timing is wrong."

"I can't afford to wait until someone discovers it. I'll just have to get a job."

Memories and Miracles

Leaving Jonathon's office, Katherine Kahn descended into the lobby of the French building. The gold filigree office doors shut quietly. She walked past the Hoffritz store for accoutrements for the home. She looked at the knives. They shone like tiny thin mirrors. "Am I ready to kill myself?" Katherine asked. "Of course not" said the tiny surviving voice inside her that chimed like a bell. "So the insurance company didn't work out. So what? You were not really in *love* with the company concept anyway. You just wanted something to do that would make some money and give you your own office. Time to give up all these schemes my dear and find yourself another way to make money."

*

Out in the snowy streets, Katherine Kahn felt immensely relieved. Even happy. "There's something about the failure of things that is enormously liberating. You get rid of one thing and you start again."

She walked up Fifth Avenue. The fake Santas were not out yet. There was just the bustle and mystery of the shoppers. What was this enormous ritual of buying and giving? The holding and grabbing of objects had nothing to do with Christ who preached freedom. If Christ were to reappear in New York at Christmas time, would he go shopping at Saks Fifth Avenue for a terry-cloth robe? All the sadness of the twentieth century gone wrong rang from the grave-groping at the department stores. Christmas-in-seed, in-seed at zero, thundered through the town. That was so kind of Jonathon to invite her to join him and his family in Florida. Wouldn't the girls love it? They loved the sea. But she couldn't accept his generosity—it would be too much. Or would it? With two hundred dollars in a savings account, and two hundred dollars arriving from Mr. Jaksforth it would be wise to think of employment not vacationing. Goodbye little insurance world. Little actuary world. World of life and death and tables of the law. It was a good thought but it didn't work.

The traffic was green and red lighted—the cars stopped and started—Katherine walked down to Madison Avenue and took the bus. Crowded between the bodies of the shoppers she felt happy at last. No money. But the wonderful girls at home. Two beautiful faces—she'd surprise the girls with a present. A wonderful present! Some oranges from the fruit store. Wrapped in white tissue paper. She'd bring home some oranges and light a fire and everyone could listen to Bach and Vivaldi. It was going to be a dingle dongle evening of children and oranges. She'd show the girls the Cherry Pit. They loved to see mommy when she was in Eighth Grade. Their favorite Cherry Pit—the funniest yearbook—was the one from nineteen forty-nine. She'd take that one out. She enjoyed it as much as the children. "Where are you—where are you mommy?" they asked, jumping on top of each other. There I am. Katherine Sue Kahn. (A picture of all the miserable little Eighth Graders.)

They would start at the beginning of the book again. First the Senior Advisors. Bettie Lee Craid. *Oh I loved Bettie Lee most in the whole school*—and a quote under Bettie Lee from Terence—"I am a woman, and nothing human is foreign to me." The quote. How much it meant to Katherine now. And then Mr. Harold Bally—Katherine's English teacher—with his little blue handwriting "To Katherine—you merely have started to realize your potentialities—try hard next year and you'll be one of the best"—but what are my potentialities? she could hear herself asking after Mr. Bally signed her yearbook. And then all the pretentious seniors—Barbara Hur, Giovanna Bautermanns, Chickie Fendler, Peter Colen and Joseph Yamale—all of them. She was in love with both Peter Colen and Joseph Yamale. She remembered being in Eighth Grade and wearing a pink angora sweater and dancing with Peter Colen. Oh it was wonderful to feel him hugging her tight. Her breasts against his chest. Pete wrote in her yearbook "To Katherine—Love that boy!" What boy? What's the difference? Love Pete—did he mean that she was flirting with everyone? Well perhaps that was true. Joe Yamale wrote "I still don't think there's a cuter little girl at Boarding School.—Be good and stay as beautiful as you are and watch out for all the boys." She knew the yearbook by heart. The girls made her read every inscription. And show pictures of Dr. Lindstrom and the boys' house and the manor house and the Athletic Field. Hyacinth days. Athletic Field hockey days when nothing mattered except flirting with boys and trying to "live up to one's potentials."

The bus stopped. She got off. Katherine took the crosstown.

So the insurance company didn't ever get back together. It humpty dumptied apart. So what. Did she really want to train in-home salespeople? No. NO. It was just another flopped scheme. Another one of her brilliant ideas that didn't work out. There had been so many others—well she could write interviews. That's what she would do—go back to interviewing people. Questioning. The occupation of a poet. To question. It wasn't much of a living. But suddenly Gertrude Stein's what is the answer what is the question came into her mind. Would Gertrude Stein have started an insurance company? Certainly not.

Snow falling on Central Park West. The churches looked like towers. A bird in the air. Manhattan in Winter. It was good to be alive. Katherine Kahn heard footsteps on the pavement as she walked towards her building. She stopped. Was someone following her? A mugger? The paranoid nausea swept through her body—the anxiety of a person who lives in the city. She turned around.

"Hello Katherine."

She couldn't believe it.

"I followed you off the bus—I was trying to catch up and surprise you."

It was Mike O'Neil from Hong Kong.

"God it's good to see you" she cried flinging out her hands and throwing her arms around the dark little man who stood laughing on the sidewalk. "This is the best surprise. I'm taking you home for Christmas."

"Where do you live?"

"Just one more block. Eighty-sixth Street between Amsterdam and Columbus. Will you join me for dinner? I want you to meet my girls. I have two big girls now—aged eight and ten. You'll love them."

"Isn't this a miracle?" O'Neil asked.

"It is."

*

They sat in her living room. Katherine made a fire. She buried herself in the past and remembered meeting Michael in Hong Kong. She had first seen him at the Mandarin Hotel. They had gone out together–had a dinner on top of the Mandarin. But she had married Mr. Jaksforth. What was the point of thinking about mistakes? Life had an odd way of changing and bending. Now Mike O'Neil was here in New York. He looked so young and full of joy. He hadn't aged the way she had. There was no hostility in his gentle face.

"This is a wonderful accident" he said. They were both drinking brandy. The girls had been introduced to Mike.

"He used to be a jockey?" the oldest girl asked.

It's your turn she said to the baby. They were "wishing."

"I wish I could be magic. I wish I could turn day into night and night into day. I wish my daddy was here. I wish I could grow up fast. I wish it wasn't windy. I wish no-one died. I wish I had new crayons."

Goodnight wishbones!

*

Cooking in the kitchen Katherine had Mike sit on the stool while she told him about her recent life. The marriage being bad. The nights in Westchester. The divorce. The money running out like a stream of water. Odd guys–people she had slept with. Friends. Silences. Studies. Teaching. Then the insurance company. How it hadn't worked. How suddenly in the middle of her life she felt frightened. The responsibility! How life had changed. How suddenly having children had changed it all. No more lofts.

Or running around. Or running away. The backpath life over. Now it was schools and bills. The children so beautiful. She'd lie in bed at night and weep sometimes over how lucky she was! Other nights being afraid. Afraid of what? Dissolving images. Hardened passions. Bills. Sweet blue hyacinth twisted over her soul.

"Come here" Mike said. She went close to him.

"I hadn't seen you in so long. I was afraid to call you. I heard you and Jaksforth were divorced. But I've changed so much too. Stopped riding. Turned into myself for a while. You know what? I've begun meditating. And studying religion. Oddly enough I became interested in the cabbala. From a jockey at the Hong Kong race track to a study of Jesus and then Hebrew mysticism. Not bad for an Irish boy from Manhattan who ran away from home."

"It's really lovely to see you."

"Yes. Yes."

And he had told stories about horses, riding slender horses at the race track. And the colors. And the race. The whole exuberant world of it came pouring out of his mouth. Nobody wanted to end things with sleep.

And the girls had been happy. They liked him. He knew their daddy. They liked that. And they were now playing jockey and horse in their bedroom. "Ride a cockhorse to Banberry Cross to meet Mike O'Neil upon a white horse," one of the girls sang.

"My knight in shining armor is a jockey." They both laughed.

Katherine left the fire and put the girls to bed. Bath. Soap. Stories. Kisses. Double-decker angels tucked into their pajamas. Snowflakes on the window.

"Will it be windy?"

"No. It won't be windy."

"Are you going out tonight mommy?"

"No. I'm staying home."

"Good."

"Let's make Christmas wishes. Let's make thirteen Christmas wishes."

"Who'll go first?"

"I will" said Katherine. "I wish I could keep my two girls close to me forever and ever and we can always have as much fun as we're having now."

"My turn. I'm the oldest."

"Go."

"I wish I had a fairy. I wish my mommy was fat. I wish I had an angora sweater like mommy used to have. I wish animals would never die. I wish I had a camel for Christmas and we could go to France. I wish I had a gardenia plant. I wish I could help all the poor children of the world."

"That's it? All your wishes?"

"Those are *some* of them."

Katherine stood in the kitchen wondering for a moment if he wanted to make love with her. God knows—she missed touching. She almost wondered if she *remembered* how to make love.

"What are you thinking?" he asked.

"I was thinking about—if I remembered how to make love."

"One doesn't forget those things."

"I wonder. Sometimes—well I don't have that much opportunity Mike. I used to find all sorts of love affairs and all sorts of men. Now my head is into so many other things. Body rights. The whole investigative aspect that hasn't been discovered yet—about our economic destinies."

"What kind of job are you going to be doing now?"

"Reporting again. And you? Are you going to be staying in New York for a while?"

"For the holidays.—Katherine I want you to be honest with me for one second."

"I'll always be honest with you Mike."

"I want to make love with you. Do you want to?"
"Yes."
"I don't want to while you're home. It's inhibiting with the children. Will you come to my hotel tomorrow morning?"
"Yes."

*

After the children were in school Katherine took a cab to Mike's hotel. She rang the bell. Two moments later they both had their clothes off and were in each other's arms.
"I'd forgotten" she said.
"I did too."
His mouth kissed her. He began to hold her so tight she felt she couldn't breathe. It was almost as if he were hungry.
"I'm going to eat you up" he said. He began swallowing and eating her mouth, her breasts, her thighs. They came in each other's mouths. They kissed as the sun pierced through the window.
"This is the way I've always wanted to make love with you Katherine."
His body was short. Dark hair was all over his body. "I love your dark hair" she said.
"You're shaking all my roots. It's as if I'm a tree and you're shaking my roots so that I want to grow on top of you. I'm tangling my tongue with yours. I'm tangling my arms with you. I'm tangled in your body. I don't want to leave you. I want more. It's as if I was always with you. I love the body of a woman. But I love your body most. The white hills. The white thighs. You're my world lying in surrender."
"I was alone in a room until you came. I was wandering through the days of my life. Thinking about work. Thinking about my children. Thinking about my childhood. The way

things used to be. Years in my mind. Years jangled in my mind. It was truly as if when I married the second time I˙experienced the death of the body. Or was it the death of the soul? When my babies were born I felt so alive inside my womb. I wanted always to hug from my guts. But there was no one to hug. He–didn't want me."

Mike looked at her and she thought he would cry. "I want you Katherine."

"I think it's too late. To survive I forged a certain coldness like a weapon."

"I want you. My whole body aches for you."

"I'm wary. And weary."

"Not for what we have. But first I'm going to make love to you again. And again."

*

After leaving Mike O'Neil's hotel room Katherine went home. She took a bath and looked in the mirror. *For the first time I feel like a woman again.* Then despair. The sadness that came after so much joy. She would have to be careful.

The phone rang. It was Michael.

"I know what you're thinking," he said.

"Do you?"

"Yes. You're frightened of me. You're in the middle of a life struggle and here I am out of the past making love to you. And you know what? I'm putting on my clothes and I'm going to make love to you again."

*

"The house is a mess. I'm about to start writing letters."

"You're not going to write letters this morning. For the first time in a long time you're not going to do all the things you *have* to do. You're going to make love with me."

They were in bed again.

"I want to tell you what it feels like to touch you Katherine. My head blows up so I feel like a balloon. And I'm floating. But it's not helium—it's something else. I feel all the newness of life. The newness of being myself and happy."

"You're a wonderful plant. I feel that I'm growing into you."

"Then kiss me. And then let's take a nap. And then let's go out and have a wonderful lunch."

"I make the lunch."

"First love. Then lunch."

Katherine Kahn felt whole. And good for the first time in a long time.

*

Over lunch they ate apricots. Life began spilling out. Michael told Katherine about what he was doing.

"I'm writing a book about my life. A sort of autobiographical memory book. Sometimes I think my own life is all I have. I have a small house on Lantao Island. I'm going to take your kids there and you there. You're going to come with me Katherine."

Suddenly anxiety in the stomach. "I can't" said Katherine. "But I wish I could."

"I want you to come back to Hong Kong with me" Michael said.

"Don't be silly. I can't do that."

"Why not?"

"Because of the girls. They're in school now. I can't just uproot them and take them into another environment."

"They have schools in Hong Kong."

"It's not only that. I left Hong Kong a long time ago with my dear ex-beloved. I can't drop everything all over again. I've done that two times. First Paris and a whole new life. Boulevard St. Germain. The bowling alleys of the world. Thinking each day I was five years old with a new window to discover, new cathedrals and paintings, old wood, tangled shadows of Proust and Rimbaud—I left in the calendar of the sun—it was lovely to have a new life then. And later—meeting Mr. Jaksforth and starting all over again in Hong Kong. Pottinger Street. The slopes of the peak. The coastline and the side streets filled with kids—me on a sampan—it was thrilling. But I left there a long time ago. Left the consulate. Left the teas for the wives of the consulate. I couldn't go back there now with *you,* with anyone. I couldn't make another life again. I'm stuck with this one. I'm too old. I can't be somebody's wife or mistress any more. I can't have my world beginning again. I'm too old Mike."

"You're not too old."

"At my age you don't start again. You take the life you have and make it work. The best you can. You live from one day to the next. You don't tangle yourself up in the shadows of someone else's solitude."

He held her in his arms. "Don't say no to me yet Katherine. I see you in a life-change."

"I couldn't deal with hope again. Because I couldn't deal with disappointment. It's not that one becomes afraid of marriage. It's that one can't stand the thought of another divorce. Can't stand the thought of layers of layers of untangling the knots one takes such care to make. Maybe there's just too much wildness in me to *give* my life up to another person."

"That's ridiculous. Why do you have to give your life up? Haven't you been telling me about mutuality?"

"Yes. But then one day one person grows tired of the other. It doesn't happen suddenly. One day you notice that your love's breath smells and you debate whether or not to say something.

The creases in his face begin to annoy you. So does his way of leaving pennies all over the dresser. And you want so desperately to have lunch with *someone* else. The feeling that nadired the sun inside you—that made you feel anticipation makes you feel annoyance. The crack in the plaster begins to upset you—and it collapses. The beautiful wall you created falls. It can kill you."

"Why live in perfections? It's human to be annoyed at someone. I can't imagine ever being really annoyed at you Katherine."

"You would suffer getting accustomed to me. My getting up in the middle of the night to read. My things that I like to leave on the sink. The unorganized way I have of doing everything. My passion for new projects. My enthusiasms would drive you mad. My exaggerations kill you. My love for people—new people—would drive you mad. Your hours of solitude would drive me crazy—and you like to be alone. You'd be living on Lantao Island like a monk and I'd think continuously of inviting other people over. No. It wouldn't be possible for us to be happy."

"And are you sure? I could see us on the Archipelago between Hong Kong and Cheung Chau. I'd take you to an archipelago and never let you have the problems you have now again. No more bills. No more demands. No more dreaming up ways to take care of things. I have such a lovely old house. It used to be a temple. We could live there so easily."

Looking at him Katherine suddenly felt very tired. Very old. In the mail would come Con Edison Bell Telephone Dr. Turppin—all the little requests for money that came under the crack of the door every day. Money. Madness to live like that. And suddenly it was so tempting to think of running away—away with Michael—her two girls under her arms like loaves of bread. No. It was impossible. Perhaps she would sit in the sitting room of her apartment on the West Side and become an old woman in three days. There it was—closed-door panic. No. She could not go.

"Let me think about it" she said to Michael.

Then, in the midst of a cold winter Manhattan morning they fell asleep.

*

Out on the street Katherine thought suddenly "I must look ghastly."

She took her dark glasses out of her pocketbook and put them on. Once safely back in her apartment she listened to some music and thought about Michael. She was suddenly excited again. She was only very sleepy, horribly sleepy, the way a child would be after a long day. And it was still only morning. Twelve o'clock.

She looked at her appointment book. *The* Jerry Rubin the angelic troublemaker and genius had called and wanted to have lunch with her. He had just "blown" into town and wanted to start a newspaper. She adored him and couldn't say *no*. Katherine had met him at the nineteen seventy-two convention in Miami—when she was a delegate. He had been for McGovern and had said "If this country elects Nixon it will be death. But if McGovern gets elected a whole new energy will be released. The crazies, gays, hippies, intellectuals will all have a friend in the White House." She had liked him—his energy was demonic. He was a tiny packed gnome who in some odd way reminded her of Dylan Thomas—the Thomas she had never known but who she had heard about. He had read at Bennington one year before she had entered. *The* Jerry Rubin was her soul-buddy. She loved him deeply.

She called Jerry's "message desk." He had left a message that he would meet her at twelve-thirty at the Russian Tea Room. That would be fun. To stop worrying for twenty minutes or an hour about bills. To stop thinking "Should I go off to Hong Kong with Michael?" To enjoy the energy of a tiny media-magician who had captured the imagination of the world by chanting "The

Whole World Is Watching" during the Humphrey fiasco. Now he had been prosecuted with the Chicago Eleven, had turned himself into a student of philosophies and a knowledge seeker. She liked his acceptance of things. They were almost the same age–he was thirty-eight–she–forty–from an odd time–the fifties and sixties. In some way they bore a resemblance to each other. A certain paranoid enthusiasm and curiosity. He had said to her once in a car "When I was born my parents say that I was born asking *why?*"

"Me. Too."

"I would have made a wonderful prosecutor. I ask so many questions. I wish I could have prosecuted the Chicago Eleven."

He was waiting for her at the table she always reserved.

"I'm sorry I'm late" she said. "I've had a difficult morning."

His hair frizzled above his head–a halo of brown curls. His eyes were happy–elf's eyes. He was a life sponge. He soaked up everything moment to moment to moment.

"I liked waiting for you" he said. "I love to look at people. And I love when they recognize me. Who's that man?"

"Which one?"

"That guy. That guy over there going to the bathroom."

"I think that's Bob Silvers."

"No that's not Bob Silvers. You mean the guy from the *New York Review of Books?* Naw. That's not him. Look. Look there he is–look he's going to a table."

Katherine looked at the large fat comedian walking down the aisle with a smile under his moustache. "That's Lou Jacobi. I'll introduce you to him."

"Who's that?"

"He was in the movie that Louis Malle made years ago called *Zazi dans le métro.* I saw it when I lived in Paris and fell madly in love with his humor. He's my favorite comedian. Woody Allen had him in his movie *Everything You Ever Wanted To Know About Sex.* He played a transvestite. So funny I thought I'd die. He also played in *Diary of Anne Frank.* He's an artist. He drew caricatures of everyone in the play and they put them in the front of the theatre. Frankly I preferred his caricatures to the play. He was in a Carol Burnett musical written by Comden & Greene and sang 'There's Always One Step Further Down You Can Go.' He lives on Central Park West. His wife is an intellectual and was studying modern theatre criticism with Harold Clurman at Hunter."

"That's what I like about you, Katherine" Jerry said. "You can really give a thumb-nail sketch."

"Thanks. It comes from years of being an investigative reporter. A sort of *deep throat* for every place."

"What do you know about her?" he said–pointing to a slight, frail woman with glasses and blonde cropped hair.

"She was born in New Jersey. Her father was a laborer. She became a lawyer representing women in divorces and other legal matters. She is the author of the *Tenant Survival Book.* Her name is Emily Goodman. When they write about her in the press they call her the young Portia. There was an article about her recently in the *Voice* called 'Portia Faces Life.' She's concerned with the basic dilemma of how women can gain enough money and power to literally change the world without being corrupted, co-opted and incorporated on the way, by the value systems they want to change. She wrote an important book called *Women, Money, and Power,* with Phyllis Chesler."

"You should have told me that first. That would have made it a better thumb-nail sketch" Jerry said. And then added–"I'd like to meet her."

"I'll introduce you" Katherine said. "We're good friends. She was the lawyer that I would have had representing me on the first women's insurance company."

"What company?"

"It was a company I wanted to start. I had the idea to call it Woman's Life."

Katherine ordered a Bloody Mary. Jerry was drinking ginger ale.

He looked at her with a smile.

"So you really think I can start a newspaper? I think New York is ready for it. And I'd like you to help me. You have great ideas."

"I'd like to help you. God knows I'd like to do something that would make me some money. I'm practically broke."

"Broke? I thought you were rich."

"I would be if I lived alone. But I'm supporting two children. My income doesn't go very far."

"Do you have a car?" Jerry asked.

"Yes. It's so impractical. I realize that. I'm selling it. I kept it to run the girls up to the country on Sundays so we could look at the leaves and get out of the city."

Suddenly she realized what a manipulator and operator this guy was. A divine angelic operator.

"Where do you think I can get the financing for a newspaper?" Jerry asked.

"It depends on your target market. You have to identify it. *Rolling Stone* makes a million dollars a year or more. The target market was identified at the perfect time. Kids into rock. Then came *Ms. Magazine*. Nobody thought there were any feminists out there. Everyone said 'One or two issues and then just dykes will read it.' It's the publishing success story of the century. Actually it's doing better than the *Ladies' Home Journal*. There are no more ladies. If you know what I mean. The women's revolution was invisible until someone saw it. The odd thing is that *Ms.* sells better in Iowa than any other magazine. Then *High Times*. No one knew so many people smoked dope. That's the market."

"Yeah. I know. *High Times* is doing so well the editor calls it a License To Steal."

"Every day a new magazine is born. *Working Woman* is a new

one that just started based on the idea of professional women wanting the kind of magazine that reaches them where it counts. Financially. They asked me to write for it—but they wanted to pay me a big two hundred and fifty dollars for an article. Don't you love it? They write about successful women and how important it is to get equal rights and equal pay and they niggerize the women writers. I told them to go fuck themselves."

Katherine ordered a chef's salad. Jerry ordered blini.

Katherine said "How about a newspaper—a weekly newspaper called NOTHING. Or NADA. Because if you identify the fifties—it was the art scene. In New York anyway. Surrealism in Paris. And sowing the seeds for political change. The beatniks. Ginsberg. Pot. The dark ages are not as dark as everyone thinks they are. That was the first lesson I learned at Cherry Lawn—my boarding school—about history. If it wasn't for the dark ages we wouldn't have had the Renaissance. If it wasn't for the fifties—no sixties. Then the sixties. You were in the middle of that. So was I in a way. I was hanging around Warhol for a while. Between marriages. The first film he ever did was called *Lips*. They were my lips."

"Your lips? Crazy."

"Yes. But I didn't say anything. It wasn't until recently—that I felt I had anything to say." Katherine laughed.

"Lips without a message. I could get off on that" Jerry said.

"Now. About a newspaper. What I would like to see is something aesthetic. Beautifully and simply done. That addressed the seventies. Called NOTHING. That's what the seventies are. So far. Nothing."

"Hey. I see that. When historians look back they'll see nothing. In the Buddhist sense. Less is More."

"Nada y Nada y Nada."

"I get it. But do you think we could get financing for NOTHING?" Jerry asked.

"Seriously? No. If you ask someone for a million or ten million dollars you can't tell them it's for NOTHING. They will want something. And that something has to be more defined than nothing."

Katherine had another idea. "Hey Jerry. Listen to this idea. You know all the pornographic magazines on the newsstands? *Screw. Hustler. High Society.*"

"What's *High Society?*"

"I write for it sometimes to make some money. Under a pseudonym of Andra Nom. I type up some fantasies. It pays bills. I'm a secret pornographer. Anyway *High Society* is a beaver magazine that makes *Hustler* and *Screw* look like *Family Circle.*"

"No kidding" Jerry said.

"It's all ass-holes. Recently between pictures of tushies and the insides of cunts—so largely photographed you couldn't even recognize what they *were*—they had a piece by F. Lee Bailey on what it was like to defend Patty Hearst. Anyway—my idea for a new newspaper—is an ANTIPORNOGRAPHIC PAPER CALLED .... CAN'T. Not Cunt. Can't. For people who either can't get it up or don't feel like all that bother. I mean—I think people are really fed up with cocksucking and cunteating and rimming and putting liver around your cock and rubbing your cunt with applebutter or whatever. I mean how much chocolate vaginal cream does anyone want? I should imagine after wiping someone's behind with your mouth for a couple of years and sucking on cocks until they all seem like jelly apples—those people would change their market. Impotents need a paper too. So give them a newspaper called CAN'T. Then there could be articles about how to play with yourself—or not play with yourself—in a rocking chair. Frankly the target audience would be people tired or bored to death with sex. It would sell an awful lot of copies in New York."

"Are the guys really impotent in New York?"

"Not all of them. But a lot of them are working so hard to be successful that the work becomes the thing that gets them off."

"Any other ideas for a newspaper?" he asked, smiling.

"Only I'd really like to see some good journalism. Mailer Bellow Emily Goodman Mimi Sheraton Woody Allen Joyce Carol Oates Lillian Hellman Flo Kennedy Gloria Steinem—there are fabulous writers around—just use them. Get Brassai and really top photographers to take photographs."

"I like it" he said.

"And—a whole section for health food nuts. That's another whole market. Gays. That's a market. The lesbian market is the fastest growing market in the country. It's just beginning to identify itself. And the nouveau poor. That's me. A whole section not on good living—but on how to save money. And don't forget gossip; also political gossip. And throw in a column by Andy Warhol. And something on modern music. And Feiffer cartoons."

"Why not put in a living supplement. You know they have TV supplements—this could be a living supplement just the opposite."

"I see what you mean. I'm conceptualizing all this. We have to think it over and put it in a proposal before we actually go for the financing."

"Sounds like fun. To start a new company. That's my specialty." Katherine laughed.

After lunch at the cloak room Jerry heard his name called.

"Jerry Rubin. Jerry Rubin."

Two women were sitting at the front table.

"Your groupies?" Katherine said.

He smiled. He was *the real angel of the meridian* and was always ahead of his time. *Jerry* they called. But they weren't groupies. Old friends. She wished she could stay. But she had things to buy for the children. She kissed Jerry goodbye on the forehead.

"Whatever you do. I want to help you. I feel as if you're my satellite brother who just dropped into New York out of the sky."

"Thank you," he said smiling. "I feel good about you too."

She went out the revolving door.

*

In the cold afternoon Katherine walked down Fifty-seventh Street and wondered about the future. She wasn't an operator. And never could be.

Katherine walked past the stores. Life is so short, she thought. Why not go to Hong Kong with Michael? He was a miraculous little person. He was aggressive and contemplative. He was immensely sensitive. She liked making love with him. He was beginning to occupy her time. In her mind. He occupied a lot of her imagination. Perhaps in Hong Kong she could find that secret part of herself that would create poems again.

"I really didn't want to start an insurance company" she said out loud. "I don't want to start a company."

Helen and Katherine

Katherine decided to see Helen.

"My life is so involved with metaphysics, money and kindness. That's it. My odd life" she heard herself telling Helen over the phone. "I think I'm a tycoon of the imagination. A tycoon poet. That's what a poet is anyway. Always an exaggerator. A schemer to get-rich-quick. The only riches are imaginary of course."

Helen said "Of course."

Katherine was lonely. She wanted an old buddy to talk with.

"I'm coming over Helen" she said. Helen was better than no-one. Drunken Helen. Katherine was lonely for someone or anyone.

*

And so Katherine Kahn–height five foot eight–size seven shoe–size thirty-six B cup when she wore a cup–waist 26– favorite color green–favorite flower–Poinsettia–favorite song– "I'm in the Mood for Love"–favorite composer–Bach–favorite playwright–Marlowe–favorite poet–Robert Lowell–favorite painters–Jasper Johns and Botticelli–went in the cold. To see an old friend. To see and talk to an old friend.

*

Helen suggested to Katherine that they go over to her apartment. She was taking a week off from work. She arrived at her house and it was still the remnants of the Bennington Bohemian Helen–wicker baskets, wicker furniture. Plants were everywhere–African daisies and pink carnations. The same Segovia music she had loved in college was playing through the apartment–baroque music–Segovia playing Bach. She poured herself a drink and looked at Katherine.

"Don't be mad at me Katherine if I have a little drink. I need it. I hate Christmas."

"So do I. It's always been like an auto-da-fé for me."

"How's my tycoon poet?" Helen asked.

"Ready to give up tycoonery" Katherine said.

"What do you mean?" Helen asked.

"I'm thinking of a sea-change. A whole change in life. I'm tired of the pain and the suffering of being a divorced woman in New York trying to bring up two kids, trying to make money, trying to get laid. I'm fed up Helen. I just can't do the things I used to do. I need a change of life. A new port. For the past few years I feel as if I've been crying at my own funeral. I've been lonely. I've been looking for love and not finding it. I've been trying to bring up two children by myself. I've been trying to write poetry. That failed. Then I left the world of imagination and went into the world of companies. Like most poets, for me money and kindness and metaphysical life got all mixed up. I tried to be a tycoon. First I tried to found an insurance company called Woman's Life. Now people with start-up companies are coming to me. Jerry the angel just asked me to help him found a newspaper. But you know what? I'm tired of looking for financing. I can't even finance myself. The fact is this: I need a change of life. I want to go deeper into myself and find out—at last—who Katherine Kahn is. Have I had a death of the soul? Or am I in the process of remaking my own life?"

Helen finished another Scotch. "I'd like you to be still for one moment and then tell me how you plan to get away from all this reality?"

"My knight in shining armor has just arrived from Hong Kong. He was a gentleman I got to know when I was visiting Hong Kong for the first time. Before I married Mr. Jaksforth. He's rich. He's an exile from America. Part Irish. Part Chinese. Believe it or not he was a jockey when I met him. Now he's given that up and he's living in a temple. Studying his inner consciousness. He wants me to come back to Hong Kong with him."

"Is he ready to hire a governess for your children?"

"He said we won't need an amah. But if we do it's easy to find one."

"Do you see yourself with an Irish-Chinese jockey?"

"I see myself with anyone that I can love. And who can love me. I'm tired of staying here and slugging it out. Trying to be a fortune-maker instead of an intellectual. I've spent my whole life learning to love and learning to write poems. Love is short. Forgetting is long. I think I'm ready to put the past away and start all over again. It's the children I have to think about. I'm not making a very good life for them in New York."

Helen poured herself another Scotch.

"What do you do about pain?" Katherine listened to her. She continued talking. "What do you do about pain?"

"I deal with it" Katherine said.

"How?"

"I confront it. I talk about it. I analyze it. I wash it. Dry it. Hang it in the sun. Fold it. And put it away."

"I read an article recently" Helen said. "I want to show it to you. It's about this ordinary man who had cancer. He had a good job working as a newspaper editor. When he got cancer he left his job and started shoveling snow. His family withdrew. They were all so depressed. Everyone knew he was going to die. Just no one could talk about it. He became depressed. Cut off. So did his family. This death that he had not only grew inside him but grew inside his family. One day this guy was riding with his wife in a car. He pulled up the car–turned and said to her 'I've got cancer goddamn it. I'm going to die. Let's talk about it. Let's not be strangers. Let's talk about my cancer for godsakes.' Since then he's founded a little group which is blossoming into thousands of little consciousness groups all over the country. It's for people who have cancer and are going to die. To talk about it. To live whatever is left of their lives with dignity and *saying* what is wrong."

"Why are you telling me this Helen?"

"Because you can talk about things. That's why you're going to survive. You have a cancer of the imagination. You were born being a poet. That means that you have always lived two lives. One life just going through the world. The other life *writing* about it. It's that other life that keeps you from dying. The poetry life. You can't give that up and go into the insurance business. My point is this: If you have the opportunity to change your life again for godsakes do so. I'd be so relieved for you to go to Hong Kong. What kind of man is this Michael?"

Katherine took a drink now. She spoke slowly.

"He's a good person. A good lover. He's lost. Like most of us he's still trying to find out who he is. He has quite a bit of money that he doesn't use. He's trying to write a book. About himself and the cabbala. He's quiet. A mystic like you. Like me. He reads a lot. He loves music. He rode horses because he loved them. Never been married. He grew up in a fancy school. He never spent much time with his parents. He is talented, a good person. In goodness there are all kinds of wisdom. Sometimes I think that he's in despair. But it's not despair really but a certain life loneliness which I understand. I don't know if I love him. Maybe I love him. I thought I loved him when I met him. Then I met Mr. Jaksforth. Then—when I was divorced I thought about him. And now—suddenly—he's arrived back in my life. And he wants to take me away with him. To change my life. Am I ready? How do I know? I want to take the risk. To change my life one more time."

"You know what I do about pain?" Helen asked.

"No. I don't."

"I block it out."

"I understand that. Though I have never been like that. The poet in me always wanted to feel more. Not less. I was always so open. And vulnerable. Even as a child. I feel like that man who said 'I have cancer'—all my life I have been congregating my feelings and examining them. And now? It's time to withdraw."

"Will you come back?"

"I don't know Helen. I don't know."

"So what else is new?" Helen said—her eyes getting redder as she drank.

Katherine was enjoying the whiskey now. "I'm so depressed by hassles. Everything has become a hassle."

"I know what you mean."

"I don't even look good any more. I don't look healthy. Time is passing. And I have such odd feelings. The other day I went to a party given by Robert Indiana. He's a tycoon. A tycoon artist. I met him years ago. I remember him as being a miraculous and quiet young man with curly hair. I loved him. We were both so frightened of life. Now he has a six-floor loft. He's made millions from his Love sculpture. Only in America can you tilt the o of love and have it make millions. He's become—so important. I heard him saying 'I have a new sculpture that's going to Israel. I want to put it across from the Wailing Wall.' Can you imagine Helen?"

"Oh?" said Helen. And then added "I can imagine. Love across from the wailing wall. So what will you do?"

"I think I'm going to go with Michael."

The Nightbird

What happened to Carole? Lois? All of us?
Helen took one more drink.

The clatter of ice mountains. A tiny Ant-arctica of Scotch and ice. Helen was my own version of Rimbaud. Other friends had become running-away hausfraus—Candides of the kitchen. Helen was a feminine Rimbaud who escaped into the Africa of Manhattan. Grinding, crumb by crumb, our own lives were grinding down to the grist. After forty the grist became apparent. What was that? Closed-door panic again.

"What got you into tycoonery?" Helen asked.

"I don't know" Katherine said. She leaned back on a wicker chaise lounge and smoked a cigarette.

"I think what happened was that I figured out that money was the end of the Revolution. First I began with street theatre. You remember the demonstrations when Chisholm was running for President? Then, from what I called *Grill-her* theatre–I did the first feminist demonstration in front of Henri Bendel's called *Why Are We Afraid Of Growing Old*–I moved on to divorce. Then to searching for myself. I went into all sorts of investigations. I went to San Francisco and tried–Yoga, health foods, sex therapy, learning to forgive myself, rolfing, bioenergetics–everything. I came back to New York City. And you know what it all leads to–the Revolution? Making money. It gives you that ability to tell everyone to go fuck themselves. Not to mention how convenient it is to raise children. Besides, that's what all the revolutionaries are *into*. Not wood-carving. Tycoonery. Just surviving doesn't interest them. Jerry Rubin would like to make millions. So would–I'm sure–Jane Fonda. For the right purposes of course. Money to be sent to South Africa to counter the apartheid program. Money to be sent to Chile. Or just money to be used to start a newspaper. Or waged in a political campaign."

"Why not?"

"It's been odd."

"Whose life isn't odd?"

"Mine. It's bizarre. Not odd. Me the tycoon."

"Tell me about Carole" Helen said. Her words were a little slurred. Again the Picasso woman with the many eyes–a seamaid singing a strumpet song came out in the life-interview.

"All right. She left Bennington and became a dancer. But according to her her legs 'buckled under' and her knees gave her a lot of trouble. So she became the next best thing to a dancer. A poet. And poets need to work. To travel. To do something of value. She obtained a grant and went to the jungles of Borneo. In Borneo she began to translate the songs of the indigenous people of Sarawak. Translate their songs and changes and chants. She spent three years in the jungle and then two years in the Sarawak Museum."

"What was it like?" Helen asked.

"She did something amazing. She made the first systematic collection of songs of the Sarawak people. Humbly she began a huge work—of trying to save the Sarawak cultures for future generations. She went into the jungle with a translator and took simple songs and, working with the translator, learned about how the people feel and behave during their lives. That's what *art* is. Just ordinary feelings. Put down in everyday language. In images. The sources of the images, she told me, are found in the Sarawak everyday lives. Jars, gongs, mats, blankets, plants, animals, birds, rivers—all of this goes into their song cycle. She told me that by experiencing as much as possible—threshing the pods of padi underfoot—climbing upstream to go tuba fishing—trekking in the padi fields—the rhythms of all of these activities enter into their songs. There's one song that she repeated to me. It's called 'The Nightbird Calls.' Of course I don't remember it all but it keeps repeating over and over 'The Nightbird Calls'—and then it keeps saying 'What a pity.' "

They continued talking. "Somehow I was able to give up my sexual desires and satisfy them with thinking of becoming a billionaire. It hasn't made me rich of course. In fact—I've been a flop at tycoonery. But that doesn't matter—the *high* of trying has been most satisfactory. It's much more fun than being a whore and trying to squeeze money at last out of a man."

"You've never done that. Your father made it possible for you to be independent."

"Yes. But a lot of women become tycoons of the orgasm. The bed becomes their office. Instead of making deals they're sucking cocks. Men too of course. But women are the traditional hookers. Their *thing* is to satisfy their desires. Too often satisfying others is not the path to self-fulfillment. Everyone is always trying to satisfy themselves even if they say it's through satisfying others. I had omnipotent daydreams trying to be a tycoon."

"Kathy—you're a poet not a tycoon," said Helen. "Tell me—don't you remember in college when we used to talk non-stop until twilight. What's happened to us?"

Katherine said "I've had an artist's life. I've been looking for myself. In Paris and Hong Kong. Hanging on to men. Trying to avoid the self I'm looking for. And Shirly has four children and is writing a paper on dying. It's part of a movie she's doing on death-training. Joan is studying mathematics and living in Connecticut. She's still beautiful and has a darling child and a good marriage. I visit her sometimes. Her house is like a haven at the end of the woods. She's a suburban intellectual. And Carole—you won't believe what her life has been."

"Joan in suburbia. Carole in the jungle. The nightbird calls. What a pity that time passes so quickly. One moment we are bathing in Bennington. Tara! Tara! Another moment time has clicked by."

"The whole thing is to make time *work* for you."

"How?" Helen asked.

"By changing. Changing with life. Not letting everything else *change* without you."

"And you? How will you change, Katherine?"

"I don't know. I think I'll move away." Katherine was tipsy. She had to leave Helen's house.

Katherine Kahn went home and made some instant coffee. She began reading some of Carole's translations. They were all in the Sarawak Museum journal. She read to herself one of the nightbird songs:

> The nightbird calls
> Heaving with sobs, the plank carved into a hornbill
> weeps for a nesting place where it can sleep:
> The nightbird calls.

"Weep? Was it time to weep? Or to laugh?"

Katherine Kahn stood in front of a mirror and laughed at herself. Big belly of a woman. Mother. Endangered species. Tycoon-poet. Every poet was a tycoon of sorts. The problem was getting a job. The problem was being a gifted, healthy, happy, joyful woman. The problem was postponing physical disintegration. The problem was calming the mind. The problem was being Katherine. But could she run away? One more time? Would it be running? Or finding?

Michael telephoned. He wanted to come over and visit. Why not?

*

"Are you coming with me?" he asked simply.

They were sitting in the kitchen amidst the pots and pans. The stove was on. Katherine was baking a chicken. It was the girls' favorite. Among the potholders and the whisks and the pans he said again—

"Will you come with me?"

"I want to. I think it would be fascinating to run away from everything all over again. What kind of life could we have?"

"What kind of life would you want?"

"Fame and money are so elusive I don't want them. At the heart of every famous person is a groupie. And inside every billionaire is a holy beggar waiting to come out. And vice versa. I don't know. A quiet place to live in. The tropics. A place where palm trees bend in the sun. My daughters growing next to the palms. Swimming a lot and not wearing heavy clothes. My two angels with me growing and joyful. A place to live where the life-mask drops and the money machines are rusty because no one needs them. A place—away from the worldliness. The battle against the worldliness—"

Michael walked over to Katherine. He started taking off her clothes. First he unbuttoned her sweater.

"I want to talk about this with you in bed."

The Bed

Katherine felt sometimes that she had lived her whole life in a bed. The history of her life was a history of one bed after another. The bed was her first memory. The bed on Riverside Drive. She would stand up in her crib—the little prison bed with the iron bars then made out of wood—and call from the top of her lungs for mommy and daddy. She would throw up in bed and no one would come down the hall—to the bed to rescue her. Sometimes Uncle Eddy would come. That bed led to the bed in Florida. The bed where dreams would bother her. Turn to one side and see Hitler. Turn to another side and see hats. Hitler or hats? The dream of a four-year-old in a little cot in Miami where she went with her mother. And later still—the bed in Riverdale. The bed with the lovely bedspread that mother had bought for her. Yellow taffeta. The yellow taffeta bed. In bed she could imagine that she would grow up. Ride white horses. Ride white horses as dangerous and swift as airplanes. Dream of puppets. She would be the sleeping beauty. A prince would come–

Sleeping Beauty: I'm too old for you.   \
                I can't be your wife.

Prince: We are equal in love
       For the rest of our life.

Rhymes and dreams in the Riverdale bed. Later a bed of tears at grandparents' house. Bed in a maid's room. Then the bed at Cherry Lawn. The boarding school bed on a cold porch. Dreams of Nazis. World War II dreams haunting her head. Different beds in boarding school. Musical beds. The beds with lovers. Husbands. Odd people she had slept with. Now this bed. On this bed she had made a child. Gotten happy. Gotten heavy. Her husband had spent so many nights not-touching in this bed. Had left this bed. Others in this bed. Sleeping with the girls in this bed. "Help me mommy–I can't sleep"–and now in bed with Michael. The same bed. She had heard that John Lennon and Yoko Ono received people in bed. So did Hugh Hefner. The bed as throne and working table. Bed me. Sleep. Most of her life was rounded out beginning and end in bed. Now warm air filled her mouth. The air from Michael's mouth.

His tongue glided over her body. His tongue greased her body. She entered into Michael's arms.

Katherine nuzzled into Michael's arms. "I've never been closer to anyone" she said. His fingers were rough fingers–fat rough fingers with calluses. She liked the way they felt over her skin. His fingers rubbed between her legs and inside her legs until moisture poured out like rain. They fused suddenly.

"I can't speak" Katherine said.

"Don't try" he whispered.

She kissed him.

"You know all about insights and distances," he said. "How did you learn these things? In what magical place did you learn this patois of the body?"

"I don't know. I learned it—here—in bed. Everything is learned in bed. Or from hurts."

She looked at him with a bewildered expression and shook her head. "I can't leave with you Michael."

"Yes you can" he said. His teeth bit her lip and he began kissing her breasts and stomach. "Every day is a new day."

She looked at him with a bewildered expression. "Well—perhaps—perhaps you're right" she said.

*

Michael was sleeping.

Katherine began to dream back over the recent past. The love affair—could it be called that? with Dino Mackenzie came into her mind. It was upsetting to think of him. And yet she couldn't block it out—shut it off. It was like a light at the back of a door that you see when the door is still opened for a crack. Some things could be shut out. Childhood. Cherry Lawn. Bennington. Paris. But for some odd reason she saw Dino. And was almost obsessed with him. The oddness of it all. She had first met Dino after her marriage broke up. She had been desperate. Helen had taken her to a party and had introduced her to a painter. Dino was a tall man—with a thick Italian accent. He told her that he was married but his wife was "out of town." His wife's name was Anne. Poor glorious gloryful Anne. How Dino loved her. The love he had shown by fucking other women and talking about Anne. He came back to her house after the party. He made love to her talking about Anne. Then he went away only to call the next day. Would she come down to his studio?

She took a cab and rode through the streets of the city. The closer she got to Soho where he lived the higher her spirits became. He waited for her at the top of a flight of stairs. One flight? Seven flights. All these stairs. She climbed them and suddenly it seemed as if she were climbing a huge mountain to reach sexual perfection. Paradise. Up the stairs. Dino stood at the top of the stairs watching her climb.

Dino had a studio that was filled with enormous blue paintings. He was painting blue on blue paintings.

"This reminds me of Yves Klein in Paris. So many years ago. His blue world."

Dino laughed. Ooooooooops. Be careful. You said the wrong thing Katherine.

"But this is Dino's world. Not Yves Klein's world. I have not been influenced by him at all," Dino said. He was hurt.

Don't compare. ·If you *compare* you'll walk out of here unfucked. Suddenly she wondered why Dino was giving her the privilege of a fast fuck while his wife slaved away at her job. Was it because he thought she was a tycoon? Was it her contacts? Or her cunt? The New York question. Cunt leads to contacts. She looked at him and there was something of the gifted gigolo about him. He was tall and dark and looked like Michelangelo's David— a statue.

Well—she had come to get laid. On with the show.

"Are you hungry?" Dino asked. He had a bar in his studio complete with salamis and cheeses and white wine. Also nuts and fruit. She sat on the barstool while he fed her. She watched his long brown legs (he wore shorts to work in) clump clump against the painted white floor. There was a large green tree in the room. And a huge heater that warmed the loft. And blue on blue everywhere. His feet moved across the white floor. He was a giant. She followed him.

"You are a writer, yes?"

"Yes."

"I feel that you are also a catalyst. You seem to me to be more of an idea-person."

"You're right."

"I'm glad to take you out of your upper middle class environment. I identify with poverty and I feel more at home in my own environment."

Katherine thought—a gigolo—talking about poverty. That's New York for you.

"I am glad you are here. You want to make love. Yes?"

"Yes."

And then—with the heater blowing on both of them—the huge generator—they made love. It became a ritual. His huge bed. Heater. Afterwards the shower and the soap on a piece of rope. Then going uptown. He—home to his wife—who had an apartment on the West Side. She—the emptiness—home to the two girls. A year of Dino and his blue on blue paintings. Recently she heard that he had dumped his wife in a cruel way. And a new wife—who looked exactly like the old wife—had replaced her. What was it he used to say when he no longer needed her—oh yes—he would call and say—"I can't see you this week Katherine. I am having my difficult moment."

He was always having *difficult moments.*

And yet she had divided her life into those weekly rituals—Dino—downtown—fucking—blue on blue paintings—the heater—his legs walking across the white painted studio—his leaving for Italy—his difficult moments.

Her difficult moments hadn't interested him.

She had done what he wanted. She had brought different patrons and painters and a conglomeration of people to his studio. They had climbed the stairs. Who knows? Maybe Dino would fornicate his way to the ultimate stardom in the art world. "I paint with my penis" Renoir had said.

So did Dino.

She had heard that the Pace Gallery was now giving him a show. How odd. Blue on blue Dino. With his opportunistic penis. It was nice though. She had enjoyed it. Again the bed. Dino's bed—it was hard to enjoy coming and orgasm when all she could think about was—I owe one thousand dollars for Jeanie's tuition—two hundred for braces—three fifty for piano lessons—one thousand dollars to the Venice Market—fifty dollars to Doctor Turppin—it was hard to have orgiastic pleasure when you were the head of a household.

Finally she stopped seeing him. She didn't want to become dependent on an Italian gigolo. Or any other gigolo. And yet here in her bed was Michael. Her lover that had just come into her life without fanfare. He wanted her to come with him—to work on a book about the cabbala with him. To explore mysteries. She would go.

At Agatha's Party and Parrots

Agatha gave a Ship of Good Hope party. It was held at her Beekman Place townhouse.

Katherine arrived with Michael. At the door was the coatrack studded with gleaming hangers on which hung sagging animal pelts—minks and sables. "Do you want some brochures?" she was asked by a young man when she entered. Another man in a black suit who was creating publicity greeted her at the door. Agatha, dressed like a colorful parrot in a long blue and red chiffon dress, arrived. She looked unbalanced.

"There she is. The most talented and brainy woman in New York. Katherine dear—I've been telling them about the cruise—

but you can put everything into words so much better than I can." She moved away into the swirl of guests.

Some people were talking Greek. Others were talking French. Katherine entered the room. She chatted with the maid. Agatha employed a French maid whose life was devoted to creating delicate small meals—all on a piece of tiny bread. "I marinate my own salmon" Agatha said confidentially to Katherine as if this were her philosophy in life.

"The usual smoked salmon is disgusting don't you think? I marinate mine in white wine and then I use dill."

The pâtés, the floats of mousses made out of caviar, the delicate sandwiches and pearls of rice wrapped in marinated vine leaves were passed on trays. Katherine was having a good time. She felt at home amongst the vine leaves and rich people who didn't remember each other's names. It was a pleasant purgatory.

The cocktail party was noisy, decent, elegant. Candles burned around the room discreetly—throwing off a scent that made the atmosphere voluptuous. Everything Agatha collected or arranged was beautiful. The flower arrangements—lilies and tulips, the Rembrandt drawings, the urn that came from Greece—brown and black and mounted on a lucite column—all the best money could buy. On one wall was a large Roman wall painting that came, Agatha had once said, "from a villa at Boscoreale, built in the midst of the first century B.C." Like all the buildings at Pompeii, this house was also buried by ashes from the eruption of Mt. Vesuvius. Three sections of the wall painting were cut out of a larger wall. "My wall shows a Woman Playing a Kithara." In casements in the living room Agatha's collection of Roman glass glistened from the candles. Lemon leaves in modern Venetian vases were placed everywhere and her great bronze modern Brancusi which dominated the room seemed polished. The butlers discreetly circled the guests.

"It's a lovely party, don't you think?" Agatha asked. She looked lost at her own party as if she was desperately trying to keep busy to keep from drowning in loneliness.

Katherine held onto Michael's arm and suddenly into the room walked the Neibergers. Lola Neiberger had been a friend of Katherine's at Beaupre and later lived in Rome. She had a lovely Botticelli face and long red hair. She ran over to Katherine to tell her what she was doing.

"I'm sculpting now. My show is going to open at the Fischbach."

Katherine remembered having been invited several times by the Neibergers to their home in Montauk.

Suddenly a time-change passed over her. She remembered Montauk. She was living with Mr. Jaksforth in their apartment. The girls were spending a weekend with their grandparents. It was hot. The children gone made the house seem empty. She was sexually frustrated. Suddenly she felt so empty and tired and used up. Unconnected to anything. Was it lack of energy? She sat in the large green chair in their bedroom reading a book. There was no air conditioner and the apartment was oppressive. The phone rang. She remembered not even wanting to answer it. She remembered her husband saying "Get the phone Katherine."

The phone call! The Neibergers—invited the *couple* to the Electric Circus. She was no longer Katherine—it was always "we" and "us" why don't "the both of you" and *the Jaksforths*. And her husband on that hot evening said "You go Katherine. I don't feel like it."

And she said "You don't mind if I go alone?" Getting out of the green chair.

"Of course not. You should do more things alone."

And Katherine had gone. And at the Electric Circus was a young actor named Barry. Barry had danced with her; his dungarees were like a second skin and she could feel him getting excited and wanting her. And she had wanted him also. "I'm

married. I can't leave with you" she had said when he suggested
that they go to his apartment which was on the Lower East Side.
"But I'm flattered" she had said. "You're not flattered. You're
hungry. And you want me as much as I want you." And she had
left with him and gone to his apartment. He told her about his
life–how he was orphaned–and suddenly his eyes seemed to have
that aquamarine color that you see on Islamic pots–she entered
into his eyes and relaxed there.

How lovely it had been to throw off her clothes and lie down
on a furry blanket that covered his bed. How lovely to feel his lips
covering her with kisses. His love-making was pagan, complex,
inventive. Slowly he buried himself inside of her. She had been
faithful until then. Returning home she had not slept all night–
looking at Mr. Jaksforth and wondering how long she could stand
sleeping next to him. But she had no choice–the children. She
couldn't hurt the children.

And the weeks that followed she had dressed in the morning as
quickly as possible and run down to the actor's house–Barry slept
all day–and she crawled into the furry bed with him and slept and
made love. Her enjoyment was that of a child.

And later still–a weekend at the Neibergers' house. In
Montauk. It was so empty. All that talk about children's schools.
Dalton. Collegiate. And summer houses. And workmen. And how
much everything cost. And what it cost to build a pool. Until she
thought she would go out of her mind.

And she realized lying on the blanket on the Neibergers' lawn
something quite simple. "I am a sensualist. I am. I am." She had
thought of Barry coming out of the Neibergers' house in his tight
blue dungarees–as if he were a beast caught in a jungle. How
terribly *unsensual* upper middle class living was. *They take the balls
out of life*–and there she was–in Montauk–with dripping thighs
thinking of Barry–while the conversation swirled around her head
about the Collegiate School and about television programs and

how awful they were—and all about maids—and all about pools—
all about bulkheads, and all about tennis—while she lay on the
grass looking at the sky thinking of Barry's lips and his body
looking fresh and clean on the fur blanket—and how she spent her
mornings when she was supposedly studying at the "New School"
in Barry's apartment—that hot summer. And Barry had gone to
California. And Barry had gone away. And suddenly the marriage
was gone too. And she had not seen the Neibergers—and here
they were. At Agatha's party.

"Michael," she said, "let's leave and go home."

"What's wrong?"

"Nothing. I'm just tired. Everyone here looks like a parrot."

As they were putting on their coats there was Elena Feesee. She
had met her twelve years ago at a party. Wasn't she the first
person who had said to her that she feared "Schluss Door Panic?"
Now she understood what that meant. Closed-door panic. She
would become a dead parrot. She was experiencing it again. An
anxiety in her stomach. A cold tiny bit of perspiration around her
forehead. And then—suddenly—it came on her again almost like a
virus—like a stomach flu—she was getting older. Michael was
going to leave. The future? What was the future? Would she be
an old woman writing poems by herself in an old room where the
wallpaper came off the walls?

"What are you thinking?" Michael asked as they went down in
the elevator.

"I'm thinking about—what it's like to grow old. No place to
go. No place to hide. I'm thinking about parrots."

"Stop that nonsense," said Michael. "You're not going to be
old. And you're going to be orgiastic at seventy-five. You'll write
poems and cook dinners and make love—or you could die
tomorrow."

"I know. I mustn't think about the past. Or the future, must
I?"

"No, it doesn't help."

"What am I frightened of Michael? I don't want to be a parrot."

"I don't know. But whatever it is—I'm here."

Schlomo and the All

"Consider yourself at home" Schlomo said.

Schlomo was a mystic, a talmudic hippie rabbi who had a congregation on the West Side and was an underground cult figure. Katherine had first met Schlomo through the poet Alan Ginsberg. He had given a reading and come back to her house with his father and a few of his friends. They—Alan and Katherine—were old friends from the hip singing days of the Village when they had sparred and joked with each other.

"I saw the best minds of my generation vacuuming" Katherine had said once to Ginsberg. Then, he had brought into her life a holy beggar—Schlomo—and they chanted poetry and Schlomo had played songs on his harmonium. Schlomo had remained Katherine's friend. Michael had met him also—independently of Katherine. They called on him in his cave-like apartment on the West Side.

"Schlomo, you outmagic the magicals" Katherine said.

"What does that mean?"

"That you make everyone so comfortable. Your home is warm—and your love." Katherine looked at Schlomo and her mind wandered back to another evening when she had heard the word "prayer." That evening she had gone to a large cocktail party at the Democratic Club for George McGovern. She had watched McGovern smiling to those who came to shake his hand or talk with him about the United Nations or the Senate or his last campaign—and she had been looking at the tall dark smiling man and thinking how decent he was and how the history of the country might have been changed if he had been President not Nixon—wondering to herself how McGovern and his wife Eleanor must have viewed Watergate—the emergence of Carter—why hadn't he won—she had stood there and suddenly Johnnie McCoy had come over to her and slapped her on the back.

"Do you have time for a nightcap with me?" he had asked.

"Sure" she had smiled at him—she liked Johnnie—one of the great movers of the democratic power not only because of his money—but his energy—he had been one of the standbys to McGovern—shadowed him like a brother—and suddenly she had taken a cab with Johnnie and they were back in her apartment. His large blue Irish eyes had deep-sea blueness to them, his face was the face of a hero—and his good-hearted way of kissing her on the couch—laughing and having fun at the same time—made her feel good—when he drank he started talking about sex—

"I want to make love with you—not fuck you—make love with you."

"And me with you."

"Someday I'm going to spend a whole night with you."

"Someday—what's wrong with right now?"

"Well right now I have to go home."

"We just got here—"

"I know Katherine. But I have to leave. But one day I'm going to pray over you."

She remembered her head spinning. Lying down on the couch. "Someday I'm going to pray over you." She wondered how many people he had used that line on. She thought she had heard everything. But *pray over you* was a new one.

"Is that what you say to a nice Jewish lady? I'm going to pray over you? Here I am—fat and forty—and I'm dying to make love. Sometimes I think if I was a hooker and charged it would be easier to get love out of the eligible men in New York—you have to pry them open with can-openers before you get one jot of love out of them—"

"Just now Katherine I love you."

"I love you too Johnnie."

"Isn't George a good man? Don't you think he would have made a great President?"

"I want to get *laid.* I don't want to talk about George McGovern. When are you going to pray over me?"

It all seemed so silly now. And there was Schlomo—saying all those Hebraic religious words. He was praying over her. She wondered if he still fucked around. That would have been marvelous—to have had a passionate person like Schlomo—to live with—to share things with—Michael. Was he passionate?

"I don't write any of my songs. They just flow through me like a channel," Schlomo said.

"Trying" blocks everything. She wouldn't *try* to love Michael. She just would.

*

Talking to Schlomo.

"Michael and I both love you. We see you as not only an orthodox rabbi but as a mystic, a schlemiel-saint—a secret spiritual leader—an oddball godball."

"I love you both very much. It's just too bad Michael isn't Jewish" Schlomo said.

He wore a tiny white skullcap. His beard was gray. When he intoned the prayers at his temple he was king. But sitting around on the pillows of his house—he was a cabbalist jester. His wife and child were upstairs and he sat with a huge grin on his face—hugging Michael—and hugging Katherine.

"So both of you have finally found each other? You love each other. Then go and be together" Schlomo said. "When a man and a woman find each other special things happen. Very special things happen. It is as if you both spent your whole lives looking for your All. You look everywhere for your All. But you don't find it. Then one day—a miracle happens. You find your All. That's what both of you have done."

Katherine wondered what this Hassidic saint would say next. He was truly a holy beggar. Or was he a musical troubadour who was trying to take the bullshit out of mysticism?"

*

That was it! Katherine thought. I'm going from childhood and Inferno, to adulthood and Purgatorio, and onto some miraculous Paradiso. Lantao Island would be paradise. No more money problems. No more creepy guys. No more trying to get laid. She would become a holy beggar! She would tell Michael yes.

Another Party in the Life of a Tycoon

The girls had pinworms. Christmas was coming. Her bank account was empty. Anxiety mounted. Michael was now at the point where he insisted on an answer. Life was a joke. Michael wanted to stay at Katherine's house that evening. He felt he should be with her as much as possible but Katherine said No— Jeanie was having a sleepover. And she had to stay with the girls.

The sleepover was a child called Lois. She was in the same class as Jeanie and all the girls were going to sleep in sleeping bags. "I don't want to sleep in a sleeping bag" Lois said. "That's because I'm fat."

"So what if you're fat? You can still sleep."

"I like coming to your house Jeanie" Lois said.

"Why?"

"Because your mommy doesn't yell at you. My mommy yells at me all the time. I like my mommy if you know what I mean. But I don't love her. Or I love her but I don't like her. I get it all mixed up. Once she hit me and I promised myself I'd never talk to her again. But I forget."

Lights were turned out. In the dark Lois kept talking. Her front teeth were buck from her thumb-sucking. She was frankly curious about the girls' life.

"Where's your father?" Lois asked in the dark.

"He's in Ethiopia" Jeanie whispered. "Where's yours?"

"I don't know" Lois said. "We still get letters addressed to him at the house" she continued, "but he and my mommy were divorced when we were young—I mean I was only six months. I haven't seen him."

Do you miss him?"

"I do. But I never see him. I don't like school, do you? The teachers are so mean. I'm on the sour lemon list. When I grow up I want to be a teacher. But a nice teacher."

"What would you teach?"

"Poetry."

"Poetry?" Jeanie asked.

"Yes. Like your mommy. You're both lucky."

"Why?"

"Because you get breakfast. My mother is always in a hurry in the morning and we never get breakfast. That's why I'm so hungry in school for lunch."

"We always get breakfast. Bacon. Eggs. French bread. Sometimes hot chocolate. It's nice."

"My mommy doesn't really want me around" Lois said. "Because when we have company she always locks me in my room. Or sends me off for a sleepover."

Katherine found herself spying on this conversation. Often she felt like a spy in her own home. Listening to the girls talking. Listening to their friends. She remembered that Michael was waiting for a phone call. She called him and they spoke for an hour over the phone. She promised to call him in the morning.

*

The next evening she invited Michael to a dinner given by the Oltovers—he had been an advisor to Kennedy. She loved the Oltovers' house—it was a form of perfection—a home where things used and old blended with paintings of hills and lakes done by Alissa Oltover's mother—a Cushing and a great painter of animals and shells and landscapes that were dreamscapes. The party itself was like a dreamscape. Eleanor and George McGovern were there. So were Paddy Chayefsky, Jason and Barbara Epstein, Antonia Frasier and Harold Pinter. She had arrived after Pinter and Antonia Frasier and had seen Alissa Oltover graciously bending towards Pinter and telling him how she enjoyed his play.

"It was the best play ever."

"Thank you" he said.

There was a pause. A bit uncomfortably she had been standing there and was sure this was true—Pinter said "What a lovely home."

They were shown into the drawing room. A fire was going. A white shaggy rug looked comfortable. Flowers. "It's lovely here" she heard Pinter say again.

Katherine found herself next to him in front of the fire. He was a relaxed intellectual man whose eyes were intently dreaming although his mouth seemed humorous and practical. An owlish man, he had an excellent tailor. She sensed that he had been taught by someone—his wife that he was now divorcing perhaps—

how indeed to live well. He struck Katherine as someone tutored in the finer arts of talking and dressing and manners and taste. The arts which befit an artist.

"Are you a writer also?" Pinter asked Katherine.

"Sometimes. I'm a poet."

"That's interesting. I'm a poet too. I began writing poetry," Pinter said. "I would like very much to see some of your poetry." He added thoughtfully, almost majestically, "it would give me great pleasure to see what you're writing now."

"I'm not writing now. I've gone into the tycoon business. I'm trying to make a great deal of money quickly. First it was trying to form my own film company. But I couldn't get the financing. Then it was trying to form the Woman's Life Insurance Company. But again the financing was difficult to come by. Now I'm designing sheets. Poetry sheets. I have an agent called Pearl Beckman who represents Gloria Vanderbilt. I'm trying to convince the domestics people that letters—particularly beautiful words—original poems—would be interesting to sleep on. From sheets to scarves, dresses, umbrellas, jumpsuits, pocketbooks is just a small jump."

Silence. Pinter looked at her as if she was mad. "Is that so?" Pinter asked.

She wondered if he understood what she was talking about. Of course he did. Behind that mask was a nice Jewish boy who understood shmatas. Shmatas were a form of poetry anyway. As she was talking to Pinter she kept hearing Lois—little fat lost Lois talking about breakfasts. The poor kid.

"And whose poetry would you use on the sheets?" Pinter asked.

"My own."

There was a long silence. It was almost like a Pinter play. Just then a man came to interrupt the conversation. He began to talk about tennis. A subject that both could talk about elegantly.

Katherine moved on to the other guests. Michael was having a marvelous time talking to McGovern. He felt at home with the atmosphere of interesting high-powered people. He had missed that in Hong Kong. Lots of talk passed easily in New York for excitement.

She stood by herself in the corner of the living room thinking about poetry sheets. She would cover the world with them. Instead of being remaindered in Marboro or unread in libraries she would be laundered—and dried—and held up to the air to be dried, poetry sheets, something clean and aesthetic and useful.

Why didn't Lois get breakfast? Why did Michael live in Hong Kong? Why was Helen a drunk? And why was she invited to this dinner? All of these passed in her mind. She watched Harold Pinter and decided he had worked terribly hard at not appearing vulgar. Which was really too bad.

*

Michael came back to her house. They had both decided it would be all right if he "slept over." Often she told the girls she was "sleeping out" and they would always ask "are you sleeping home mommy?" It was the cross the divorced woman with two children had to bear. She could see it inked on her tombstone. "Are you sleeping home mommy?" And yet Katherine admitted to Michael that having men sleep "over" had its problems.

Not many people could experience an orgasm while two little girls were banging on the door screaming "Mommy. Open up." When she arrived home with Michael it was late and the girls were sleeping. She stuffed the key-hole with Kleenex. She and Michael took off their clothes and got into bed. Just as they were about to kiss each other a noise on the door sounded.

"See what I mean?" Katherine whispered. She called out "What is it?"

It was Jeanie. "Can you leave your door open mommy? It's windy and I'm afraid of the wind."

"No I can't. I have a sleepover."

"Who?" came the demand from behind the door.

This was now an inquisition. Jeanie was the Grand Inquisitor:

Grand Inquisitor: Who's in there with you?

Katherine: A friend from Hong Kong; his name is Michael.

Grand Inquisitor: When is he leaving?

Katherine: In the morning.

Grand Inquisitor: Does he like turtles?

Katherine: Yes. I think so. Why?

Grand Inquisitor: I lost my turtle. I think it's in your bed.

Katherine: Good. We will sleep with the turtle. Go to bed. It's very late. I'll see you at breakfast.

Grand Inquisitor: Where were you?

Katherine: At a dinner party.

Grand Inquisitor: Why do you have to go out?

Katherine: Because I can't be a prisoner all my life. Go to bed. I beg of you to go to bed. Please. Pretty please go to bed and let me sleep.

Grand Inquisitor: All right. Good night.

Katherine began to hold Michael. Surely to be a divorced woman didn't mean you had no life any more, or did it? Would it ever be any better—would it be better in Hong Kong? Or anywhere?

The doorbell rang. It's Jeanie—Katherine thought. She got out of bed and put on her bathrobe. She put on her slippers. Unlocked the door. It was Jeanie. She had rung the bell to get attention. Truly this was a play by Pinter. No it wasn't. "This is my life" she said to herself as she scolded the little girl for being naughty.

"Did you fall down from getting drunk?" Jeanie asked. She certainly knew how to hurt a girl. Motherhood!

"Be quiet sweetheart. Mommy will sit by your bed until you go to sleep. Mommy will sit on your bed."

When she went back to sleep—Michael was sleeping.

*

Yes, life was a joke. Sometimes she felt she was walking on the walls. Could she really move back to Hong Kong with Michael? Reality was so much more bizarre than fiction. Could you imagine really having a life where there was never privacy? Could she really move back to Hong Kong with two turtles, three goldfish, a dog, a cat, two children—what would her analyst say? What would her friends say? What would the girls' piano teacher say?

"Darling I love you I want you to come with me."

"Is it possible to get a good piano teacher in Hong Kong for the girls?"

"I want to take you with me and we will start a new life together."

"With a baby-nurse?"

Yes. That was it. When you were divorced everything came down not to romance but to baby-sitters and baby-nurses. During the time she was married to Mr. Jaksforth a sage called Marietta had said to her "No matter what happens hang on to your baby-nurse"—and now her life had been governed by governesses and maids. *Help!* My life is a help-problem.

Maid madness. That was what she had participated in. Maid mania. There had been Lili, and Joli—and after they were gone there had been Hazel from Jamaica who greased the girls' hair, and Ursula who ran up hundred-dollar phone bills to Vienna and cooked strudel with the baking equipment she had forced

Katherine to buy—and then there had been the health food freak
called Dina who didn't like Katherine's "life-style" and asked if
she could walk around the house barefoot. She had kept live
oysters in her room, and collected buttons. She didn't really like
children she confessed—no—she was just working to make enough
money to open a button boutique at a flea market—there was Mrs.
Googie who had a Catholic cross and tried to teach the children
about salvation, there was Kookoo who had a high voice like a
hyena, there was Nelda from Chile with sad yes yes eyes who
stole—there was the old woman from Estonia who had never
worked as a governess but had worked at the Dixie Hotel as the
head of the linen department—who wore a wig—once she had
come home and found her wig on the couch—a great big yellow
wig—she had always been afraid that a baby-nurse would commit
suicide when she was out of the house and for a moment she
thought that the wig was the woman's head—there was Olivia
who cleaned with all sorts of "new" products and had a gold
tooth and she had loved Olivia—who couldn't sleep in—and nurses
and housekeepers and maids had come and gone—telling them her
life story she had heard theirs—they had exchanged living together
in the odd way that governess and mother relate to each other—
each fighting over the love object—which is the child—it was all a
nightmare.

"Some day" Katherine said—"I'm going to write my auto-
biography. It's going to be called 'I married a Jewish lawyer to
live with a Nazi baby-nurse.'" Now it was over. She couldn't
afford a baby-nurse. Her accountant was lending her money for
the psychiatrist. Soon she would have no sanity at all. Tycoonery
was failing. Even Bronfman was having business problems she had
read recently in the *New York Times*. With thirteen million
marijuana smokers the liquor business was falling off. He had
been quoted as saying "Let's face it—business isn't what it used to
be. But we still have things on the back burner." If Bronfman was

having business problems—how about a divorced poet? A Jewish divorced poet? With two kids? She would run away. That was her fantasy. She would run away from the creepy dates, the mad maids, the understanding psychiatrist, the dinners and intellectuals, she, a divorced poet who had failed at poetry and tycoonery would run away.

"Somewhere I know another world exists where women are not walking the walls" she said to herself. No. She would write. She would try to write. "Can't you think with us around?" the little voice asked. It was Jeanie. Hammering one of her toys. Jeanie was banging heart and soul on the piano. The noise! The noise! "I am a woman who hates background noises" Katherine said to herself. And she knew that once more she must change her life.

Pinter had just written *The Last Tycoon*. It was all Pinteresque. What did he really know about tycoonery? *Nada.*

Cool

"I'm obsessed with earning money—I always need money. But money and poetry don't go together." Katherine sat talking to her psychiatrist about dollars. He was a bearded Freudian who had spent a great deal of his time studying in Vienna. He specialized in children. Once, during a career change, he had contemplated becoming a jazz musician. He had written the definitive book on Schizophrenia and Music. Katherine found him to be the only person in the world she could really talk with on an intimate basis. He understood her roots and complexities.

"Why are you so interested in money?" he asked.

"Money—I know what you're going to say—is shit. I mean Freud compared it to doo-doo—but frankly it's the doo that makes things do if you know what I mean. Money is a way of having a high. You can give it away—you can have fun with it—it's the key that opens doors—it's bread—green manna. It's terribly helpful if you have to pay for things."

"Umm," said the doctor. "But why a tycoon? Aren't you happy writing poetry?"

"No. Poetry is a form of talking to yourself. The whole idea of a poem is to teach you how to write another poem. I'm not a worldly person. I don't think poetry has anything to do with money. It's an aesthetic that is simply a way to lead your life. It's a way of breaking bubbles. It's a way of saying I am angry boom boom boom. Or I am joyful. But you can't sell it. Because if it's good—no one wants it. Poetry is the one thing in the world that isn't bullshit. It's the only language left that tells the truth. I don't get poetry and money mixed up."

"Interesting," said the psychiatrist. "Then what way do you think you're going to make money?"

"I don't know yet. I tried movies—that didn't work. Fund raising and distribution in the hands of the Mafia. I tried the women's first insurance company. That was practical. A possibility. But an idea that was too much too soon and then too late. It was a rim of a vision. I saw women protecting themselves—writing out the contracts for their own lives. Selling to themselves. Creating their own job force. But that didn't work. I played around with creating events. A new kind of yippie oriented happening at Macy's. But the management wouldn't hear of it. The PR of the angels isn't what corporate structure understands. Then I thought of cloth—poetry sheets. You know—the whole world wrapped in my poetry scarves."

"Umm-hmmm" the psychiatrist said.

"Me too. Only it didn't happen. Then I thought about it and I thought—why not make another documentary movie—called *Remember the 1980s*—a movie about the future. The superstars of the future are those who communicate. Talk to the communicators. Mao Tse Tung's wife–put in a lot of good music and dream sequences–and make a movie like *Woodstock*. Only it would be Wood Stop! That's another concept. I don't know. I guess when I read King Arthur I was more interested in Merlin the Magician. I'm interested in the magic that's around. Where's the Queen Arthur? Gwen is out making a living. You see King Arthur and Gwen got a divorce. She got the kids. Arthur went off to find himself. She had to get a baby-nurse. But she couldn't afford one. Being a lady she had just so much scratch. But she needed to be pumped up. She wrote to King Arthur. Her lawyer wrote to King Arthur. But even though he was a knight–he kept writing back these wondrous letters saying 'God send you good deliverance' but no scratch. The acts of Arthur and his noble knights had nothing to do with his lady, Gwen, and the divorce. Gwen goes into consciousness raising. The things they say about knights shouldn't even be printed! Gwen experiences Jewish guilt. She can't give her kids away to a boarding school. She went to one herself and she knows they are full of shit. She can't just give them up to Arthur. She can share them but not give them up. So to be a mother, and still do Gwenish things, she has to make some bread. Merlin has no idea what she can do. His magic does not extend to Gwen's pragmatic problems. That's why I want to be a grownup. And you–are Merlin. Any ideas?"

"None. Except I'm proud of one thing. You are giving up being infantile. That's all that psychoanalysis can hope to accomplish. You're becoming a woman–which means you are taking responsibility for your own life. You're finally becoming a grownup. You are using insight. I'm proud of you."

He shook her hand. "Go back to poetry. Forget tycooning," he said.

The analysis was over. After all those years. *Goodbye Goodbye*.

Katherine went home and cried like a baby. In secret. Always in secret.

Sunspots

"Tell me about Schlomo" Katherine said to Michael.

"I love him" Michael said.

"Besides that—"

"Schlomo was born in Berlin—his father was a rabbi. In former days being a rabbi was a high profession—according to Schlomo his father was very high. In 1938 he left Germany and came here—he wanted to be the greatest scholar in the world. I learn from him. From his warmth. From his friendship."

"He is warm. So many people—it's hard to say this—but so many people are difficult for me to relate to. They come in and out of my life like sunspots. Schlomo is a rabbi in a time when holy men are discredited. I'm not Jewish. And yet I see his holiness."

"Tell me about your lovers" Michael added.

"You tell me about Schlomo. And I'll tell you about my lovers. What do you want to hear?"

"Who was your favorite lover?"

"My favorite lover is a mad-man who's Italian. He owns a restaurant and spends his time between here and St. Moritz where he has another restaurant. He's a sort of guru fucker. He knows what he's doing. He's an expert. And he enjoys older women."

"What's so unusual about that?"

"A lot of older men want to be with young girls. Because they don't know what they are doing and they feel more comfortable with them. But my favorite lover—call him Nino—I don't want to tell you his name—he understands women and he has a sense of humor, he's sensual and he knows that making love isn't a sin. It's a pleasure and for some it's an art. Sensualists have to seek each other out in the dark. Like sperm whales. There are very few sensualists left in the world. I'm afraid they are a dying breed. I've been fucking with Nino for the past fifteen years–perhaps twenty. I first met him when a friend of mine who was a Greek shipping king took me to his restaurant. Then he called me. And came to visit. I was very young then and I remember looking at his body. It was beautiful to look at. Everything looked beautiful. And smelled beautiful. I liked his eyes. They were clear. And his skin was a golden color. He looked healthy. That was it! There was something so healthy about the way he kissed me. I remember thinking that I could not enjoy making love with him if I was conscious–so I let myself stop *thinking* and just begin feeling. I felt his tongue gliding over me, inside of me, and I remember something odd. The feeling of moisture–as if I were under saltwater as he came in my mouth and I came in his mouth. The seaspray of semen and salt. It was all too quick. I felt that I wanted to take hours hearing his voice, being with him–I knew that he made love with most of the attractive women who came to his restaurant. But that didn't matter. And then I saw him aging–as I aged–but it didn't seem to bother him. In fact–in an odd way–he became a better lover and so did I. When I say better I only mean more relaxed. There's a holiness about the body that I experienced with him. The excitement of the breasts–of the secretive parts of the body–of the blood inside you which you can feel. Sometimes–I want to get this across to you–making love with Nino seemed so natural. As we stayed in each other's arms and came in each other's mouths–it seemed as if making love was the most natural thing to do. You see with most men–it is often a very *un-natural* act. But sensuality is a mystery. But only with you can we start talking about rabbis and end up talking up jubilant curious things like coming in Nino's mouth–breasts and thighs–a lover with gray hair–the more I live the more I want to love. I guess that makes me a sensualist. But aren't holy people–

fanatics, addicts, furtive rabbis, artists—just inside-out sensualists. Sensualists with lonely childhoods? Isn't that what a neurotic is? A sensualist with a lonely childhood? The more I live, the more I wonder about the sensual part of me."

"You mean—does one want to give in to that part—or run away from it?"

"I wrote a poem that ends:

> A poet is a breakneck
> Boss who doesn't want green bucks,
> Mommy bucks, cant make it
> In the conglomerate Mogul world
> where everything is worth
> fighting for. Time is not time.
> Money is not money—
>
> Time is exaggerated—time is nothing
> Real—except what once was funny is
> Now becoming ridiculous—
> And I am on call back and yield
> My eyes to whoever wants tongue and eyes.

you see—it's a poem about time. And money."

"You want nothing for yourself that's personal—do you?"

"What do you mean Michael?"

"You write your poems. You have all these odd responsibilities. You move in and out of parties and people's lives like sunspots. Can't you give this up? Give up the structure?"

"How can I really? Can you imagine my taking my life and putting it at your disposal? How can I? To start all over again—following a man. To take two little girls and trek them across the world and start them living like new plants in a new soil—it's hard to think of it. And yet—I feel so much that I am in transition. That I don't want to be afraid of growing old. That I don't want to be out looking for lovers—and being told no-thank you. I have the heartache of wanting to have more then being on my own. I want the jubilation of giving myself away."

"Then give yourself away to me."

"It's not just me anymore. It's me. And two children."

"I know. And a dog and a cat and a baby-nurse."

"And anxieties. And dreams. And frustrations. And jubilations. And wanting to write. And wanting to make money. And too much wanting. I've never really had a *career*—I've gone from teaching poetry to writing articles to trying to start various things. Nothing has really worked. So here I am. In the middle of my life. Lying in bed with you."

"Are you happy here?"

"Yes. Because I can see being your friend. I can see myself going away with you. And talking with you in the morning. And sharing things. I don't want to wake up one day in my old pajamas and feel that I missed doing what I wanted to do."

"And what do you want to do?"

"Go with you Michael."

"What about your affair with Nino?"

"Nino can't fit me into his prime time. Forget it."

"What do you mean?"

"Well Nino services so many women in New York. All the women who eat in his restaurant he gets to fuck. But—with all the horny women in New York—he hardly has time to fit them all in. He called me last week and said he was available on Monday at four o'clock in the afternoon. I said I couldn't do it at four since I was working. I explained that I was now writing an article and I didn't have afternoons free. I told him if he couldn't give me prime time to forget it. And you know what? He got huffy. I suppose I'm at the age now where Nino can pull his huffiness. But I didn't call him back. Just then you came into my life."

"I'll give you more than prime time. I'll give you all my time."

"That's what rightly or wrongly frightens me. I have an evening to spare but to tell you the truth–I don't think I have a year or a lifetime."

"Nothing is sure. I am as frightened as you are. It's difficult for me too. To start a new life and to risk not only living with a woman but inheriting her family. Maybe your kids will hate me. Maybe you won't be able to really give up the action of New York to be isolated. Hong Kong is an island you know. It's not like Manhattan. It's not the place. But I'm bringing you into a whole new way of life. Living with me. I'm a new person."

"I've lived with a new person before. But never with a family. I'm not the Katherine who I used to be. I have appendages. Wings. Feet. Arms. That don't belong to me but that I carry with me. I'm not one person. I'm now three people."

"I want to take three people with me back to Lantao Island."

LANTAO ISLAND

Lantao Island

Michael lay down beside me in bed. I, Katherine Kahn, unraveled myself, took down my hair, touched his face and wept.

All that I could think of was how goddamn fucking sad it was that the new is the old lived over and over again. Once, ten years ago, I had left New York City with Mr. Hinkel Jaksforth. I had left my friends, my job teaching poetry at Fordham, my Tai Chi Chuan teacher, my mirrors and books, my apartment, analyst, my free-lance writing assignments—all of it to go and live in Hong Kong with a man I didn't know. How had that all happened? Now it was happening again. Only this time it wasn't Hinkel Jaksforth, the diplomat, in Hong Kong asking me—the father of my children—it was a dwarf—a mystical talmudic jockey who was lost and rich and part Irish—who was an outsider—a person who was, more or less, like one of those endangered species—an odd-ball animal, last of its kind, who had to be protected and in that odd way that everything you *save* is able to save you—he was saving me too. In some odd way we were both endangered species—myself the artist—the odd-ball poet who grew up with too little touch—a hunger to write the world down—words freed in my mouth like apples—the poor little rich girl who was rich with a lonely childhood who had learned the difficult lesson of surviving through art. That was it! Art had been my life-shield. It had been the way I confessed, I got the anger out, I released secrets—it mythicized my life—through poems I was able to turn my own life into a legend. Into the writing workshop I had gone at eight. Out of the writing workshop I had come at forty—a battered woman but still a survivor. Art was my mystery, my identity, my life-line, my hookah pipe, my one way that I stayed sane. Art—or whatever you wanted to call it—poems—kept me from suicide many times—made me into a life survivor with only poems locked in my hand as a weapon. How many times—how many times had I wanted to wound myself, round out my life with death? But poems kept me confessing, pumping out the hunger. I trained my imagination the way a body builder trains his muscles. I worked out in the life gym. Yes. I wrote out everything—opening myself up with magical pencils—to the world of paper where I was in control. Writing had made it possible for me to be in touch with my secrets and feelings, language enabling me to spit out my life. Poems had bloomed out of my skin enabling me to grow. Epidermis of hurt. Breathing mechanism. And then when all of it was too much—marriage to Hinkel Dinkel. Mr. Jaksforth.

A poem begins in my mind as I lie next to Michael.

Now like the flow of traffic
In a huge city
I hear the waves coming in and going out—
Waves of loneliness—
I think of all the men I've loved
And none of them loved me
The way I want to be loved. Totally. Tenderly.
Here, lying in bed with you Michael,
Short king of mystic remembrances
I lie in a room filled with carnations and roses—
Candles—my hair falls over the pillow—
Your mouth is on my mouth—tongue in my mouth

You lie over me—your spit drips in my mouth—
Your warm arms—strong muscled arms on my back—

"How do you know I like that?" I ask—
"Because I like that," you say.

And suddenly my own mouth goes down into the earth part of you—not the heaven part that reaches to the stars—your chest—your arms—but your earth part—and there I take your light brown cock inside my mouth.

And hold it in my mouth—holding, sucking, swallowing, breathing, chewing, plowing, planting up and down in the earth rhythms I love—until your seed runs all over my face—and I swallow. Tears run down with the sperm. I love this cock. I hold you now—my feathered friend—for suddenly you are all feathers—you are the precious whooping crane—

An endangered species.

Who I must protect and keep alive. Here. Feed on my love. In secret. In secret I am with you always. You. Michael. The funny little man I never noticed—now my hero. Kindness is everything.

Now it's time to let my secret out.

Kindness is everything.

Kindness and the joy of the sexual feast. I eat you again. And you eat me. Slowly your tongue glides over my arm, my nipple, my thigh, into the deep eye.

We taste each other over and over again. I want more of you. Suddenly you fly into me—swiftly—again again—it is too much—stop all this ecstasy—milky sperm mixes into my own watery thighs. Now our body floats in water. The water of my liquids in my thighs. My belly is a mound of water. Spit. Seed. Tongue in my legs. My mouth in sperm. Wet. We are both so wet. Rolling in our own rain. We have perspired and rained and come on each other. The new is the old lived over and over again. Like the flow of traffic—my heart makes these odd sounds—noisy greased up tire

songs–songs of wires crossed and tires used out–songs of blood
and gasoline on a peak in Hong Kong and why I didn't know
you–although I used to see you walking on the streets near the
Mandarin Hotel–short–sexy–stocky–well dressed–your black
hair shining in the sun–I noticed how the girls looked at you–
wanted you–I had traveled all around the world to be near you
and I didn't know it. You said to my husband once–I think it
was at a dinner party at the Cheungs–"I've made all my long
trips. Now I think I'll make my longest trip. Into myself. I've
decided to become a psychonaut. And travel deep into my psyche.
There's so much there to find." You were always happy to be
different. You queer thing. You who rode horses–

What were you doing in an odd place linking your life to
Hong Kong?

What made you move there?

Look at me my love. What were you doing in an odd place like
Hong Kong?

"I wanted to run away," Michael said. "I was certain that if I
stayed in New York I would be destroyed. I couldn't find
anything human there. My father wanted me, of course, to enter
the corporate structure. You can't imagine what it's like to be a
skinny boy, short and always a mess, part Chinese, whose father
wants you to be a general–someplace. Anyplace. As long as you're
a hero. You know what? The country of the hero is the heart's
size. I felt I couldn't breathe. After graduating from high school I
lived in New York City in a tiny room without windows. I
climbed seven flights of steps. During the days I worked as a
waiter, then a bartender. Finally my old man insisted I go to
business school and I enrolled at Columbia Business School. I
remember the cobblestones of Columbia, I remember the cold
mornings in the library when I studied penalties for violation of
the Federal Chartering Act when I wanted to be studying Pablo
Neruda. I'd read about taxpayer rights for about three hours, until

Chinese silk and red and orange Chinese silk from the mainland. His favorite colors. My favorite colors too. There are plants inside our home. Huge green fronds in Ming blue and white big bulbous nose pots. Pillows and plants. On the walls are the huge metal sculptures created by Cheung Yee, the Chinese painter and sculptor who Michael discovered living in the New Territories, whose work was so odd no one would buy it. Except I. A long time ago. So he has bought many Cheung Yees and hung them around the house. How can I describe them? The Cheung Yee sculptures are like huge metal shields.

Oh Katherine.

You've played a life Bingo.

You've won.

To be here, on Lantao Island, with Michael. This peace is everything you could ever hope for. You are free of ambitions.

*

Insight.

And mornings.

Love.

And study.

My own room of silence.

New words on paper.

Children home from school.

Kisses. And soap. Music. And a dinner to be eaten.

Palm trees. And telling time by the sea.

To live with love.

I have always wanted this.

But never believed I could find it.

Study. Writing. Lack of ambition. Cold water. A hand held. A body next to me in the dark. Laughter. And the odd dull sensation that I always knew this would happen. At forty to be born again. Here in Hong Kong. To inherit joy the way you inherit a fortune. I lived a Torah-less life. Suddenly the Torah is taught to me by a dwarf. I lived a loveless life. Suddenly love is brought to me by a stranger. I lived a greedy stupid life. I couldn't cope. Suddenly I am on an island where I become what I am. I am living through all the ages at once. The Age of Belief and the medieval philosophers, the age of adventure and the renaissance philosophers, the age of reason and the seventeenth century philosophers, the age of Confucius and the Chinese philosophers—the ages of ideology and analysis—and the Torah—it all dances in my head. Starfish without spines. I am my own philosopher. My own goddess. My own Amazon of the oddball imagination.

Tell me miss what is your name?

My name is Katherine.

You are the first winner. Thank you for everything.

What have I won?

Life Bingo.

You had the right combination. We called your number.

You are a winner.

B 4. o 70. 7. zero. seventy. n 32. Life Bingo. You have won my dear Katherine Kahn once frightened of everything. n 36. You would never believe that you could be happy like this?

To live on an island.

To live with Michael.

To escape the life that wasn't really reality. People only said it was.

You were the one without hope. You were the one without echoes. Suddenly you came to this distant place. This oddball from Hong Kong who studied the Torah and had an income and lived once in Oklahoma and was just four feet nine inches tall who read her poetry and said "I have become attracted to your style" and bit her breasts—who inspired interest but little sympathy because he seemed so sure of himself. A little jock jockey from another world. Who wanted to have her change her life one more time and run away with him.

I think it over.

Why not be childish again?

Why not laugh it off like a cosmic joke and leave?

Leave New York. Leave the towers of numbers.

And start still one more time.

I dreamed of things we could do together. We could take the Hong Kong ferry and watch the blue water.

We could climb the Peak.

We could walk hand in hand in the New Territories and watch the birds circle in the sky.

We could eat dum sin with chopsticks.

We could hug in front of the Mandarin Hotel and take the elevator to the top and dive in the pool like two dolphins.

We could take the tram to the top of the Peak.

We could get lost among all the Chinese merchants selling oranges in the dusty Kowloon streets.

We could ride horses innocent as pandas.

We could study Tai Chi Chuan.

We could live. We could breathe. We could leave.

And that's what we did.

One night, when no one really cared, I left New York with Michael and my daughters.

I had stored whatever furniture and books meant anything to me in the womb-like tomb of the Manhattan Storage vaults.

I was free.

To own things had never been one of my great desires and I had packed everything I wanted in one large green canvas knapsack. I felt like Huckleberry Finn with daughters. If Huck had run away with two children both of them his—that would have been me.

I had bought the girls wicker suitcases.

The three of us stood standing in a cluster of light at the airport while Michael strutted through the lines of supplicants and arranged the tickets.

We waited.

The girls were joyful.

This was an adventure.

Hong Kong was another part of the world they hadn't seen. Like Vermont. Or New Hampshire. They had found it on the globe I gave them for Christmas. They knew their mommy had met their daddy in Hong Kong so it was a place of good omens. Actually in their secret hearts they hated New York and Sesame Street and Radio City Music Hall and ice-skating lessons at La Petite and piano lessons and violin lessons and Saturdays in the Park and their boring little bratty friends. They were happy to leave New York City. They were assured that they would never have to have another lesson again.

I had bought us all straw hats.

I don't know why I bought straw hats.

I thought it would make us look more festive.

I thought straw hats would be nice in Hong Kong. So we stood in our winter clothes, bundled up to our ears in sweaters and coats and boots and mittens and straw hats. Three little Indians. Three little adventurers. Three girls. We are leaving. We are going with Michael. What will Hong Kong be like? ask my girls.

It will be crowded and sunny.

It will have a lot of fruit.

It will have lots of Chinese people. And lots of Chinese restaurants. It will be like the Tunnel of Love.

*

Part of me is shocked at part of myself.

Part of me did not believe I could run away. From what? From my psychiatrist. From my friends. From my career–(What career? You call making two hundred and fifty dollars for an article a career?)

From my hairdresser. From my lawyer. From my odd dates, acquaintances, buddies, from the streets I knew.

Don't be silly, says a voice.

The earth is a planet among galaxies.

A place where people live on sampans, where people fish oblivious to who you are–where–over there–on the island of Hong Kong children sell sunkist oranges in the sun–in the central market–ducks hang like tennis racquets from a rack–where snake bile is sold, where the Hong Kong bank stands guarded by sleek turbaned men–where people drive around town–working–living–breathing–dying–where children in uniform go to Saint Stevens School and learn English and Chinese–where the British crown colony runs its British flag–where tailors create suits for the overnight tourists–where garments are sold–where the embassies shine in the sun like tombs–where the singsong of Cantonese spills over the luncheon counters–where boys put on new shoes and walk out in the sun–where another life begins and ends. Here you have come again–not to take place in all that activity. Not to have suits made by overnight tailors, or to pour tea, or to be a wife. But to be–on another island–a life student.

You have come back here to learn.

To learn what?

To learn what it means to know nothing. To discover an inner life that you have neglected. To be, if you must put it that way, a psychonaut. An endangered species. The artist in you that would not die.

To go into the adventure of your own imagination. To go into consciousness and explore yourself.

But what will I find?

*

Arriving home from my visit to Kowloon on the Lantao ferry. A letter arrives from Agatha. I open it. Michael takes the children and they play tag in back of the temple. I sit at a straw table reading the letter.

"Darling"–Agatha says–

"I miss you so much in New York. But you were damn right to leave. It's cold. It's snowing. And I feel depressed all the time. Is it the cars? I don't know what it is. I feel suddenly that I'm living in a terribly condemned world. Part of myself is shocked to see that I am getting to be such a pain in the ass to myself. I miss you and hope that you and Michael are happy. I feel in my old Greek bones that you are. Somehow I am always with you and I feel that you have found the contentment so many people blab about but so few have. I know that I talk too much even in letters so my darling I'll sign off by saying that you have found happiness–I know it–now don't let anything or anyone steal it from you. If you need anything let me know. I love you darling. New York is a million light years away. Love, Agatha."

*

Happiness.

Is it only all this: Michael next to me. The straw tables. The children playing tag. Wu in the kitchen making dinner. The sea.

The palms. Books to be read. Mirrors on the wall, Kong. Hee. Fat. Choy. Happy New Year.

I'm living on an island in Asia.

I at last have found what I thought I never deserved. That was it—years spent feeling like nobody—though I never deserved all this love.

And then—after the second divorce—the incessant need to be successful. How stupid. ME? Running an insurance company? Woman's Life? Bizarre. And yet truth always foreshadows what's coming next. In some new way I have found a woman's life. Found it with Michael. I think of all the times I said "I don't need a man"—well it was true. Not just A Man. But someone. Someone to love. Living all those years with explosions of loneliness inside of me.

*

Michael makes love to me all night—every morning. He won't stop. He is charged to insanity heroically divided into dreams and pressing his tongue against me until my head falls on the pillow and my legs relax. I am crying. I don't know why. It is too much. I am empty. Then his body is on top of me. His hard body is now pushing into me. I turn my stomach around and around—as if I eat him with my stomach—he is on me and up and down—long kisses—upstream—in the midst of all these waves he screams and looks at me—I can feel that his body has grown so hard inside me it's going to burst—I send out red flags like signals to a lighthouse—"Come" I say to him.

"Come."

And in a moment, quickly, then slowly, he yields in my arms and falls on top of me as we hold each other so tightly and my words are tiny like the tracks of gulls on the beaches—tiny little tracks—I remember when I was a child.

"You came, came, you came" I whisper. Kissing his arm.

*

We are on the junk that Charlotte Horstman lent us. It is a huge junk, with a Chinese captain, and all the pillows are silk. Because she sells antiques all the eating utensils are blue and white china. And blue silk pillows. It is the ultimate sampan. We bob in the sea.

"I want you," I say, taking his mouth into mine.

Michael says to me, "Do you know what I sometimes shout in the afternoon? When I'm taking a long walk around Lantao Island by myself? I shout 'You are mine. You are mine!' I shout this into the island's wind. I shout into the sea. I feel a certain insanity when I THINK about you. You're like a fish infinitely hooked onto my soul."

I look into his eyes.

It's myself I see there. Katherine born. Katherine loved. His hands which are always rough—still rough from taming horses—slide over my back. The rough palm on my skin. He kisses my breasts and my stomach. His tongue glides over my stomach so that I giggle. I am also mad with happiness. Laughter and desire always alternate—are all mixed up. His tongue goes over my fold of skin and he is lifting his tongue up and down over my clitoris. He will not stop. Odd fantasies go through my mind. He is kissing me. An old boyfriend Danny is kissing me. Dorothy, a beautiful woman with large breasts who I once adored in college, is kissing me. Electric currents. I am going out of my body and lifting higher. A short pain begins. Ecstasy pain. If he stops now I will kill him. The sour smell of our naked climate. His tongue still lifting me up higher into another place. Hardened by his tongue lifting me I go mounted on my own wave. In music I have heard horns blasting like this. Lunar. Solar. Burning. Cold. Michael's love-making has pushed me to insensibility.

*

Mae and Peter have invited us for a drink. That means a Hong Kong party. They have asked us to come without the children. Mae is afraid of children. So we leave them behind with Mr. Wu. We take the ferry. "Mae is allergic to children. Actually they remind her too much of her own dead child. It upsets her," Peter says.

I understand.

Peter and Mae live in a large white apartment on top of the peak at Victoria Court.

Their apartment looks over the mountains of the New Territories.

It is furnished with Charlotte Horstman antiques–Chinese screens. Blue and white Ming vases. Bamboo furniture. It is beautiful. The guests are Americans from the State Department. Colonials from Australia. Businessmen from Scotland. Millionaire shipbuilders. K. C. Paou is there. The great Chinese shipping tycoon. So is Run Run Shaw the film producer. So are the Cheungs–he is Hong Kong's outstanding lawyer. Kayin Low, the beautiful publicity director from the Mandarin is there. So is Ken Moss who runs the Hilton. A smattering of Chinese artists. Businessmen. And Chinahands. Journalists. They are all there. I have met almost all of them in my other incarnation as Hinkel's wife. I am happy to see them. Do they find me changed? Not really. Anna Thornhill left and went to America to become a painter and sculptress. Pat Tow left and lives in Hawaii. Her husband has become a laundry king–automatic laundry machines–in Singapore. Michael Thornhill has married a Chinese woman and has a baby. He no longer plays golf. Charlotte Horstman is still with Gerald Godfrey her loving business partner. She is still the most intelligent woman in Hong Kong. Maria Louisa de Romans has left Hong Kong–many years ago–with the Italian Ambassador, Boola, and now lives with him in Mexico City. The Wong sisters have all divorced. I hear the gossip. Cheung Yee the sculptor is there smiling and happy to see me. We embrace. He still doesn't speak English. I still don't speak Chinese. We hug talk. The party is elegant. Mae still gives the most elegant parties everyone says. I wonder why I really didn't get to know them well the last time I lived in Hong Kong. Seven waiters in white jackets pass the hors d'oeuvres. The amahs sit in the kitchen getting the trays ready. The women are elegantly dressed in the Chinese fashions copied from *Vogue* over in Kowloon. All the shoes are Charles Jordan sold at the Mandarin Hotel. I am happy. I am like a drunk. I am a new person in Hong Kong who is an old person. I am drunk to see my old friends. Everyone asks politely about Hinkel. I tell them as much good news as I can lie about. My old friend, Rosamund Brown, the painter, has come down from her own temple on Pollock's Path. She has gotten older. So have I. Everything is right. Michael holds my arm. He loves these people without needing to see them very often.

He submits to worldliness.

Michael who is the least worldly person in the world submits to worldliness the way one submits to having one's fortune told. But he is glad to leave.

So am I.

We walk into the night. We have kissed the others goodbye.

K. C. Paou has offered us his yacht.

Run Run Shaw has asked me to write a film.

Peter has asked for the thousandth time if Michael will stop learning his mumbo jumbo and go into business with him.

Winnie Wong has asked me to lunch at the Mandarin.

Rosamund Chew has asked the children to visit her child.

Loretta has invited me to bridge with Donald Cheung.

Cheung Yee has asked me to look at some of his new drawings.

Willy Woo has asked Michael to do some public relations for Hong Kong in America.

Kay Howe has asked us to spend a week at the Mandarin with the children.

We have said *maybe* to everything.

We leave to go back to the temple on Lantao Island. There are books to bring us wisdom. Things to be learned. Words to write. Children to give our arms to. Suddenly everyone you once wanted to see becomes a shadow play. The riff-raff of moments spent talking to others.

We have so little. We have so much. We have time together. We have now. Michael and I take the ferry home hugging.

Will it all disappear?

Who cares I say to myself looking at the sea. I have the present. I have a pleasant smell of frying sausages in the morning. I am a woman over forty who loves her life and her future. I am a person who doesn't miss New York. My eyes look at the sea. I am filled with the sea colors. I lead a watercolor life. I'm the watercolor poet I always wanted to be. I feel humble. I know that the end of life is the worm. Michael has taught that to me. I will die. I will become nothing. But while I am alive I can live with my senses wide open. I am filled with joy. I celebrate each second of life. I am exactly where I should be. I want nothing. I care for nothing more than I have. Both of my children look at me. They see a mother who is content with her own life. I wonder if they are too. I feel that they are. They listen to Michael as he reads to them. He reads to them Irish folk tales. The Talmud. He reads to them in Chinese. They love him. They follow behind him as he walks through the house like two little shadows. They don't cry. More than that—I don't cry.

I have forgotten depression the way hill people who came out of the sea have forgotten undersea landscapes.

I have forgotten money pressures.

I have forgotten being afraid to grow old.

I have forgotten worrying about my breasts sagging. And wrinkles.

I know that some day I will go again to a modern airport and be again waiting in an airport lounge with fear in my stomach and the same old knots inside of my stomach. But for the moment I have come to the good party in the fairy tale. There is magic. There is possibility. I have found it here in Lantao Island. I can babble about the sky and the fish and braid my long hair. I don't have to think about fate. I don't have to think. I can just be. All that I wanted when I once wanted everything was this: to be allowed to name things.

Each morning I sit in the room of perfection.

I sit in the silent room writing down odd things that will mean something or nothing to strangers. Depending on what they are looking for.

Actually I am writing a way to protect yourself.

I am writing a guerrilla book for people who know that love doesn't have to be scarce.

I am wiring a new light bulb. I am saying writing is everything. It's a shield. It will protect you. I am saying write everything down. So it doesn't get away. Write down moments. The artist is the only historian. Write about despair. Celebrate with words. The stratosphere. Forget. Recreate. I live with sun. Sea. Love and palm groves.

Here. On an island.

*

And yet one morning I wake up and say to myself "Katherine
—what are you doing with this little man?"

Everything has changed.

I realize that it is just my desperation that has convinced me
that I love this man.

I love him because truthfully I am tired of the others.

I love him because I do not believe in happiness any more.

I love him because night after night in New York City I have
looked out of the windows at the huge buildings and felt in some
odd way dwarfed myself. I have felt loneliness. I have been afraid
of old age. More than that I have been afraid of not being able to
cope. I have allowed babies and money and lack of success in my
work to freeze me into the refrigerator of my own soul where I
am no one.

I am alive and not writing poems. May goddesses and gods
forgive me.

I am not writing.

I have not become the Katherine Kahn I should have been.
The real Katherine Kahn, that girl who went to Bennington
College and lived in France and Hong Kong and looked at
pictures on the walls, that girl who wrote her own screams on the
walls, that girl who looked for samples of love but never got
enough, that girl who became a woman with her first husband
leaving her in vague hotel rooms so that life beamed out utterly
cold waves of energy from a frozen sun and she woke in the
morning freezing because marriage had become irrelevant and love
was at best a sample—that girl who had so much courage and
picked herself up and started again, started life again so many
times with one man or another was now tired. She was tired of

movie stars, violinists, shipping kings, lawyers, primitive would-be gigolos, Armenian architects, men in the food business, men in the medicine business, yes she was tired of medicine men, tired of grocers and singers and composers and violinists and writers–god she was tired of goddamn fucking unpublished writers, tired of hairdressers and insurance kings and sailors and pilots and editors and revolutionaries and historians and cartoonists and gurus and the new awareness–she was just tired of every man she had ever married, gone out with or fucked or sucked or listened to or fantasized about or had as an asshole buddy who tired her and turned out to be just an asshole. And now here she was–like a little kitten cuddling up to the sun–making love with the oddest ball of them all. Making love with Michael.

Anguish and oblivion. We have not drowned. We have found each other. That is the miracle. Just as I thought there was no place to go no place to hide–just as I thought my life was over–just as I was tired of all my life mistakes–tired of money–tired of trying to be a success and not being one–trying to be a person I could never be–the way nets cannot hold water–suddenly I am a golden girl fugitive in a new place where I wake every morning singing, where a man climbs to my mouth and presses his mouth on my mouth, where every morning I wake and celebrate joy.

I sing. I burn. What is this quietness that comes over me all at once?

My sad tenderness.

Am I saying "Katherine you do not deserve this joy" because I am afraid? How hard it is to accept joy. How hard it is to really feel free to love and be loved without anxiety. Without feeling bad for being alive. I have reached the first true moments of joy in my life. I am loved. I love. I am not ashamed of the solitude I have always known turning into soundless delirious joy. I am marking time. It can't last. It doesn't matter.

*

I don't want to be protected or protecting any more. I want to escape the prison of our relationship. What was once love becomes the shiny bars of a love prison. At night I lay awake preparing my escape. MY DEPARTURE.

That has happened with every man I know except Romano.

I wonder if it will happen with Michael?

Is it possible it will happen with Michael?

I suddenly get frightened.

I walk around Lantao Island looking at the blue sea. I stare at the palm trees whose great green eyes stare back at me. Will boredom replace ecstasy?

The indoors and the outdoors have become part of me.

I love Michael.

I love my daughters waving goodbye as they go to school in the morning and running to hug me when they come home.

I love Mister Wu waddling down the road like a great big Chinese duck.

I love myself in the morning when I wake and I feel like the Katherine I never was. Katherine the great lover. Katherine the queen. Katherine who must have been a good person to deserve such happiness. Katherine who eats butter and jam and no longer cares about losing weight because Michael swears he loves me as I am.

Katherine the fey.

Katherine the loving. The no longer unhappy Katherine.

Yes, I have found contentment.

*

Michael studies each morning the translations from Hebrew to English. He is particularly interested in the Chinese Jews—a tribe that escaped to the China mainland and kept the Talmud. He believes that the Talmud has entered into Confucian thought and later into modern Chinese thought. He sees in some ways that I do not yet understand a bridge between the Talmud and Mao Tse Tung. He studies Rabbi Akiba. He sits all morning drinking in the words of the Torah. His favorite maxim is "Keep far away from an evil neighbor. Do not associate with the wicked. And do not shrug off all thought of calamity." The evil neighbor, he has explained is one who is evil to mankind and womankind, who is not a good person. The wicked refers, he says, to an evil impulse which dwells at the opening of the heart. When a person seeks to commit a transgression, the evil impulse bends all the limbs over which it rules to that end. Isn't it odd? Michael spends all morning studying about love. A man must love men and women. "In the scroll of saints it is said: if you wish to attach to yourself a devoted friend, do things for the friend's welfare."

Holy people have no desire to wipe out the world. That is what Michael studies all morning. How not to hate.

"One who is not always striving to improve will come to an end, that is to say, the very memory of that person will vanish." Hence the sages have said that one should always be adding to one's learning. Even if that person learns a number of things, that person should go on learning.

Michael has made me into his disciple.

He has said to me:

If I am not for myself, who then?

And being for myself, what am I?

And if not now, when?

I think of all the times I was not for myself. I sit in my own room writing out my own loneliness and joy and celebration and childhood. I celebrate my girlhood. But I was not for myself then.

*

At two o'clock Michael stops studying. He comes into my room and we kiss. It is time to go out. We take long walks on the island. Michael talks to me about what he is studying. One morning we talk about the meaning of Cheerfulness. What does it mean? To receive all people with a cheerful countenance? As we walk Michael talks about a teacher who gave his students all the good gifts in the world with a downcast face. Scripture says that he gave nothing. Then scripture talks about a teacher who gave everything with a cheerful countenance. That teacher was remembered as if he gave all the good gifts of the world.

I now have a happy face. "That," says Michael, "is the opposite of arrogance and anger."

Michael is my lover. He is also my teacher.

This is what our mornings are like.

Mr. Wu is up at six and takes the girls to their new school on the ferry.

Michael and I get up at seven. We love. We love each other. We wash. We use big towels to dry. We put on an LP record. Some days it's Jean-Pierre Rampal playing a jazz flute suite. Other days it's Bach. Or Horowitz playing Chopin. Some mornings it's Chinese wedding music. Or the sitar. We bathe and listen to music and eat fruit. We drink hot instant coffee. My soul wanders. Happy. Sad. Unending. I can't believe my luck. I am with my life-friend.

At about eight-thirty Mr. Wu returns. We go into our separate rooms. I sit in my room of silence and write. I write anything I like. I just let life come pouring out of me. I don't think of what I have to say. It's there. I don't look. The words come. It's not like the interviews I used to write. I sit in my room of silence and make things up. I let all the words out of me. I breathe them out.

I write like a child. I tap tap tap tap tap on my typewriter the way my grandmother from Russia once tap tap tap tapped on her Singer sewing machine when she was making dresses for me. She sat in front of her little black machine all day—I spied on her—and made blouses and skirts and little hats and tablecloths—she sewed the world up. That's what I do on my own machine. I too make blouses and scarves and dresses out of words. A word wardrobe. I write about ordinary things. Write about dancing elephants. I write my Asia love poems. I write my love poems. I write a poem in praise of men. I write a poem in praise of Michael. I write a poem in praise of the body of a man, white hills, white thighs. I write about how I was alone—like someone lost in a forest of dinner parties and buildings and people who meant nothing to me. Kind strangers. I was alone. I write about how a small man with the body of a giant came into my life. I write about his voice which was slow and sad. About his strong arms. And his eyes that looked for me. I write poems in praise of Michael. Of his body. And his mind. I write these poems and I never get tired of writing them.

I write about the light around Michael's body. I write about light. I have always been—in some odd sense—light years away from who I am. Suddenly I am with a man who is like a small electric bulb. The light wraps around him. He has his own flame. Around his body is marvelous light. I write about Michael. His illumination and his color. His aura. And his flame. I write about light.

I write about the vastness of the sea.

I look at the China Sea and I write about the sea. I write how, as a little girl, I heard the sound of the sea the way you hear the song of a bell. The gong of the sea in my ears. Waves breaking. A solitary bell. When I was a child I always stared at seagulls. I felt sorry for them because they were not able to sing. As beautiful as they were—as free as they were—they had no voice. They were free.

But could not sing. And I, in my girlhood, dreaming about being a poet, dreaming about naming things—I pitied the seagull who could not sing. I would watch them a moment before flight taking their time and then slowly lifting into the air—to fly in the cloud. But what difference did it make—I asked myself—their flight—if they could not sing?

Often I wanted to give them a gift of sound.

I imagined a long soft remote voice that could come from their sea-bird throats.

I sit in my room of silence and write about seagulls. And freedom.

I sit in my seagull room and sing.

I sit in my room of silence and write about the morning itself. A morning on Lantao Island filled with sunshine and the sound of insects and birds. I write about the clouds passing from the New Territories over Lantao Island on their aimless way to Hong Kong and Kowloon and the rest of the world. I write about fruit going to seed in a huge bowl. I write about the secrets of fruit. I spy on fruit. I watch, each morning, the fruit as it decays and comes into something else. That is what I am and what I must always be. A spy who looks at death and tries to understand its changes.

I watch the death of custard apple.

First it is picked and put inside the bowl.

It is fresh and round and green and ripe and firm. Then slowly it begins to sag. It is no longer firm. The skin breaks. The white tissue inside comes oozing out. The seeds begin to fall out of the custard apple. The skin shrivels. In a few days it's almost all moisture. That is death. How wondrous it is that I can write all this down. That is all I ever wanted to do. Write about birth. And death. That is enough to devote my life to I think.

I write not only about death. And mornings.

And sea. And the body.

I write about magic so that someone I don't even know will hear me. I write like a chubby aborigine in some odd room all the chants that I know. I throw them on paper for strangers that I don't even know. I write so that strangers may hear me. I, who lived on books, for whom books were the only way to survive when I was a child, know that at one time in my life—I was the stranger who received words from others. Words saved me. And kept me alive. And so now I write about magic to strangers. I write about the magic of gulls and beaches. I write about necklaces, and orchards and train stations. And I watch my words from a long way off. They fell out of my suffering. I write about the magic of mouths and blood and chants. I write while next door to me my friend studies wisdom in his own room.

I remember myself as I was.

I remember myself as a little girl.

I remember always wanting to find an island where the sea was blue, there were green trees, and soap was sold at the general store. I have achieved all this. I have achieved all this in my room of silence.

While I write. While I tap tap tap my dreams. Michael sits in his own room. Studying.

*

If I could look through the walls I would see Michael. What is he doing after breakfast?

He is lost in his own world.

On this island, on Lantao Island Michael is studying wisdom. The Talmud. The Law.

Michael's window looks out at the blue water of the China Sea and the palm trees. Michael is his own ambassador of the imagination. Who are you? Michael. Out of Ireland and Galway. Out of New York City and a Chinese and Irish parentage. Out of military school. Out of Manhattan and ranches. No wonder you like the Jews. You are like a wandering Jew who one day wandered into the city of Hong Kong and never went back. Sad blue eyes. Long lashes. Straight short Roman nose. White alabaster skin. Tight muscles. Tight chest. Here I love you. In this odd temple that you share with me away from the world I love you. We are far away from childhood. Far away from divorce-land. Far away from fights and divorce lawyers. Far away from New York City. And bills. And cash flow. And crowds. And restaurants filled with bored people who lift little pieces of celery to their lips. We are far away from administrations, and election campaigns, and movies, and literary agents and fuck papers and the Rolling Stones and hostesses and hosts and Off Broadway theatre. We are far away from that odd civilization that never fed me. Whatever we are we will always be. We are living in this odd cocoon where I read and write in my own room and you read and write in your own room and the children go to school and we watch each other's faces for signs of pain. But there is no pain. We have skated away from the other skaters.

We are here alone.

But what does Michael do in his room?

Michael is looking for himself.

Not in a convex mirror.

In a book.

Michael reads a book to look for himself. He is voyaging not across the world but across the pages. He is voyaging into himself. He's a tiny Rabbi of the imagination trying to understand things. He is buried deep into the voyage of his book. The book he reads in the Talmud is called *The Wisdom of the Fathers*—Michael—who never really knew his father looks for himself in the wisdom of the fathers in the Talmud. He is reading the teachings of the Jewish sages on the conduct of human life and thought. Here—a tiny Irish American Chinese oddball—with a warm large heart as large as the universe–studies the Talmud. In his own temple he reads the archives of studies and debates conducted in the Palestinian and Babylonian academies for more than seven hundred years, from before 200 B.C. to the year of 500 on our calendar. Here, on Lantao Island, Michael is studying a new translation of the Pirke Abot, one of the treatises of the Talmud. He is reading Pirke Abot–a collection of the sayings of the Synagogue Fathers, maxims which summarized the anguish and joy and understanding that the Synagogue Fathers experienced in their study and practice of the Law. The sages quoted are men who lived sometime between the latter half of the fifth and the third century before the Common Era. They are descendants of Rabbi Judah the Prince, who lived in the third century of the Common Era. Their maxims are their poems.

Michael studies wisdom.

"Give thy ears, hear what is said" declares the Egyptian Amen-em-opet. "Give thy heart to understand them. To put them in thy heart is worthwhile." Let them rest in the casket of thy belly that they might be a key in thy heart.

Michael studies what Zeradah says: "Let thy house be a meeting-place for the sages, and sit in the very dust at their feet, and thirstily drink in their words. But in much wisdom is much vexation and he that increaseth knowledge increaseth sorrow."

*

Locate me first of all in a tropical country. Locate me in a place where thousands of people run up and down the streets–but I am far away from them. Locate me on an island. Where the trees are green. Where the fruit is ripe. Custard apples. Avocados. Lichee nuts. Where love is not scarce as mercury. Locate me in a house with a lover who lies in bed with me at night and releases all the secret juices from my body. Locate me with a man who is all tongue. Whose tongue goes in and out of my mouth and thighs as if I was his fruit. Locate me with my two children—my two twigs—my bosses and blossoms my loves. My two little girls who are in love with the island. They run naked in the house. They ride on a ferry to school. They have a prince of their own. This prince is a man called Mr. Wu. Mr. Wu is a houseboy, cook, comedian, sage and wisdom maker. He is about sixty. He wears a white coat, black loose pants, and velvet shoes. His face never changes except when he smiles and then you see he has perfect white buck teeth. His skin is brown and has wrinkles like weeds around his lips. I think he is blind in one eye so that one large brown eye is open and one large eye is almost closed. He does not speak English. He does not want to speak English. He speaks smile. He and Michael talk in Cantonese which is the language he speaks. Michael has a telephone in his house and until I arrived Mr. Wu's only company was the telephone. He still gets constant calls. I hear him chatter in soft Cantonese with his hand over his mouth.

*

I listen to his telephone calls. I think he is a bookie. He shuffled to the phone the first day I arrived and spoke in his singsong Cantonese in a soft voice very quickly. He spoke in a whisper because I think he thought his phone calls would bother me. But nothing bothers me. Now he runs to the phone and speaks in a normal Cantonese voice. I mean to ask Michael what Mr. Wu is talking about.

I am delirious.

I do not get phone calls.

No one knows where I am. And no one cares. I care. I care

because all this joy was just waiting for me on this earth. I just didn't know it. Love you see does not have to be scarce as uranium.

In the mornings I wake and hold Michael very close to me. I examine his eyes and ears and nose the way you examine a fortune. He has become very precious to me. He wakes. We look at earth and sky and moons in each other's faces. We touch. We wake. I go marking the atlas of Michael's body with my fingers. He goes marking mine. We whisper stories. I who lived for so many years in cold harbor from which I loved no one–suddenly I am here in this quiet and calm place with my love. Dream and silence cross. Soundless, delirious, between motionless teachers who approve of my new knowledge of the body, I go marking his body. I mark it first with my fingers. Then with my tongue. Between my lips and his voice saying "Katherine" as if it were not my name but some wonderful new word that he had discovered this morning.

*

Love gifts for me.

Michael has bought sculptures in the New Territories. New Cheung Yee sculptures for the living room. I stare at Cheung Yee shields. What are these objects? They are sculptures of protection and they are like harmless turtle backs. They are made of steel. Also on the walls are Chinese Scrolls. On the floors are plain woven straw mats. In the children's room is a parrot–a green and blue bird that is friendly. I live in celebration all day long. And best of all Michael has given me my own empty room. My room of silence. My room without objects that stand in the way of dreams. My own room without old things. Michael has given me my own room which I call the room of perfection. Did I ever dream that I could be so happy? That someone would give me my own room? Here I sit all day at a desk with a typewriter. And empty paper. And a chair that is made out of wicker and has a yellow silk bottom. This chair I love more than anything in the world. It was a gift to Michael from Charlotte Horstman who owns an antique shop and is part Chinese and part German. She is a fascinating odd woman whom I had known once before the last time I lived in Hong Kong. Now I sit on her chair. For me it is a throne. I can sit in my own silent room of perfection and look out the windows. I see grass. And clouds. And birds crying down at me. I can sit and dream all day about everything I was and everything I want to be. I can sit and luxuriate in the now. Everything I wanted when I once wanted everything was this–to be able to sit still and name things.

To write about flowers and blood as if I had invented them. To enter into names. To be a little Noah for every animal. To sit in a room creating words.

*

"When I first came to this temple" Michael says, "I stood up in my room studying. Poring over different books of wisdom. The more I studied the Chinese the more similarities I saw that the Confucian thought had to the ancient Hebrew sages. I found similarities. I also found similarities between modern science and poetry. Between knowledge, drugs and understanding. Suddenly I began seeing similarities in everything. I studied the Talmud because it was the basis of Law. I felt if I understood the ancient laws I would understand the basic unit of Western thought as an indivisible entity whether metaphysical–which is BEING or psychological which is the SELF or social which is NATION, CLASS AND POLITICAL BODIES. The model for all of this I found in the ancient Hebrew laws which were also in some odd mixed-up way the current Chinese laws used in the Peoples'

Republic of China. If you make a study of Mao's poetry and laws they correspond almost exactly to the laws of the Talmud. The basic units are interchanging. The archetype of Maoism, the basic intellectual framework, is all found not in Marx only but in the wisdom of the fathers of the Pirke Abot. The ethical principles are the same... In one philosophical thought worships god, in another philosophical thought dissolves the god and replaces god with the good for everyone, but basically the position of the leader in the superstructure is the same. In talmudic thought, as well as Maoist thought, and even, by the way, Tantric thought, there is one particular feature: God is almost always accompanied by consorts. Duality, a basic feature of Hebraic thought–good and evil–or Tantrism, or Maoism as we have come to know it–shows that all of these religious or semi-religious systems are based on the pure and the impure."

Michael doodles, writing the Chinese ideogram for *freedom*.

"The divine society is a place where everything fits together. The divine is not the godhead. The divine is a society that follows laws, a tissue of relations, a magnetic field, a phrase. The God becomes many men which function as elders or wise men–which in turn are almost like a fluid throughout the society, something like the atoms, the cells or the phonemes of the divine. The question is: who is divine? The answer is always–the human being. The wisdom of the fathers–or the Torah–teaches, as do the Tantric Buddhist scrolls, Hinduism, that Nirvana is inside us. In Sanskrit zero may be spoken of as either Sunya–empty–or purna–full. Anyway–I'm just a vagabond seeking liberation. I take wisdom wherever I find it. Right now I find it–in the lost world of the Torah. And I find it in being with you."

Michael walking out of the bathroom.

Hugging me.

Both of us falling on the unmade bed.

Time, technology, drugs, poetry, language, revolt–all of this exists in our embrace.

*

"Strive every day to do the Will of God with a perfect heart and a perfect spirit" Michael said. He was shaving. He was standing in the blue bathroom. Our room was painted blue and the bathroom was also blue. Michael stood there with a white beard of soap. His clownlike pink smile.

"Were it not for the Torah no man would be able to achieve perfect ethical behavior" Michael said, bringing the razor down across his right cheek. I stood there naked with a blue towel around my waist, admiring him. He had become miraculously beautiful to me. When I first saw him his body was short and his face too angular. Now all that I saw was a perfect body and great luminous eyes. He had become on the outside what I had sensed he was inside.

"How did you come to study the Torah?" I asked.

"I was living in Hong Kong" Michael said–"and I was riding horses at the track. In the evenings I would go out to the discotheques, fool around at the different bars–like any bachelor in this town. I had enough money to live on and I kept feeling that this was not only the time of my life to have fun, and enjoy myself, but to learn something. I guess I've always been studious– like you sweetheart–and learning has been fun for me. I started studying Tantric Buddhist scrolls. I began by studying different kinds of Buddhism and teaching myself Chinese at night. When all of Hong Kong was sleeping and all you could see was the fishermen's boats on the sea."

*

On Sundays we ride on a junk. Lazy sea Sundays.
My children run up and down on the boat.
They have never been on a junk.
And this is a fairy-tale junk.
A lovers' junk.
This is the slow boat to China, with huge red sails, that they read about. Silk cushions. We take white porcelain spoons and scoop wintermelon soup out of bowls. And eat chopped scallions and bean curd and long green bean pods with our chopsticks. Checked blue and white tablecloths flap on the pillows. We laugh and wipe our mouths. Mr. Wu runs up and down. He brings Michael a flute. Michael plays the flute. He plays Chinese music and Mozart. We are mesmerized by him. We laugh. The boat sails on the green China Sea.

We have sailed away from the world, but we are in the world. I can't believe that this is real. But it is real. We see the towers of Hong Kong—the island in the distance. I can pick out the Hong Kong Bank, the hotels, the buildings and the Peak. I see Hong Kong. But we are out on the sea.

I was once a form in search of myself.

Now I found myself.

My hair blows. My blouse is open. The children are making drawings with red and pink magic markers. I brought my straw hat. I wear my straw hat on the sampan and lay it aside and lie down on Michael's arms. Thank you Michael, I always knew I would be fulfilled—I just didn't know when. Now, at forty, just when I thought nothing good was possible, you banged into my life like a bright gong. A stranger I met you—remet you and suddenly I am here. Sailing on a junk.

We drink vodka on the rocks.

The boat goes slowly.

It's Sunday.

A lot of junks are out on the sea. We sail away from Lantao

Island. We eat. We kiss. We place ourselves in the hands of the sun and lie back and sunbathe. A picnic on the China Sea. A piece of fruit falls on Michael's pants. It spatters his white pants. We laugh. We eat the fruit. Something buzzes in my ear. It's almost a bee. But it's only this: I am truly what I always knew I could be. Katherine. Secure. Without despair. With the children. With Michael.

The sea is calm. The boat bobs up and down so slowly. I wish I never had to return. I wish I could draw out this moment forever. Beyond all desire is this moment.

Can I draw time out? Can I make it go on forever? The boat sails slowly on the sea. The junk bobs and the sail moves with the wind. This is a nameless day. A day without volcanoes. Or LP records. Or bright memories. A day without despair. My only day without despair. Anxieties gone.

I always knew time could stop.

Time dies. I sail on the junk. I hate for the first time in my life—the sunset.

When we sail home.

Even the children are disappointed. We wanted this day on the junk to never end. But of course it does end.

Of course it does end.

*

At night I would have nightmares of the past.

I would sleep in our bed and suddenly have odd dreams—I dreamt of my first husband visiting me. In that dream I still loved him deeply but he was with another woman—I kept wanting to say "She's too young for you" but I could never get near him. In that dream I would meet a handsome young Frenchman but he would ignore me. Then a group of old friends—my Greek friends—would be going to a party and I would never be invited.

It was a party at Arthur Schlesinger Jr.'s and everyone I knew was going to be there but I wasn't invited. "Oh god, another evening alone tonight in New York" I thought to myself. Then the dream ended. The dream ended and I was in Michael's temple without many things, without datebooks and telephone numbers and things that hang on the wall only to become the walls themselves. Michael was sleeping next to me. I had a terrible desire to take him in my arms and hug him. It was real! That other city, New York, that other place where the eternal thirst flows and wariness follows, that place of the infinite ache was no longer my city.

I walked like an Indian, careful not to wake him, barefoot into my room. There I looked at the white paper that lay on the table and out the window at the palms and the sea. The sea knocked my eyes out with its blue. A sampan was sailing on the sea. A large junk was passing my window. I wanted to go on a junk and Charlotte Horstman, the little German part-Chinese woman with white hair and understanding clever eyes had lent Michael and me the junk. It was Saturday. We were going to go on a junk-trip. Mr. Wu had packed a picnic in the wicker basket. The girls had been looking forward to this all week. But the house was still sleeping.

I sat down at my desk.

Hong Kong and Lantao Island.

Are you really all this?

A bright morning.

A mango eaten in the sunlight.

The blue sea.

Cold water. And soap. And my own room. My own room where I sit down on a bamboo chair covered with yellow silk and write about my joy. Lantao Island where I reach the peak of my life. What does poetry mean? I think, as I sit in front of the white paper. Poetry has been likened to mysticism and eroticism. But this isn't quite true. The most important difference is this—the mystical experience—or the experience that Michael seeks in studying the Talmud and the Tantric Buddhist scrolls—is a search for coming close to a constant good. The object of mystic experience is to merge symbolically with some meaning. The object, I think, of poetry is essentially language. Someone who writes poetry is more concerned with words than what words delegate. That is not to say that the world of the poet lacks meaning—or that meaning is peripheral. It is only that in poetry *meaning* is inseparable from words, whereas in ordinary conversations, or conversations of mystics, the meanings lie in what the words point to—a meaning beyond language.

I look through my notebook at the love poems I have written for Michael. Poems that remember anguish and the past.

The inert lifeless mass calls out into space.

It is called memory.

I write of memories. Of calendars of the sea. Of my love for my children. Of Michael's body. This is another world. A life that Michael has given me.

Michael has given me my own world. The odd thing is that Michael has taken me out of the frantic race to the gates of hell and allowed me to find paradise in a small room.

Love Poem for Michael
What I wanted
Was to be myself again
On a Monday morning, to
Wake and wash with cold water
And soap, to dress
Swiftly and walk without
Thinking
Where I came from, who I was,
To be silent and

Saved
From the long days of myself.
It no longer mattered
If I burned, bursting
Then catching fire. It
Was enough to have
Known the war within
Myself and to be tired—
To be sick of the
Boundaries—to have
Lived in the calendar of the
Brain where one meets
One's self each day in a talking
Mirror and says, "How long
Are you here for? When
Will the war be over?" I wanted
A sea change, a place
Where things grew into
Secrets of color,
A place I imagined of festivals,
Rocks, brilliant
Reptiles, trees
And serious things—wind bells
That chime—a place
Where I could be useful.
We moved, quite suddenly,
To the Colony.
I saw ancient women
In their tennis suits
Playing all afternoon. Their men
Played Business, Journalist,
General—others were
Involved in Domestic Monopoly—

And some played
Sailor on the sea. I lived
In their fashion,
Going in and out of the
Moments. If it were not
For the fish
And melons,
For the queer atonal
Music and Water slipping
In the cracks of houses,
Olive fresh-water snakes,
The strangeness—
I might have
Become a part of the Colony,
Seeing myself in that life
In which all things
Are at the height of themselves.
I might have eaten mangoes,
Had my picture taken,
Written postcards to friends
Announcing my recreation, gone
On gaping at bar girls
And bargains, and having
Coats made by
Overnight tailors.
But I must tell you this:
One morning I woke up
And entered life;
I ran quite swiftly through the mountains,
Passing the palm trees and civets,
Watching harvests
And children
All in the ripeness of summer. It

Was then
I inherited joy
The way one inherits a fortune.

Love Poem for Michael
This ancient Chinese man with white-,
Blue-, and red-striped socks, white
Shorts, hat, white hair, old skin,
Moves quickly on the court,
Looks across the net, and says,
"Each time you move your racquet
It is
The closing of a door. Lifting
The racquet, moving it across
Your chest, across your heart—
The closing of a door.
The closing of a door."

I move across the grass,
Awkward unathletic,
Thinking of the past.

As the swift game continues
I drive strokes past
Camps and boarding schools,
Japan, three years in France,
All the voices
In the flame trees saying,
Love me. Use me. Use me
To see everything, as
One by one
My ghosts sweat and work out
Beside me,

Swinging
Their helpless arms
Into the sky.

Love Poem for Michael
The
White bird
Circles over me
Wearing a crown. He
must have escaped
From a country where
Chinaberries dangled
From the green trees
Against yellow
Skies, where ebony spleenworts
And branches
Were dazzled by the wind
And where
His great crown
Was made. O bird! I exhale
And inhale your secrets—my
Heart beats now like
Yours
As I lead you home alive.
I am quiet
As I move through
The twigs as if they were
Clouds—I am what
I always was—a child
Leading
Birds out of the sun.
The weeds are quiet now. I
Listen to imaginary

Woods and grasses–gullies,
Trees, ponds–
None are as real
As your white pearl feathers
As we fly
Through the parables of
Trees while I call to you, "Bird! Bird!"
Crying again
To be so young.

    Love Poem for Michael
We wake. Our day
Starts on the Peak: we are
Singing and burning
Our secrets. All night
We turned in the same sheets
And now we share the day.
We dress, lace our shoes, run
To find the end
Of each long walk. There is none.
Up on this high wild hill
The dangling birds
Open black fringed umbrellas
And bob
Invisible through fog–blackbird
Umbrellas,
Shielding gods.
How free,
How easy, our life
Here. There's not
Much to do
But read or answer
The doorbell. Our

Long talks,
Like water blending into
Water, have
No end—and no
Start.
Old loneliness
Goes flying with
Birds down
The green hill.
I have achieved a life that is natural.

Love Poem for Michael
Women peel
Thousand-year-old eggs
By scraping off mud
From the colored shells. Under
Great fish heads bleeding
On a string, we
Are discovered walking
Hand in hand
In this market where
Everything's possible.
We have arrived
In this human place
Of sea-horse medicine
Where sugared kumquats
Shine in glass jars
And spiders and rats
Parade through vegetables. Here,
In this winding street,
A lazy boy
Holds Chinese oranges
Inside his hands

And spends all morning
With a rubber stamp stamping
Them "Sunkist" so
They'll sell for more. Here we
Touch elephant horn–black
Tusks and ivory–
Here we touch thin private scrolls
And rims of porcelain,
See wizards carve flowers
In white Mah-Jongg cubes. My
Senses open wide
And make me dizzy. Water bugs
That will refuse to drown
Burn on our sandals. Vendors
Show their teeth
Of golden stones. Suddenly, ducks,
Pressed with sleepy eyes,
Hang over us like rows
Of tennis racquets. Snakes
Are pulled out of
Baskets to be eaten. And the sun
Presses against us. Starting
From where we are,
Let's go down, down, down under cabbage and
Ginger, let us escape
These ducks and taste our lives. Under
The blood of animals
Let's turn our own lives inside out,
Throwing away petals
We cannot hold–
Families, deaths, marriages–
Discarding our histories,

Those exits and entrances
We cannot explain, mistakes,
Odd people, countries
We have slept with,
Throw ourselves
Down under dragonflies, broccoli,
Under the pythons, crushed medicines,
Spices,
While our silly tongues scratch,
Our new bodies touch,
And we are always ready to be born.

Love Poem for Michael

Love
Opened my eyes to the amulets
Of trees—
Green leaves, falling miracles,
Falling, one by one,
On the street. In Japan we bought

White porcelain tipped into palm-eyes
And icicles, pots shaped like
Peach stones and glazed in sky blue.
We touched the rims of the world's glaze
But arrived without anything. Then

You gave me my own room without old things,
Without decorations, without paintings
That hang on the walls
Only to become new walls themselves, without
Shapes that interfere
With what I must be.

My dreams were unshaped and unpainted. I
Lived with the fantasy of the sea–shaped
Always on the verge of words. You–
Looked for emptiness the way lovers seek sleep,
Burned currencies
And seeds of your own beginnings. How easy
For us to change into firebirds, fly
Past history, oceans, striking against the sky
With our own new wings. Now–
Shall we return where we came from?
You be the brush that strikes.
And, burning inside, still burning, I'll
Live as the flaming kiln that shapes the pot.

Before Michael nothing was original ... Love? A harpoon to
enter the odd whale of life.

*

I remember the time I met Marlene.

The time I tried to become a lesbian. "I'm gay" she announced
with her sorrowful voice. She was a revolutionary and was always
sorrowful.

I took Marlene to Chile. I was writing an article for *Travel &
Leisure* and my air fare was paid for by Lan Chile.

I had three commissions from three magazines–I was worth
more in Chile than I was in America. I told everyone "Hey–listen
to this–I'm worth more dead than alive." Allende was then in
Chile.

Pablo Neruda had called me from Paris, where he was then an
Ambassador, and asked me "Linda Poet" to see his Chile. He gave
me an introduction to Allende and a letter to introduce me to a
woman he called Glorious Gloria. She was Mrs. Allende's

secretary. I asked Marlene to come with me. She was unhappy in New York because her girlfriend was living with a younger girl now and she was more or less left out of the ménage à trois. I was in the process of breaking up with a hairy horrible man with whom I had been obsessively in love since my divorce. I had enough money from all of the commissions to invite her to come with me—I arranged to get two free airplane tickets.

On the plane Marlene told me about all the famous lesbians of the world. I was amazed to see the world through her eyes. EVERYONE WAS A LESBIAN. The President of the United States was a lesbian. The Pope was a lesbian. The great movie stars of the thirties and forties were all lesbians. On the flight to Chile I wondered if I was also a lesbian. Marlene had asked me in a whining voice to experience her body. I told her I would experience her body when I had the urge. I had no urge though. That was the trouble. We had different life-urges. I was lonely. That was it. And I liked Marlene's company. Back at my apartment she had been wonderful with the children. She had known how to fix things. Goddammit she could fix my towel rack when it broke. She knew how to put Band-aids on the record player so it actually played. She could open the terrace doors and hammer them so they actually worked. But although I liked her company we went to Chile with the understanding that we would be just friends. She was interested in meeting Allende. I was interested in seeing Chile. She calmed me by assuring me I would have a simpatico companion.

But it was a disaster.

From beginning to end.

Marlene and me.

From the beginning, from the very beginning it was a fucking mess.

First of all I was not fucking Marlene. That was the trouble. Even if I was interested in kissing Marlene's cunt I wouldn't have been kissing Marlene's cunt because Marlene for some reason or other had never heard of soap and water. She smelled. Also, for another reason (which I will never be able to understand why) but Marlene wore a little dirty white undershirt. Under Mexican peasant blouses. Creepy dirty jeans. Filthy underpants. Socks and hiking boots. Even if she had been Warren Beatty in that outfit she wouldn't have turned me on. She had long brown hair which she never combed. And a soft whining voice. She was also a poet. She had written one fucking poem in her whole life. It was about the Queen of Sheba being a lesbian.

Wherever we went in Chile I was asked to read my poetry and I would always insist that Marlene read her poetry also. I heard that fucking Sheba poem all over Chile. It was about the wonders of lesbianism.

Let me tell you about the wonders of Marlene.

To begin with we checked into the Santiago Hilton which is up on a hill and where the manager gave us a room for free because I was writing for *Travel & Leisure*–also because of the revolution there were very few customers.

Marlene immediately became sick.

She needed a doctor.

She was dying.

Her tumor was bleeding.

There I was nursing a lesbian in Chile. Paying doctor bills. The doctors kept saying she had no tumor and nothing was wrong with her. I sensed that Marlene was just annoyed that she hadn't met any lesbians. If I wasn't going to sleep with her and nobody else was going to sleep with her she might as well get sick to cause attention.

In desperation I wanted to dump Marlene. Our friendship was a mistake. But how could I? She was "a sick comrade."

I could not leave the Hilton Hotel for fear that Marlene would say I was deserting her. There I was—with Glorious Gloria arranging for me to see Allende, to meet members of the revolutionary MIR, with introductions to all the outstanding historians, revolutionaries, artists–people waiting around the clock to greet me in their homes, tell me their secrets, take me into their confidences–and I couldn't leave the fucking hotel because of the sick lesbian I had paid to come down with me and keep me company. I was a prisoner not of Allende or of anyone else. I was Marlene's fucking prisoner.

I picked up Alverro in the hotel lobby. (Marlene didn't mind if I went to the lobby for half-hour periods as long as I came back to the room to check on her ulcer.) In the lobby I spotted Alverro.

He was a tour leader.

He spoke English and looked bored with the tour.

He was simpatico and had a charming smile. In some ways he reminded me of my great love Romano. Alverro came over and talked to me. I liked him immediately. He had a good smell. He bought me a planter's punch in the bar. He told me that Allende's life was in danger. That another revolution was about to take place. "This time it won't be peaceful." He tells me he is a lawyer. He is a socialist. He lives with his mother. Details about a sister. He takes me upstairs to one of the rooms in the hotel. We make love. I am worried about Marlene. I promise Alverro to meet him for dinner. I can't come. I am too worried about my companion.

That evening Marlene says she doesn't really have a tumor. She admits she just wants attention. I am allowed to go out of the hotel.

I wander alone in the streets of Chile. I prepare to take a trip to Zaballar. I am going to go to Antofagasta to meet Allende.

But Marlene won't let me leave.

"See this? I am sick" Marlene says. She shows me some blood. She has diarrhea. I can't leave her.

We stay in the room listening to Violetta Para records.

Next door a celebrity is staying.

Teeno Gomez.

Great Mexican American superstar singer.

Teeno at the Village Gate is a Golden Record. Teeno is in the hotel. He is making a movie in Chile. No longer a superstar he is now into "other projects." Teeno has a henchman called John Looper. John shields Teeno from the world. He tells him which fork to use. Who to see. How to belch. Where to go. It is as if Teeno is blind and John is his seeing-eye dog. Teeno has a gigantic cavity in his personality. He feels inferior. He is afraid the world will not see him as the classy act he knows he is.

He is afraid the world will not recognize his class. John is there to provide the class. John is a combination faggot, gofer, sycophant, secretary, courtier, pimp, gossip, teacher, classmaker, momma, hangeroner, jackass. He takes Teeno's crap. He also gets paid handsomely for doing all this. He is a paid craptaker. He loves his job. There is a sado-masochistic arrangement. John is the masochistic and Teeno is the sadist. Teeno orders John around. But actually John puts Teeno down. Their blessings and bruises are all mixed up. They are products of American Hollywood illness. Teeno and John are perfect candidates for an asylum. They are both insane. They don't know it.

Because Teeno has been a superstar he is not considered ill.

He is considered rich.

He is a hunk of ex-glamour.

He was once famous.

He once recorded seven golden records.

He saved his money.

He bought a supermarket.

Therefore he is still rich. He can still sponsor his own projects. Kick John around. Support his Mexican mother. Hang out with Frank Sinatra and pick up his own tab as well as everyone else's (in the kingdom of the newly poor the tab is never picked up) and Teeno can still get a second-rate kind of celebritydom.

Although he does not make news any more in America—although he no longer has the number one bookings—consequently rather than be a lounge act he only makes "personal appearances." He is still a superstar left over from the sixties. He once created the new Latin sound. Still can be met at airports. Still have flowers in his room. He is still "interviewable."

Ho Ho. John found out I was in Chile. He had radiated into my interviews and articles. He knows I mean possible publicity for Teeno. Flowers arrive. Marlene is upset. Who is sending me flowers? Is it Salvador Allende? Will I leave her and go interview Allende in Antofagasta?

Her tumors hurt again.

She radiates annoyance. If I was gay I would never leave her. She is sick. I am her sister. I must stay with her. More Lilith poems. More poems. More talk about Violetta Para who was the voice of Chile and killed herself. More diarrhea.

Who are the flowers from?

Are they from a lesbian?

Have I actually rejected her cunt and her breasts and her mouth and found breasts and cunt elsewhere?

She sits up in bed and raises her arms over her head so I can be turned on by the hair in her armpits. She puts on her best Mexican peasant blouse. She tries to whine but all she can do is accuse.

"Who is your lover?" she asks in our little hotel room.

"No one. Teeno wants to be interviewed."

"You can't leave the hotel. I have ulcers," she pouts.

"Well Miss Smartass he's right across the hall. So I don't have to leave the hotel."

Marlene gives permission.

I go down to the pool to meet Teeno.

John whispers in my ear "He's turned on by your breasts. He thinks you have great nipples."

Sitting by the swimming pool John is whispering in my ear things Teeno only says presumably in Spanish or when he is not being watched. Teeno is a jackass. This is a midsummer's night dream but it is taking place in Chile before Allende's revolution has a chance to work. IT IS WHACKY. My daughters are being taken care of by their grandmother. I am traveling with a lesbian I do not even know. I am picking up her tabs. I am trying to make three thousand dollars by writing a piece about Chile for the *New York Times, Harper's Bazaar* and *Travel & Leisure* but I do not have the leisure to travel because Marlene won't let me. She is playing on my guilt. My concern for Marlene is now artificial. I hate her. I hate her because she is a fake revolutionary. She would actually like to be wearing a mink coat and making out with a big-breasted woman somewhere in Sweden where no one can find her. But instead she has latched on to me. We are here in Chile and she is trying to convert me to revolutionary politics and lesbianism. But she is instead converting me to poverty. All my money is going for her doctors and perspiration and prescriptions.

"Teeno would like to meet you in his room. He doesn't care to be interviewed at the pool," John says.

I look at John.

"Where did you go to college John?"

John looks hurt. "To Harvard. Where else?

"I wanted to be a surgeon. I wanted to help people. I went to Hollywood. But instead of going to medical school I felt Teeno needed me. I used to work for Engelbert Humperdinck. Then I heard Teeno sing at the Gate. That convinced me. I do everything for him."

Now that I've interviewed John I can interview Teeno. I take the elevator up to his room. Actually I am excited because I know that I am not going to interview Teeno. I am going to make love with him. I have heard that Mexicans are fabulous lovers. We will see I think, getting wet in the elevator.

As I go to my room which is across from Teeno's I notice that

Marlene has left the door open. But she is sleeping. I close the door gently.

Then I go into Teeno's suite and wait for him to come up from the pool. I wonder if John is going to watch us. Or give directions. I wonder if he is going to be there to say to Teeno "Move over on your thigh lift your left leg and hold her arm over your head" since he seems always to be telling Teeno what to do. He manages Teeno every moment. In the room are photographs of Teeno's mother in tortoise-shell frames. She is a pleasant fat woman in a black dress. There is also a carved portrait of the Madonna. And many framed pictures of Teeno with various girls who can only be satisfactorily described as "dishes."

There is Teeno with a blonde dish. With a young dish. With a famous dish.

Finally he enters the room.

I watch him take off his thousands of dollars worth of chains, studded dungarees and handsewn cotton shirts. When he is naked I can't help but look at his body. His cock is almost as big as he is.

He turns on one of his records.

I'm not too sure I can come to one of his lousy records. I have not and never will be a Teeno fan. Most of all I loathe background music. My wet disappears. My pussy is now a desert in Baja California.

"What's the matter?" he asks.

"Can you turn off the record? I like to listen to your music when I can give it my full concentration. After all you're an artist. I have to really listen. And I can't listen while we are making love."

I am glad I have not hurt his feelings.

I have flattered him.

He comes back to the bed.

What follows is some of the things we do: gurgle, moan, suck, grease, penetrate, sssss, whop, whack, come, spit, ooh, ahh, bite, pinch, come, moan, gyrate, and other details in the sexual ecstasy act. I have never felt such a big cock inside of me. It touches my throat. I have a burning rod inside me. I put my mouth on it but can hardly cover the entire surface of skin. I go up and down like a go-go dancer dancing on his cock. As I am sucking him a ridiculous thought comes into my head—how many angels can dance on the head of a prick? I push this thought out of my mind and pretend instead that I am Linda Lovelace doing my own deep throat in Chile while a lesbian waits for me in the other room.

When I am finished making love to Teeno it is romance time. "That's the greatest blow job I ever had in my life. Give me another one later" he says. Such tact. Well I guess when John is not around Teeno is not really such a classy guy.

"Teeno I'm staying in the room next door" I say. "With a friend who is sick."

"Hey that's great. Let's all of us go to bed together" Teeno says, now genuinely happy.

I shudder.

Marlene will have a heart attack if Teeno goes near her. Unlike myself she hates men.

"No. Let's just keep this affair between you and me" I say.

"All right sweetheart. Because you're the greatest lay I've ever had. Where did you learn to suck cock like that?"

I suddenly am at a loss for an answer.

"At a cooking school!" I say—groping for an appropriate answer.

"And your tits. Man I could suck your tits all day and forget about that fucking movie they wanna make down here."

Suddenly I understand why he is no longer a superstar.

"I give you no promises," he says, "but lots of intimacy."

"Good."

"We are alone" he says.

He stands there.

I am frozen. I am also a little guilty. Had he seen me spying in his bathroom. I flush the toilet just so he won't suspect me of doing anything more dangerous than peeing.

"You turn me on" Teeno says getting to the point.

On the back of a chair, carefully folded, I see his ninety-dollar Meladandre shirt.

He has a nice chest. He put back on his chest inevitable talismans. The gold pepper given to him by Frank Sinatra. The ivory tusk given to him by Sammy Davis Jr. The Saint Christopher's medal given to him by his mother. He identifies all of the talismans around his neck. Like a soldier who has just been found and is obliged to read off the numbers on his dog tags.

"Forget the interview" he says.

"I have already forgotten" I say. His naked body is exciting me again.

"Come here."

I walk over to him. I am only partially naked.

He rubs his hand on my breasts. Slowly he takes off my blouse again. I am sure as hell grateful I am wearing one of those sexy black bras with wires which lift my breasts up and not an undershirt the way Marlene kept suggesting.

His hand goes right between my thighs.

"Your pussy's wet" he says with a Mexican accent.

My eyes go to the rug. I notice, to my complete surprise, on the rug are comic books in Spanish. He must not be too well educated. That would explain John.

My eyes travel to the night-table. A picture of Robert Kennedy inscribed to him is framed in pounded silver.

The closet is filled with hundreds of suit jackets and sport shirts.

About one hundred pairs of Gucci shoes line the closet floors like shimmering fish.

Ripe fruit is everywhere.

Nuts with nutcrackers made out of a woman's legs (my father had one of those back in the forties. I think it came from Havana).

Also liqueurs. Teeno watches his weight so he is into liqueurs. Not liquor. I wander into the bathroom spying on his medicine cabinet and personal habits. I always do this. I always look at a man's medicine cabinet after I make love with him. If he takes too many pills I never see him again. But just as I thought Teeno is into health remedies. He has soaps made out of natural things—cereals and lemon leaves. He has all kinds of tea instead of medicines. He loves mouthwash. No pills. At least a good sign. No pills. No drugs. Only soaps from the Laszlo beauty clinics. Suddenly the door is opened. It is Teeno himself. He wonders what I am doing in his bathroom. Does he know I am spying?

And so I fuck my brains out in Chile. Marlene stays sick. Allende is finally interviewed by me. He looks like George Raft. He is a nineteen-forties movie star. I love him. I love Chile. A place of sunlight and hopes.

Suddenly the trip is over.

Marlene and I fly back to the States.

Teeno gives me a goodbye present of all of his records and the key to his penthouse in Los Angeles.

John gives me a dirty look. He is jealous.

Goodbye to Chile.

Soon after I leave Allende is murdered. The Beautiful Chile disappears leaving only a violent mark in its wake. Marlene goes back to reading her Sheba poems at revolutionary meetings in New York churches. She adds to her list of accomplishments on her brochure "Read poems all over Chile at request of Salvador Allende."

And I have helped Marlene with her credits. She now shuns me. Since I will not recognize the grand fragility of my own life bound to hers she stalks off.

My lesbian affair has ended without physical contact.—I know that I have left important details out.

But I think of this on Lantao Island.

I think of my lost life.

I think of the odd people I have slept with and not slept with. It all does seem like a milkshake made somewhere else in some other blender.

My weird life.

*

Now the past rides away on dandelion strands.

Past lovers. Past cocks and conundrums. It is all like a nursery rhyme. Ride a cock course. But I did ride them. That was the trouble dear madame, general, madman. I was cock crazy. Once I started I couldn't stop. Marriage of course always put an end to sex. I don't care what people say, I know it does. Both of my husbands stopped fucking with me when we lived together for a long time. What was hard just became hard feelings. Oh of course we played around together in bed. And I came. And they came. And the RITUAL went on. But the juices dried up. That was the trouble with marriage. The juices dried up.

That's why I always got a divorce.

I didn't feel that I had to live with anyone when the juices dried up.

I always knew that I could survive. And take care of myself no matter how badly. When I couldn't make love I couldn't write either so I always left marriages even though it was painful.

I'm sure that in this world there are people for whom the juices do not dry up. Who become better lovers after they are together for a long time. Better lovers. Better friends. I am not one of those people. I get tired of someone quickly.

You have found the elsewhere that people always dream about.

Yeats called it Byzantium. Or singing school. But it's here for everyone. For you Katherine it is Lantao Island. It is the elsewhere you had the courage to find. Look at it this way. You are sitting here this morning. You are sitting in a place where sunlight filters through the window a little at a time. You are not waiting for someone. The person you have waited for is there. In the next room. So this is all there was? The obscure feeling of being able to eat breakfast and then put words on paper with a friend in the next room? This is all there was?

Do I really deserve this?

To be rid of my childhood?

To be rid of my past—the way you throw out the garbage?

To live only in the here and now?

Yes.

I am able to cope owlishly with words on paper.

To watch the sun set on my own words—sunlight on paper.

The children near me.

A while ago I was desperate in New York.

Now I sit in a room of silence. I have escaped. But it is not escape. This was always waiting for me. Inside.

How did I enter the marriages?

The first man promised me an exciting life in Paris. But it was his life I wanted. The second man promised me security. And children. But it was his security I wanted. I never wanted what it was I had inside of me. The situations always worsened.

I looked for myself in the sexual mirror.

I would stop in the midst of sucking a cock deep inside my mouth and look in the mirror. It would be me as a lifesucking angel. But it wasn't that cock that I really wanted.

To be honest I wanted to suck at life.

To suck up all the understanding and sunshine and calmness into myself so I didn't need the cock or tit any more. I got so tired of playing the sexual games. As if my life depended on it.

Cum. Cum. Come. I thought of nothing else for a while. The shadows of venetian blinds on the walls looked down on a forty-year-old woman scared to death of not coming. Of not making someone come. Stared at the great big fragile leaves of flesh.

Why did it always end in sadness?

Because I never found in the arms of another the ME I was looking for. "It's good for the skin" they said in boarding school. But my skin was too fragile. The details always upset me more than the act.

A man getting up in the morning. Looking at his wrist watch. Putting on his socks. And shoes. The separation about to become reality. His combing his hair over the sink. His leaving me in the dark. All this made me panic. Being left alone again. After lovemaking. It wasn't worth it. The aloneness was more than I could bear.

I had always to call girlfriends.

*

We sit with Peter in Doctor Wong's office on the Peak. It is filled with famous people's pictures that are his patients. They are mostly Chinese. One picture is of General Douglas MacArthur. They smile at me from photographs. Famous eyes and ears cured by Doctor Wong. Michael holds my hand and looks nonchalant. He doesn't understand why all this fuss is being made. "It's nothing" he keeps saying. Peter slaps him on the shoulder. "So if it's nothing we can all go out and have dinner at the Mandarin. Mae has been looking for an excuse to see you. She's bored as hell out here. The first year she spent all her time at the tailor's in Kowloon. The second year she studied Chinese. The third year she gave up Chinese and started inviting houseguests from the States. That drove her nuts. The fourth year she traveled all over India. But she missed me. Now she has a huge calendar on the wall of our bedroom and crosses off the days—like a kid with an Advent calendar before Christmas—counts the days till we leave this place." Peter is talking too fast.

He is nervous.

Doctor Wong's nurse doesn't smile.

She ushers us into a room.

Doctor Wong enters. He is old. And kind. He looks like an aging Peter Lorre from my childhood days of living in movies. Peter Lorre makes us leave. I feel like fainting.

We wait in the waiting room.

The real Peter holds my hand.

Doctor Wong calls us into his office. I can't tell whether he is smiling or about to cry. He speaks overly perfect Oxford English.

"Michael has cancer" he says.

"And there is no point operating. It is hopeless."

I hear my life ending. But I refuse to accept this information.

*

Dr. Wong has Michael in the hospital.

I visit him every day. He stares at me and laughs. He is studying his Torah. He has stacks of books by his bed and goes on studying. When he looks at me his face looks happy.

An odd thing has happened.

Doctor Wong has given us some hope.

Michael tells me.

"There is an odd person in Mexico. In Acapulco who has found, he claims, a cure for cancer. As I understand it he claims that he has found a supplement to cancer and its arrest. His name is Byron Jorgenson. He calls it the Byron theory. Wong heard about it from a friend of his, a doctor in Mexico City who wrote him a letter. No one will listen to this man. He has written thousands of letters to various institutes including the Sloan-

Kettering Institute and has never received a reply. He is independently wealthy and lives in Acapulco. He's not even a doctor. But Doctor Wong says he has arrested cancer in five cases. That isn't very much. But it's worth trying."

Michael smiled.

"What do we have to lose?"

*

Mae has moved out to Lantao Island to help Wu with the children. I pack a small suitcase and explain to the girls what is happening. Michael has cancer.

"What's cancer mommy? Is it a lump of something?"

"It's nothing to be afraid of" I lie. "We will be back soon."

I hold them to me.

Mae has brought a puppet theatre with her as a present. The girls play with the puppets. I can see them as I set off on the boat to pick Michael up on the Peak.

Why? Why is this happening? There is no reason.

And Michael feeling it too.

Both of us looking for each other like sperm whales in the sea. On other parts of the ocean.

And then—finding each other.

I wish I could take a picture of myself as I am now. Portrait of the artist as a forty-year-old woman in love. Wish I could take my small black camera and focus it on myself. Into the X-ray part of myself. Show what it really looks like inside—and not be afraid. Photograph of joy. Nothing can ruin this. Nothing can take away my bliss. Two sparks at the tip of the world. Michael and me on Lantao Island.

The woman who writes every morning.

Is an authority to herself.

The young man, younger than she, who opens the books of

wisdom and studies what it means to know life's laws. Studying about commandments. Studying about creation. Studying about volcanoes and philosophies. Chinese. Hebrew. Gaelic. We have our own singing school.

The children are brown as ripe brown nuts.

They speak now not with whines but laughter.

They play games with Michael.

Do I love him more for loving me? Or loving them? Only a mother with children to bring up on her own can understand and be grateful for a man who loves her children. I look at Michael through the window. He was always happy to be different. That queer thing. Michael. Short. Loving horses. Loving books. Where was he when I was a young girl in boarding school?

Where was he?

He was doing as he was told. He was putting a pillow under his head. He was living. I was living. We were living so far away from each other. No love touch for either of us. We were loved by no one. Love starved. Both of us believing "love does not exist."

But it does exist.

That's what I want to tell you dear madam, madman, editor, philosopher, wise person—love does exist.

It is strange to carry inside you someone else's body all the time. Michael is in me. I know, for the first time the joy of loving a man. And it doesn't seem to be fading. That is the miracle.

*

Michael didn't feel well this morning.

He had a pain in his back.

And a strange growth behind his ear.

A lump of something.

We both ignored it. But he didn't smile as he usually does. We still hugged. We still made love. Still washed in the shower together as we always do. But he looked strained. And didn't talk much.

*

For three days Michael has not been well. I've decided to tell Peter about this. I talk to Peter on the phone. He insists I come to Hong Kong on the ferry with Michael and see the doctor again. Doctor Wong is his closest friend. He arranges for us to go again, one last time, to his office. Michael says no. But I insist. We leave the children with Mr. Wu. It's a weekend and they are not in school. They play with Chinese friends who have come out on the ferry to visit with them. They are all making a doll house— a pagoda in the yard. I wave goodbye. I wear my straw hat for good luck.

*

Michael is dying.

ENDANGERED
SPECIES

Going to Mexico

Michael is dying. I have the impression that the life I am leading is like a dream. That life itself is the dream. Certainly I feel that way when I arrive at the airport in Acapulco with Michael. All of these events, seconds and moments are happening to me—and yet they are not happening in life but in an odd light way that one moves through sleep. We are in a feathery airport. I am the loving woman—the strong one, now joyful and full in the richness of my love Michael, my beloved jockey scholar who must not die. Michael has healed me. Has sewn up my grief. Now—here I am in this airport with Michael who is ill with cancer. The abscess behind his ear—the ear I have kissed and loved is large and not pleasant to look at. Michael has been tired. At the airport as we are going through customs Michael looks at me and says "I just don't have any more strength. I've lost my strength Katherine."

To be near a man that is sick—hopelessly sick—makes me think of being near a poor sad animal that you cannot help. I look at Michael—who—just weeks before was filled with strength and buoyancy and now is tired. His eyes are no longer that fiery Irish blue but stare at me as if they do not know me. It is always as if Michael is looking beyond me.

In the Acapulco airport our love bonds like silky ribbons hold us together. I, healthy and alive, am bound to my lover, who is dying. In some odd way it is as if I am part of his death. As if I am dying also. "No Michael. I won't let you" I want to say. "You mustn't leave life. We love life too much." When someone you love is dying you live in another time clock. The real world of tick tock no longer matters. You live in the last seconds of a human being's eternal statement. How can the body and the spirit separate like this? I want to ask. How can they go in such different directions? Never was a spirit more curious and alive than the imagination of Michael. And now the body was going the other way. Going into death.

*

In the airport. Spanish is spoken. Buenos días. Gracias. We walk around–climbing the marble stairs–past the customs–past the souvenir shops selling black velvet enormous sombreros with silver thread embroidered on them. A woman buys a huge black sombrero and has a plastic bag put on it. She wears the sombrero with a plastic bag around it on her head. She topples from the weight, wearing an enormous black Mexican lampshade. Oh my god–souvenirs of Mexico. Michael is dying. I hear my high heels clicking on the floor. This is all a dream. I stare at Michael's eyes. At his mouth almost about to speak and tell me some secret.

*

Doctor Wong has given us an idea of what will happen. The man who will take us to Byron Jorgenson is called Irving Speed. He is actually an ex-New York advertising executive, the publicist at the Hyatt Regency Hotel. According to Doctor Wong, Byron had cured and arrested cancer in five people. One of the people who was cured was a Mexican gynecologist who was a friend of Doctor Wong's and had written him an amazing document on the Byron Theory of curing cancer. Who is Byron? Is he a fake? Is he just another one of those crazy people who live in Mexico in the hills and have theories about the nature of the universe–the sun gone into their skull? What difference does it make? I think. If Michael is hopelessly ill–we have nothing to lose by visiting Byron. I stare at Michael as we enter our suite in the hotel. At his impossible mouth which is about to tell me some secret. I want to lie down with him. I want to take his body into mine. Mother him, earthmother him, goddess him, take him into me so that my body with all of its juices will make him well.

"I'm tired" he says. "You'll feel better after these treatments" I say and kiss his forehead. He is very warm.

*

Opening the bed, pulling off the heavy red and pink Mexican bedspread, I arrange for Michael to lie down. Quietly, I put on my white bathing suit. I look in the mirror at a tall heavy woman in the middle of her life. Out for a sunburn. And a discussion about death with Irving Speed.

*

Irving is waiting for me. He is friendly and talkative. He loves Byron. Is he a sunburnt serpent? His eyes are green and they slant. His hair is graying. He is an ex-water skier, ex-beach bum, ex-advertising executive, ex-genius. You can tell Irving is kind. I sense he is brilliant the moment I meet him on the sundeck. He talks quickly. Out of his mouth pour a thousand ideas bubbling at once–a thousand words of praise for Byron. He is Byron's *representative.* We have one day before Byron can see us. One day of Michael's life gone. Byron has taken a trip to Mexico City. He will be back tomorrow.

*

Irving stretches out on the deck. He is smoking a cigar and tanning his body. He tells me how he came to Acapulco.

"I was working in New York as the head of the Gillian Cigar account. I was making two hundred thousand a year as the head of this account. It was a cigar that was exactly like a Cuban cigar–everything–the leaf moistened on the woman's thigh– everything the same–only it wasn't made in Cuba, it was made in the Dominican Republic. Yeah–well I decided one day I wanted to buy the fucking advertising company. The only trouble was I didn't have the money. I went to my lawyer–a guy called Hawkins and I told him 'I'm handling this account and I want out. Or buy the company.' He said 'How much?' I said 'four million dollars.' He called a bank in Texas and said he could get me the money immediately. The only trouble was I could only have it for one day. I went to the guys who owned the company. They were having a meeting. I waited for my turn and I said 'I want to buy the company.' 'You don't have the money.' 'I do' I said. You know what? They didn't believe me. And those sons of bitches wouldn't sell. So I just collected my salary and left. I had left my wife by that time. She was suing me for alimony. The bitch. So I took all my money and put it into pesos. And you know what? I said goodbye suckers. My wife has me on the wanted list in New York for back alimony. I can never go back there. And the company? They lost the account and they went under. How's that for justice?" Irving Speed puffs on his cigar.

"I've been living for fifteen years in the sun. I'm the smartest man in the world. And the best water skier. I've been living down here and you know what my philosophy is? Just enjoy yourself. About ten years after I was in Acapulco I met Byron. I knew he was a genius. He became my only friend down here. His story is the strangest story you've ever heard."

I lie there shading my face with my hands from the sun.

Irving never stops talking.

The sun is turning me into a burning person. I can feel it on my arms, on my belly, in my hair. I don't dare move. I wait to hear more about Byron.

"Byron was also a runaway. Byron isn't his real name. Byron Jorgenson is just the name he uses. No one knows what his real name is. He came to Acapulco after kidnapping his two children. His wife was screwing around and walked out on him in Connecticut. One day he picked the kids up—who he loved—and flew to Acapulco. He was—and is—independently wealthy. Byron is the most famous man in all the discotheques in Acapulco. He loves Latin music. When he arrives at a discotheque they play his favorite *Paso Doble*. He brought his mother down here with him. She brought up the kids. They are in college now. Byron Jorgenson is the most brilliant man I know. Let me tell you what happened to him three years ago. He decided to take a mind control course. The course was held at his home. Up in the hills. You'll see it. A *gorgeous* home. He invited the guy running the course to hold it at his home. He rounded up about thirty people. He was really excited about the course. I said 'I ain't gonna pay no three hundred bucks for mind control—I have a good enough mind' I said to him. I was with my second wife at the time. Before we split. But she was interested. 'Nothing doing' I said. Byron said 'Listen—they're giving the course at my home Irving. I'm going to invite you into it free.'" Another puff on the cigar.

The sun like a bully beats down on us. We lie like mummies

on the deck on our striped terry-cloth towels. Irving keeps talking as we look out at the Acapulco bay. A fat woman is hanging from a parachute. A beach boy is pulling her in a speedboat.

"Then the most unbelievable thing happened. We went to the course. The guy who ran the course told us how we could descend into the laboratories of our minds. It's called 'going to your level.' There. On a screen. We could talk to anyone. I wanted to be a novelist. I saw Ernest Hemingway on a screen. I talked with him. I talked with Balzac. I talked with Leon Uris. They were all there on the screen in my mind. LISTEN TO THIS. ONLY BYRON COULDN'T FIND A WAY TO DESCEND INTO THE LABORATORY. He just was a failure at mind control. It made him miserable. He couldn't communicate. He couldn't reach what they call HIS LEVEL. We all went into our levels but Byron couldn't go into his level. After the course was over he went crazy."

"How do you mean—crazy?"

"He began yelling at his servants. He began drinking. He wouldn't go out of the house. He stopped dancing. Finally he had a vision. He will tell you about it himself. Through a series of numbers, he had found the cure for cancer. He became obsessed by it. He began talking to everyone in Acapulco about it. At the big parties given at the Obregón estate at Teddy Stauffer's Villa Vera—everywhere—in the red light district—at the discotheques—he told everyone about his theories. People began to avoid him. He became a madman to be shunted away. No one would listen to him but me. That was three years ago."

*

I lay there on the burning deck, listening to Irving. I imagined what Byron would be like.. Could he really cure cancer? Lord Byron in Mexico?

BYRON JORGENSON THE MIRACLE MAN

And now, presenting for the first time in my life–Byron Jorgenson–the man who discovered the other ninety percent of the brain. For the first time, in my life, I will see a psychic whiz kid, a maker of secrets a Buddha-buddy, a Mantra for all seasons, a spoon bender, a fire eater, a cosmopolitan universal star gazer. Come with me to Acapulco. Come and meet–for the first time in my life–which means for the first time in your life–Byron Jorgenson–the man who discovered:

THE ARREST AND CURE FOR CANCER
THE SECRET OF THE PYRAMIDS
AND HOW TO GET ENERGY OUT OF THE SEA

Forget your preconceptions about what can't be done. Byron Jorgenson–through his one on one relationship with his own awareness–through his own mind control–has discovered–without meaning to–without even knowing what he is doing–secrets of the universe. Yes sir, ladies and gentlemen who have tuned into this program because you want to be amazed–yes sir, you out there in the world who have turned me on because you want to meet great psychics, saints, business people, artists, magicians, doctors and cosmic saints–yes, a roonie all of you who know that Madame Blavatsky had nothing on Katherine Kahn–come with me–Mae Est–and meet my new friend–Byron Jorgenson. And now. GERIATRIC PATRICK MANTRA TANTRA–Here's–*Byron.*

*

I entered the experience of meeting the miracle man, Byron Jorgenson, with a certain intuition that I was "in for" a miracle. Of course, both Michael and I, through our life sufferings had learned that miracles do happen. Who was it who said "Don't look for miracles! You are the miracle"? Yes. It was Henry Miller. Well now–I was looking for miracles. Irving was our driver. Our guide to the miracle man. I can't say "doctor" because Byron Jorgenson is not a doctor (flash forward–the head of Squibb International going on a tennis court–saying Not A Doctor? So how could he have found the arrest and cure for cancer if he's not a *doctor?* But sir–Einstein wasn't a doctor–Madame Curie wasn't a doctor–Newton Johns' great namesake–Sir Isaac Newton– wasn't a doctor–yes–but that's different–says the president of Squibb International Drugs walking two more steps onto his court)–Irving drove us to the hills of Acapulco. I sat with Michael who was sleeping in the car. The car stopped in front of a large brick mansion. Irving had said that Byron was independently wealthy–but I was surprised at the beauty of this mansion. It was built around a large patio and garden. It was all old red Mexican brick. And the arches reminded me of a Gothic church. A church of arches in pinkish red brick. There were Byron's paintings hung all over the brick walls. Before having his experience of "going mad" Byron had been content to be an artist. Now, of course, Irving had said he had given all of that up in his effort to de- vote himself to the cancer cure. I was shocked as Byron came out to meet his guests and "patient." SHOCKED. Byron was the same height Michael was. He had white hair. Large blue eyes. An extremely trim body, just like Michael, and a soft voice that sounded like the voice of a radio commentator. Rich low tones that caught you, sucked you into the charm of his throat.

"Good evening" he said.

"I know that you have come here at the suggestion of Doctor Wong. Won't you come and sit down?" he said.

A shock of recognition went through my body. Had I ever seen this man before? His eyes were gay and crinkled so that he looked less like a wizard and more like an emperor or a sage. He clapped his hands and a graceful boy, a Mexican servant in a white coat arrived.

"Gustavo. Would you please bring everyone an iced tea? Or—" he turned to us—"would you like anything stronger—a whiskey— tequila?"—

"I'll take a double Dewars on the rocks" Irving said as he flopped into a chair. Michael and I were sitting on the veranda on a large blue couch.

"A Scotch please. And some iced tea."

The servant went away silently to get the drinks. Byron spoke to me.

"Now. I understand that you have studied some of my papers and know a little bit about what I have been doing here in Acapulco. You understand that I have cured five people of cancer. And that this is of course still in the experimental stage. That in a sense I need 'hopeless patients' as much as they need me. It is only by having these cases that I can effect my cure. And since I am working totally independently of the medical establishment—it is as hard for me to find bodies—patients—as for patients to find cures. And so I am grateful that you are here."

We sat down. I looked at the face of this wizard of cancer. This odd man who, as Irving had told me, took his children and one day left Connecticut—and settled in the hills of Acapulco. This odd and short man was going to cure Michael. It all sounded crazy. But what did Michael have to lose? Nothing.

I heard Agatha's voice in my head. I could imagine Agatha saying "My dear anything is possible. We Greeks are believers in miracles." I wished Agatha was with me. Michael looked calmly at Byron. Like a trusting animal staring. Byron began speaking.

"In 1971 I took the Silva mind control course. After the course was finished I became crazy. I had a messianic vision. The vision was of a series of numbers. I didn't know how they fit. The number that I finally saw clearly was the number 39. I believed, I don't know why, that a multiple of the number 39 would be important and produce a network so that all energy stations would have to feed on it. My background, by the way, before I came to Mexico, was in civil engineering. I understood the 39 mesh. But I was still not off the ground. Nor did I know what I was discovering. I knew that the Compton wave length of an electron is equal to point 39 centimeters. But I didn't know what that meant. I ordered several encyclopedias and I began reading them. I also ordered forty-five books at random—and I began following that number through everything that I read. I went on blindly. I began thinking of different things. For example I began fighting, in my mind, with Einstein. Einstein said that all matter is convertible into energy. I felt that this couldn't be true. During this time I postulated various atoms had different matter. There was a shorthand that I had to invent to put the graviton on existing 39 charts. I realized that the graviton is a sub-atomic particle. But that we live in an atmosphere of sub-atomic particles. I realized that it was muons which were carriers of gravitons. And that muons were in part the cause of cancer. One of the most prevalent concepts of cancer is that cells do not stick. But, I discovered, the gravitons have a glue-like quality. The concept is complicated. But I realized in short, that the main culprit of cancer is the graviton. And I was working on the concept of the unification of nature's forces. So. We are dealing with understanding—muons and gravitons."

Byron took a sip of his iced tea. We listened.

"After understanding the quality of the gravetons' weight I went back to muons. The cure for cancer, if I was correct, had to do with the fact that people die of cancer because they are susceptible to muons which can be reversed by atom smashers.

The atomic smashers can REVERSE the procedure of the muons. If it is correct that muons are electrically charged—you can correct them. You can kill them with neutrinos. What is a neutrino? A neutrino is nothing but a muon without a charge. It is like a massless neutral ghost particle which had to be coming out of a radioactive decay and was the particle that carried off energy. Fermi had told us that there are unknown particles coming out of particles that decay. What no one—not even Fermi or Einstein discovered—and which I discovered—is that neutrino. Neutrinos are masses. They are equal in weight to muons. But they have mass. Science had already discovered that neutrinos do not interact. I believed intuitively that gravitons were carried by muons and that these would correct cancerous growths. I then took the next mental jump. NEUTRINOS COULD DO THE JOB. Since neutrinos are not DANGEROUS to people—and since all radioactive elements give off neutrinos—I decided that Strontium 90—which is an isotope of strontium—you can use it—had radioactive decay which can change something unstable into something stable. I selected Strontium 90—not out of the blue—but on the basis of gamma rays. Let me put it this way so I am sure that you will understand what I am doing here at Prevado Del Venado in the hills of Acapulco. Look. Strontium 90 gives off electrodes which are small killers. It is known that electrons, as they fly through the air can have a toxic effect. But the toxic effect depends on how far away they are. Now as I was discovering all of this, my dear Katherine and my dear Michael, coincidentally the eye doctor here in Acapulco was operating on my mother for cataracts."

*

An hour later Byron was still explaining his work. We were fascinated.

"It is amazing, isn't it, how coincidences rule our lives? I explained my tentative theory for cancer cure to my mother's eye doctor and he said to me, quite casually, in English of course, although my Spanish is quite good all the doctors here speak perfect English, 'I happen, Señor Jorgenson, to have in my possession, quite illegally, Strontium 90. I use it in an operation which removes cataracts. You dab the Strontium 90, which is on the tip of something which looks like a fountain pen, on the eye, you touch the eyeball with Strontium 90 and it removes the cataract. The reason that I have this little Strontium 90 rod illegally is that in Mexico, as elsewhere, you have to take out a license to use any sort of radioactive material—and since I am a busy doctor—I do not have three months of my time to desert my patients and go up to Mexico City to get a license. I will lend you my Strontium 90.' So you see—it was sheer coincidence. Now I had to get myself a patient to test out my theories. The normal therapy for cancer of the skin was to use fluorouracil ointment. But in many cases this ointment did not work. I was going to try having the patient be exposed to Strontium 90.

"I found myself a seventy-year-old Mexican peasant . . . she had cancer of the skin and had gone for cobalt treatments. I explained to her in Spanish what I was doing. She had faith in this first experiment. And besides she had nothing to lose. She wasn't nervous at all. Her daughter brought her here, right to this house, she sat right here, where you are sitting Michael, on the couch of my patio. I made arrangements with the good eye doctor to borrow his box for the weekend. His box with the rod and the Strontium 90. The seventy-year-old peasant with skin cancer sat on the couch for four hours. She was smiling and she was very calm. I wasn't. I was quite nervous, I can tell you. I wasn't sure that the neutrinos would get through to her. I exposed her, for four hours each day on the weekend to the Strontium 90. The woman was happy to do whatever I said. The daughter was happy because the cobalt treatments had taken up all of the family's savings. And this treatment—that I was giving the mother—didn't cost anything. A couple of weeks later the woman's pain disappeared. She had a large abscess—just like you have Michael behind your ear—on her nose. The scab fell off the abscess. And clear pink skin appeared underneath it. I quite frankly was amazed. I took photographs of this first patient—which I will show you. There was a black pearly remainder around the place where the abscess had been. I think you could say it was a blackish sort of line on the skin. The solid line began to become a dotted line. The dotted line turned into a scar. You see people heal in different ways. Even though of course there was no operation, and no knife, the abscess was totally healed by the exposure to Strontium 90, a scar formed. Some people scar and some people don't. The woman was so grateful to me. She went back to the hills where she lived with her daughter. I drove them back in my car. When they arrived at their home in the hills—which resembles a chicken coop—they wanted to give me something to thank me for saving a life. The old woman gave me a live chicken and a big papaya. I drive back, every now and then, to visit her and see how she is. She is working in the fields. That was my first patient. And that, Michael, was two years ago."

Another round of iced tea was served. It was late at night. Irving had gone to lie down on Byron's couch in his study. He had heard all of this before. But we were amazed. I wanted the odd little man to keep on talking. I had never heard anything like this. And I felt, as did Michael, intuitively that we were in the presence of something like cosmic genius. A mystical madman. Who was mad enough to have found a cure. It all made perfect sense.

"Go on Byron, go on" Michael said. It was the first time I had seen his face come alive. There was hope. There was hope! Death wasn't the inevitable visitor we had thought it was just a few days ago in Hong Kong. Here, in the presence of the odd but brilliant Byron Jorgenson, we both began to see that life might be–oh please let it be–prolonged. The miracle man began talking to us again.

"Well my dear Michael and Katherine" he said, in his totally disconnected radio narrator's voice which was both human and lulling at the same time, so that at the same time that he sounded like a mad scientist he also sounded like a life artist, a life poet, chanting out his cures. As we listened. Yes. We listened to the chanting. Reaching out for facts. Hope. Information. Reaching out for more information.

"Tell us more–tell us more" I said eagerly. I was so excited I could hardly breathe. I remember sitting there on Byron's terrace having an orgasm of information. "More–More. Tell me more." And he continued in his calm voice. And we received his information. We were so amazed, so stunned at all of this I could hardly breathe. But we didn't dare move. Or speak. We sat there. Holy beggars for life. Holy beggars who had come to the life priest. Our only hope. When doctors failed. When science failed. When Sloan-Kettering and Mt. Sinai and all the other hospitals held no hope for Michael. This odd little white haired cosmic genius, life artist, or life spook, held out some hope.

"Go on Byron" I said in a voice that was almost a cry for joy. Michael might live.

*

"What happened was quite extraordinary," Byron continued. "It's all bizarre how I arrived at my theories on the origin and arrest of cancer. At about this time I happened to mention my theory to a local gynecologist. 'Listen Señor Byron' the gynecologist said to me, 'I have something quite important to tell you.

And perhaps we can help each other. I have a patient who has cancer. She is a non-operable case. And I rather like you Byron. I remember once visiting your house and seeing a plate by Picasso drop on the floor. You picked it up and put it back on the stand in its broken state. Half of the plate was missing. And you said to me, Señor I have never gotten over this, you said "A broken plate by Señor Picasso is better than a not broken plate by anyone else" and I said to myself "This man is a genius." And so I want to give you this inoperable case. I want to give you this broken person Byron.' And he gave me the inoperable case to experiment on. She came to my house. She did not belong to Social Security. She had no money for treatment. After one month of exposing her to the Strontium 90 her pains went away. It was my second case of cancer arrest. Well, I can tell you I was very excited. Perhaps the first case was just faith healing. Or an accident. But now I had cured two patients. I realized that neutrinos do interact with matter. I called the physics department of every university in the United States. I spent thousands of dollars of my own savings—which didn't matter of course—on phone calls. I was obsessed. But no one would answer my calls. Or my letters. Or listen to me. Yes. A few doctors in Mexico. But that was all. I had found a missing link. My number of 39 had led me to discover that we live in a neutrino sea. I discovered that magnetism and gravitation are all the same thing. But I was so isolated. No one listened to me except for a few doctors in Mexico. And Irving. I had gone crazy. And made a discovery which was a breakthrough equal to the breakthroughs of Newton and Einstein. But no one would listen. I was an outcast. I stopped going to parties because I no longer had Acapulco chitchat. I would buttonhole people at parties and tell them I had found the origin and arrest of cancer. People shunned me. But I had found a connection. I wrote it all down on paper. What I was trying to tell the world was that the single most significant characteristic symptom of cancer is that cancerous cells are able to *divide again and again.* Since no parent cell, normal or abnormal, can divide until it has unzipped into single strands, the premature unzipping may be part of the cause of cancer. If the neutrinos or antineutrinos do not encounter a radioactive atom or atom of deterium with which to interact, they will pass through the body with no effect. Well, all of this is very complicated and perhaps I have spoken enough about cancer and my theories. Come back tomorrow and we will begin treatment."

*

Could he cure Michael?

Byron made me believe he could. He was eccentric. He had body heat and energy, almost like stage presence. He was the Red Skeleton of cancer. He could make us laugh or cry. His routines were total life information timed as well as jokes.

I loved Byron. I loved him immediately. "He is quite mad" I said to Michael.

*

We went home to the hotel.

Michael was tired.

I was equally tired. The next morning we woke and I lay in the sun with Irving on the deck of the Hyatt Regency. Later that afternoon we drove again to Byron's home. Michael sat down in front of the Strontium 90 machine. He sat there for four hours. He was exposed to the rays. "My theory is that abnormal and cancerous cells are being corrected right now by using the antineutrinos emitted from the Strontium 90 and neutrinos emitted from Iron 55. Since Michael, who is a cancer victim, is unable to naturally destroy his cancer cells by the body's immune system, I am exposing him to a system that is his 'nonself.' I must emphasize one thing to you Katherine. Do not forget that there is no limit to the amount of irradiation by neutrinos and antineutrinos that the body can be exposed to. Neutrinos are not harmful to the human body."

*

Day after day we drove to Byron's house. I loved him more each day. Michael began to get well. He felt less weak. His abscess disappeared almost completely. But an odd thing was happening to me. I was falling in love with Byron Jorgenson. As I looked at the good doctor, who was not a doctor at all, but a former civil engineer, who had gone into his family's lumber business, and had run away to escape his wife with his children to Acapulco, and who was now an alchemist, turning sick patients into healed ones, as I looked at this man quietly reading his books, and exposing Michael to a new kind of radioactive energy which would cure him, yes, I began to love him.

*

Yes. The sun was hot. Yes. I drove every day with Irving, our guide to the hills of Acapulco. Yes, every day we went to see the miracle man Byron who had found the cure for cancer. I think that we must have spent hundreds of hours together. Byron told me about the secrets of the pyramids. He believed strongly that the Egyptians had put the pyramids on earth as a way of telling a mathematical secret to future generations. "The pyramids are no more and no less than stone books. Made out of stones they were put there to tell the future generations the secrets of the universe. The secrets of electrons and other mathematical equations. What I have discovered is that if you add the point to the pyramids–the top part which is missing–it all works out from the base to the point to a secret number of 39. Therefore my 39 theory which is also the equation four squared is the key to the pyramids. The pyramids were symbolic equations. They were there to tell future generations about mathematical equations in case the world should be destroyed. They would remain. No one understands this. They can't figure out the most basic thing. That just as poems are symbolic holders of truth and moments–the pyramids are stone poems. To tell us not only poetry. But the poetry of numbers."

*

Michael sat on the big blue couch. We drank iced tea. I remember all this. Quietly he received the treatment. I talked with Byron. And as I began to love him–this handsome quizzical obsessed little genius–who was definitely an eccentric bamboozler of the truth–I realized that while Michael was being cured, energy of love was going through my body. Another form of light. Another form of radiation. My love for the miracle man was going through my body. And his love for me.

*

I must tell you that I know how desperately Byron Jorgenson needed me. Just as Michael needed to be cured. Byron needed to be understood. To him I am the first person who understands his

Something ghastly has happened. I realize that I am not sure if I want Michael to die or live. Of course I want him to live. But I also want him to die. If he dies I can live with Byron. I could bring the children from the island and we would live in Acapulco. I see my life. I could type papers for Byron. I could help him tell the world about his theories on the arrest of cancer. I will make the world see him as the healer that he is. I would. I would be a fertile nymph. I would give Byron more children. I will love him. The mad miracle man. I would give him what he needs. Understanding. He wants me. I know that. He loves me. At least now he does. As I lie with Michael in bed in Acapulco all I can wait for is the sun to come up so we can drive up on the hill and I can make love with Byron while Michael is having his treatments.

*

I called Agatha collect to New York.

"Agatha. Please. You must fly down right away. I am here curing Michael of cancer in Acapulco."

"Then what do you need me for darling?" I could hear Agatha saying far away in New York. See her smoking in her living room on Beekman Place. Beautiful Agatha. With short blonde hair. Agatha would have been born near Alexandria. Whose family came from Milos. Agatha the Greek one. Who had married a shipping king. Who had lived in London. Who despised money only because it isolated her from others. Who hated and loved at the same time the goddamn Greeks. Who would never wear a black dress and solitaire diamonds like the "other goddamn boring Greek wives who have nothing interesting to say since their whole lives are spent making caca out of themselves for their husband. Skata. And caca. That's what their lives are. Those rich Greek women who I don't envy for one moment." That was

Agatha. Outspoken beautiful bitch in her early sixties–able to teach me all about life–Agatha who I now loved.

"Agatha, don't argue with me on the phone" I cried all through the switchboards of Mexico. "Just come. I'm in love with the man who is curing Michael."

"Oh my god. You are in a bit of a mess darling. Aren't you? Tell me. Tell me over the phone. What does it mean you're in love with him? You always love brilliant men. Maybe it's just that you're in love with his theory of metrons or neurons or whatever the hell's his theory. I frankly adore Cancer Research darling. I've worked for the ship of HOPE on the Carras lines as you know. And I find it most desirable to irradicate the cancer thing. But it's just his mind you're in love with. What does he look like?"

"What does he look like? He looks–you won't believe this– like a white haired Michael."

"Of course I believe it. Short men are your type darling. Besides I think little men are always more dynamic. Look at Napoleon. He had to have balls to make up for his lack of shoulders and height. And most of the most brilliant men that ever lived were short. Take Caesar. He was supposed to be a shrimp. I have no way of knowing if that was true. But certainly there were a lot of very exciting short men. Look at Niarchos. Look at George Livanos. Well you can't look at George because he's dead. So is Onassis. But look at what's his name? Dustin Hoffman. Now he's sexy and adorable and he's not exactly a giant now is he darling? And Al Pacino is tiny. Well all those men are terribly attractive. Oh my god. What am I talking about? Of course I'll come down to see you. What hotel are you at? The Hyatt Regency? Is it a dump? What a silly question. Everything in Mexico is a dump as far as I'm concerned. I loathe–simply loathe–cruises and tropical climates. That's why I always keep my air conditioner on. I'm the only Greek who is really civilized. But of course I'll come. Do you want me? Really? I'll come at once. I'll fly down. Hold on Katherine. Don't do anything really naughty."

*

Agatha arrived. And Michael was almost cured. At night I lay in the suite that we had in the Hyatt Regency and thought of making love to Byron and now I would have to leave. I couldn't leave Michael. But how would I leave Byron? Could I tell Michael I would stay in Acapulco to help him—that darling man who had saved his life—with his work? No. That was impossible.

"You've certainly picked a divine man to love this time" Agatha said after meeting Byron Jorgenson. They sat all day chatting about energy and psychic spoon bending and the eyes on stupas and the Greek islands and the cures for cancer. And as they chatted I knew that I had to make a drastic decision. Perhaps I should kill myself? That was absurd. You don't kill yourself when you have children. I was depressed. And at the same time overjoyed. My love with Michael had been so brief. Now it was over. It had been killed by my attraction for Byron the miracle man. I now loved Byron. Not Michael.

*

The gift to me of Byron's mind began to overflow in my body. The love I had for him came into my body. I had to hurry to see him. I felt always like an animal in heat. I couldn't wait to have him inside my body. The flames began when I thought of him. Even making love with him didn't satisfy me. My heart was not happy because I didn't have his love. He had not made a commitment to me. How could he? When I was there with a dying lover? I felt I would not leave him. Even if a stick beat me off. I suddenly remembered a poem that I had copied down when I had been to the temples in Egypt. I had found an Egyptian love song and had copied it down. It was still in my head and I could remember it as I lay in bed thinking of Byron and his body while I lay next to Michael. The poems of my life began to crowd in my head. But I could only think of the loving poem that I had gotten from this odd trip in Egypt. It remained in memory.

> My love for you is mixed throughout my body
> Like salt dipped in water,
> So hurry to see your lady,
> like a stallion on a track,
> or like a falcon swooping down to its papyrus marsh
> heaven has sent you her love
> as the flame falls
> and my heart is not yet happy with your love ...

At the Hairdresser

"As I understand it correctly you're here in the hotel to have a vacation and at the same time get your boyfriend cured of cancer?" The hairdresser bent over my head as he washed out the soap. To seek relief I went to the only place where I could think. The Hyatt Regency Beauty Parlor. There I had made the acquaintance of a fabulous friend. A rabbi turned fag turned hairdresser called Vincent. Or to be more precise, Mister Vincent.

Vincent was part Italian and part Jewish. A tall burly man, he had dark hair, a charming smile, a huge stomach, and very strong hands. Once he had been well dressed but now, even while he was working at the Hyatt Regency in Acapulco, he "schlepped" around the hotel in white jeans, an old white shirt, and blue *huaraches*. His clothes were not chic. But as he chatted on about his life there was a certain dignity to him—he became a priest of the holy roll, a seer of the scissor, a hairdresser who might, had fate been different, been a count or a king or at least a duke—but was now simply content to be part of the oasis of hairdressing royalty.

"Have you ever heard of a miracle man who lives in the hills called Byron Jorgenson?" I asked.

Vincent kept rolling my hair.

"Are you kidding? That nut? Of course I've heard of him. He's crazy. I mean really crazee. You know what I heard? He was very rich. Originally Norwegian or something Scandinavian. He lived in the States and then when the alimony got hot he came down here. Took his kids. Wanted for kidnap in Connecticut. He doesn't give a fuck though. His kids are grown up. When he first came down here he used to dance to all that corny Latin music. He was a flamenco dancer that was just crazy about Latin music. He used to dance in all the discos with a big rose in his mouth. All the whores in the red light district swear he has the biggest cock for a gringo they have ever seen. What happened to him, honey, was that he took some kind of mind reading or mind control course. He wanted me to take it. He's *crazy* about me. I think sometimes he'd love to suck my cock or be my lover. But that's crazy too because I'm sure he's straight. But anyway I told him 'No thanks' about the mind control course. And then he decided that he could cure cancer. No one invited him to parties anymore. Which is a shame. He's so much more amusing than the other dummies Acapulco attracts. He lives up in the hills. What do you think of him?"

"What do I think of him? He's curing my boyfriend. I brought my boyfriend down here dying of cancer. Now he's cured. The miracle has happened in front of my own eyes. Let me read to you from his paper on the Supplement to Cancer and Its Origin and Its Arrest."

"Don't bother. I came to Acapulco for a good time. That's all I care about. I don't care to hear about *cancer*. Here—let me finish your rollers."

"Really Vincent. He is amazing."

"So was Helena Rubinstein. She made millions by curing dandruff. I guess that's what she did. So what? She was a hell of a promoter. If Helena Rubinstein could do it I guess he can do it too. You want to know a secret?"

*

What am I doing in Acapulco hearing the secrets of a hairdresser? What am I doing in Acapulco with a wizard? With Agatha? With my lover who is a talmudic specialist who was once a playboy? It's all so odd. But Vincent continues talking.

"The beauty business is an enormous hustle in Acapulco. All the dames who come down here from the States want to look gorgeous. You want to know why women go to the hairdresser? I'll tell you why honey. They go to bug their hairdresser. They're lonely. Or they hate their husbands. Or they can't stand their lover. So they go to someone who has to listen to them. You get it? I have to listen to everyone whose hair I do. It's part of my business. But the blower has blown this industry right out of business. The goddamn fucking blower is replacing the hairdresser."

"What do you mean?"

"When a rich dame comes down from New York or San

Francisco or Cleveland she brings her goddamn fucking blower with her. It used to be she brought her big old wigs in a wigbox. Now she brings her lousy blower. I don't have the customers I used to have. Do you have any idea—I MEAN ANY IDEA—of the heads I used to do in Acapulco? I did Elizabeth Taylor who was the most beautiful woman I ever saw and still is. She'd come into the shop and the other women who were so jealous would whisper—'That's Elizabeth Taylor? She's ugly' but that would be because she was so fucking perfect. The biggest purple greenish blue eyes. And a perfect nose. And beautiful lips. And the skin. The skin is heaven. And she loves animals. Just like me. She just loves animals. So you know she has to be a great person. I mean—tell me—who ever heard of a good person that didn't love animals?

"And I did Merle Oberon. Before she left her house for a lover. But I said to everyone 'What does she need a tin fortune for? She's fed up to her ass with tin. Now she wants a good lay.' Which is all anyone down here wants in the first place. She didn't need the security of some rich guy's tin. I mean she had already *decorated* the fucking Obregón house about forty times. Now she can just have fun. She doesn't need tin. Or houseguests. And I did Greta Garbo. And I did—Lana Turner. What a beauty she was. And Rita Hayworth. Rita was my favorite client. Yes she was. She had the nicest red hair of anyone in show business. And what a sparkling personality. And besides that she was generous. She knew what it was like to get a small tip. She had been poor. Tits and ass have no class. But Rita Hayworth? Now that's what I call generous.

"I've done all the great heads. When Charles Byrd flies down here on the weekends—he has the prettiest house in Acapulco—you better believe it—with two pools—a fresh-water pool and a honey, a salt-water pool—he always brings the classiest girls. His

houseguest is always someone beautiful and he sends them here to
have their hair done. His last houseguest was Jan Cushing. She
wasn't his date. Just his guest. And what a person she was. Crazy.
But I wish everyone was as crazy as Jan Cushing. She's a good
girl's example of how to please a guy. Funny and nice.

"Anyway I don't miss New York. Do you? I think that New
York has become a dump. Muggings. And rape. And then, you
know, everything so expensive. And nobody has any more class.
The days when Helena Rubinstein lived are over. I remember
Madame Rubinstein would invite me to her house. What a casa!
You never saw such paintings. And she was very generous too. At
Christmas I always got a bonus. I hate these rollers. Typically
Mexican. So flimsy. Mexico hasn't caught up with technology
honey. Wait to see what those dryers are like. You won't believe
them. I sure love giving you a combout. You're so patient. You
sit there while I comb you like a little Spanish doll."

Departures

The calendar clock.

Time to leave Acapulco. To leave Byron. But I'll die if I leave
Byron.

Michael is well. He is anxious to see Doctor Wong. To go
home.

I must go back to my other life. On another island. Agatha is
thrilled. She is studying Byron's theories. She is going to take
them to the Cancer Society in New York when she gets back.

I tell Agatha, "I'm going to write about Byron and have the
whole world know about Byron Jorgenson by nineteen seventy-
nine. In nineteen seventy-nine it is going to be recorded that in

Acapulco a certain Mike O'Neil was cured of cancer by Byron Jorgenson. That through Irving Speed and through the offices and belief of Katherine Kahn a breakthrough was made by the human species. We no longer had to be endangered by cancer. I am going back to New York. And I am going to tell all those idiots at Sloan-Kettering–how dare you not investigate even the slightest possibility of a breakthrough in cancer? You know what I think? That up to now cancer has been just another hustle. Billions of dollars are spent on research. A person can go through their whole lifetime and be supported to do cancer research. And come up with nothing. And those conventional medical societies? How dare they not realize that the seventies is a time of breakthrough? And new awareness? How dare they not even look into Byron Jorgenson? What are they afraid of?"

Agatha agrees.

*

A small paper has been published by Byron. It is with me now as I leave Acapulco. I will just simply privately tell you how important this man is to me. He is a monster of madness. He is a saint. He is a cosmic genius. He is a life singer. He is a genius. He is a fool. He is ahead of his time. Like Buddha. Like Christ. Like me. And you. We are all ahead of our time. But what is time really? Listen to the praises of a Chimera–an impossible poet in the middle of her life. Who understands very little. But here is what Byron Jorgenson knows. Here are his secrets–direct from him to me to you. Secrets of the universe. Psychic secrets. Secrets about spaces. And energies. And radiations. The breakthrough of the seventies. Here is the paper of Byron Jorgenson that nobody will believe.

Supplement to
CANCER
Its Origin and Its Arrest
The Byron Theory
as told to Katherine Kahn, poet and journalist
Acapulco 1977

The Byron theory postulated that abnormal and cancerous cells can be corrected into normal cells using antineutrinos emitted from Strontium 90 and neutrinos emitted from Iron-55.

This theory is hereby revised to the correction of only the abnormal or pre-cancerous cells underlying the cancerous growth by using neutrinos.

The human body possesses natural mechanisms for its own protection and defense. Hence, the body's immune system should, in theory, be able to reject all foreign substances or foreign cells which are not recognized as "self." Since the immune system of a cancer victim is unable to destroy cancer cells, it is possible that the immune system is unable to recognize these cells as "nonself."

If we consider that cancer is the result of a series of mutations within a single line of cells, then each of the cells in this line may still be considered as "self" even though the progression has been from normal to abnormal to cancerous.

If we now postulate that some of the cells in the dermis are changed, abnormal cells, then the dermis is defective and may be sending out wrong signals. If we also endow the dermis with the ability to recognize foreign antigens and to be able to signal the immune system to attack, then the lack of response in the case of skin cancer may be due to the defective dermis which cannot recognize the cancerous cells as being foreign because the cancerous basal cells, being an outgrowth of the dermis, are still "self."

It is hereby postulated that if abnormal cells in the dermis can be corrected into being normal cells by irradiation with neutrinos, then the dermis should be able to recognize the cancerous basal cells as foreign and signal for an immunological attack.

However, it is probable that the body's immune system would not be able to destroy an overwhelming quantity of tumor cells without assistance. In fact, it may be the dermis which guides the immunological attack and if the dermis is only capable of short-range surveillance of a thickness of five cells in the epidermis, then the attack would be inadequate and would therefore fail. This condition may be parallel to a massive bacterial infection which requires the assistance of antibiotics.

Since any organ in the human body may be considered as having a "dermis" or layer of supporting tissue which supports any overgrowth, the above reasoning can be applied to cancerous tumors anywhere in the human body.

Therefore, whatever combination of surgery, radiation and cytotoxic drugs can be used to reduce the tumor volume and slow down the cancerous growth will increase the probability of a cancer arrest, or cure, using neutrinos. Hence, even where cancerous conditions are considered inoperable, as much of the cancerous tissue as possible should be removed by surgery.

It is recommended that cancer patients who have had surgery, radiation or chemotherapy, or any combination of these treatments, should be further exposed to antineutrinos for a minimum period of three months at the rate of eight hours of full-body exposure per week.

The recommended antineutrino source is Strontium 90 kept at a distance of 3 meters from the patient so that very few of the electrons emitted by the Strontium 90 will reach the patient. Strontium 90 does not emit gamma rays and the secondary braking radiation created by the slowdown of electrons is minimal.

It is theorized that a complete cancer arrest can be effected using only antineutrinos where the patient has had partial surgery. This is based upon two successful cases of this type.

Where a patient has not had surgery, it is postulated that chemotherapy using 5-fluorouracil in addition to the antineutrino treatment will be required for a complete cancer arrest.

Since the cancer problem is so variable, it is probable that certain cancerous conditions will require treatment by both antineutrinos and neutrinos. However, it is recommended that each type of neutrino treatment be given separately.

It must be emphasized that there is no practical limit to the amount of irradiation by neutrinos and antineutrinos because they are not harmful to the human body.

The Dream Collections

Like my soul sister Anaïs Nin—who died of cancer—I can love anybody. And everybody. Shortly before I left for Acapulco—Anaïs Nin died. My beloved goddess. But I am alive. Surviving. Determined to worship the heart not the head. As the Egyptians did. Because I know that the Egyptians, when they buried their kings and queens and citizens, cared nothing for the brain. They pulled it out of the nose with tongs and threw it away. But the heart was kept sacred. It was the heart where the Ka was, the soul was kept. With all my heart I love Byron Jorgenson for what he has done. He has built a pyramid of knowledge through energy. Through solitude. I love my children. But all geniuses are my children also. In some odd way I was put on earth to nourish genius. To be the earthmother, Katherine Kahn—for all the geniuses I meet. I find genius in children. They haven't had the secrets kicked out of them yet. They can still be magical. For them—for children—from the ages of eight—to perhaps ten or fifteen—they have a chance to understand that creativity is not thinking but being. That art doesn't have to take a lot of time. That's all in you. Art is in all of us. To be released whenever we decide. But of course the sad thing about the world—is that it only respects what is already known. It only looks for what it knows. Not for what it does not know. Imagination requires innocence. And love. And courage and loneliness. I know this. I am an endangered species. I must hide out until my time is ripe and I won't be killed. The imagination that it takes to love oneself must be given to all humanity. If it stays just stuck within yourself it will kill you. That's why technology doesn't have the dimension to make discoveries.

*

I'm back in Hong Kong.

Michael is cured. A miracle. Is he cured or dying? I can't tell. I can hardly speak.

Agatha is somewhere in New York and I can't find her. My children are off visiting another house. I am only an ear. A sad ear. I hear Michael's voice. And as I write to Byron I tell him "Your cure worked. Of course it did."

I believe that. Recently, Michael tried cobalt treatments under the suggestion of Doctor Wong. Unlike the treatments of Byron Jorgenson which did not kill, the cobalt treatments break down cells. And by killing the cells also I'm afraid the treatment is killing Michael. Such is destruction. Life is a huge and wonderful gamble. Not gamma. Gamble. It's your chance now Katherine. Go out and win without killing. What are you thinking?

*

"I love Michael. I do. But I love my children and myself more. And I must leave him. Our time is over. Our love ended. How sad to realize that the end is here."

*

Is Michael cured? He is like an elephant. He just wants to be left alone. I am living back at Lantao Island. I wait on Michael with great love. I look at his face. I wonder—is he really cured? Or will he get sick again? He just wants to be left alone in his room. Suddenly I have grown to hate Hong Kong. The places that were so wonderful and joyful are now annoying and grotesque. Could I really have found Lantao Island so charming? Mr. Wu is a pain in the ass. Peter and Mae—we are constantly spending the weekends with them—because of their love for Michael—have become so boring I can hardly stand seeing them. Mae is kind. And an absolute irritant. I detest the conversations of Peter and Mae. They are banal.

*

Agatha is here in Hong Kong. We have become best friends. I begged her to come. She is my confidante. To her I confide the fact that I am now miserable on Lantao Island. Michael in his post-cancer state just stares at me and begs me silently to leave him alone. No matter how much I do for him and want to wait on him he is annoyed. He snaps at me. We no longer make love. I don't blame him. He just doesn't feel like it. Neither do I. The children are always crying. They are beginning to resent being isolated on Lantao Island. They talk about America. They dream of eating pizza and spending their Sundays listening to *Grease* on their portable phonograph machine. "When are we going home mommy?" they ask. The love island is a fiasco. The truth is that I now hate Lantao Island as much as I once hated New York. The truth is—that it's the same over and over again. The flies drive me bananas. The servant problem is all everyone talks about when we go to Hong Kong for an occasional outing. Michael no longer wants to ride on a junk, or visit, or read, or make love, or be civil. He has retreated into his elephant land where he just lies on his side and stares at the ceiling. I now hate Hong Kong as much as I hated New York. I spend my days thinking of Byron. Of course we write letters. Occasionally I call him long distance. "How is he?" he asks. He is sure that Michael is cured. But all I want to do is to go back to Byron and the hills of Acapulco. I would like to devote myself to Byron Jorgenson, his cures, his madness, his strengths and his life. Suddenly the paradise of the temple revolts me. The ceiling leaks. The rains are bothersome. I want to be with Byron. I want to go back to Byron. I will find a way. Yes dear Michael you no longer need me. So I am packing my ghastly little suitcase with poems and dresses and shoes and scarves and I am leaving for Mexico. I am taking with me my beautiful children, who have loved you. I am taking with me Agatha, who is fond of you. I am taking with me the goddamn fucking parrot you gave me. And my books. And my shells. I am leaving you because you no longer need me and I no longer need you. Since you beg "to be left alone" I love you enough to leave you alone. For once I am going to do what I want. I am fleeing for Mexico. Running. Or saving myself. Or whatever you want to call being able to survive. I think of Byron. Will he love the children as much as Michael? Of course he will. We will live together working in the hills of Mexico. I am sure that this is a life change for the better. My last life change. Goodbye little Michael who I loved with all my heart. I'm off to another life. Goodbye old little king. Were you the straw that broke my camel's back? I am so tired of noodles I could spit. I am tired of chopsticks. I am tired of the Hong Kong ferry. Guess what? I am tired of the Talmud. I am tired of conversations from Mae's lips about clothes and servants. I am tired of Michael pushing me away from him. I am longing to be with the mad genius. To make life easier for him. To understand how I can help him and to devote my energies to him. To write. To live. To love. To laugh again. To be of some use to someone. And of course to devote myself to the children who, I am told will love Mexico. I want to stop running away from who I am. Is Byron my life partner? I think so. For a while. I believe in his theories. I love him. Yes I love him. There is an underlying order to my life. I must be swift. I have always known that Byron wanted me. I am going back to him. Finally. I want to live with a genius. To find my life partner at least for a little while and begin another life. I refuse to be rubbed off the blackboard. "You see, Agatha, my heart is inexhaustible."